... to Lisburn, Northern Ireland.

... at Queen's University, Belfast and Manchester ...ropolitan University. Shirley-Anne wrote and performed with Belfast-based arts group, Ikon, for several years and she currently lives in South Down where she spends her time as a writer, schools worker and mum.

*Also by Shirley-Anne McMillan*

A Good Hiding
The Unknowns

# Every
# Sparrow
# Falling

## SHIRLEY-ANNE
## McMILLAN

ATOM

First published in Great Britain in 2019 by Atom

3 5 7 9 10 8 6 4 2

A CIP catalogue record for this book
is available from the British Library.

ISBN 978-0-349-00332-0

Typeset in Garamond by M Rules
Printed and bound in Great Britain by
Clays Ltd, Elcograf S.p.A.

Papers used by Atom are from well-managed forests
and other responsible sources.

Atom
An imprint of
Little, Brown Book Group
Carmelite House
50 Victoria Embankment
London EC4Y 0DY

An Hachette UK Company
www.hachette.co.uk

www.atom.co.uk

For Peterson Toscano

# Chapter 1

My name is Cariad. That's Welsh for Darling. But my personal translation is 'Someone once thought you were good enough to name.' Whoever they were, I have no idea where they are now.

Anyway, I don't live in Wales. I never did. I've never even been there. Maybe my parents had never been to Wales either, who knows? It doesn't matter now anyway. That's one thing you learn when you're 'in care' – nothing really matters. *Life goes on*, as they say. And the only thing that's real is the present. This moment, right now.

That's what I was repeating to myself as I looked out over the sea.

*This moment, right now. That's all there is.*

This morning, when I'd got detention for another missed maths homework, didn't exist any more. Last night, when I'd got hammered on two litres of Diamond White and Stevie B. tried to get off with me – that didn't exist any more either, thank God.

What definitely did exist was my thumping hangover, unfortunately. But the wind and the sea exist too, I told myself. Every wave shooshing on the sand below me, every whisper of cool air breathing life into my body. The long drop between this cliff top and the sand below. The thoughts about what it would feel like to jump. The seal flipping up, suddenly, from the water. Was it a seal? It seemed too big but it was hard to tell. It flicked out of the water and in again, a sleek body, unaware that anyone was watching, showing off to itself. Enjoying itself. I wished that I could see it up close.

'Cariad,' Madge had said on one of her visits, 'you really have a hard time having a good time, don't you?'

I suppose she was looking at my gurny gob, trying to make me smile. But it was a stupid question because what does 'having a good time' really mean? Does it feel like being drunk? Having a laugh with other people? Just being day-to-day happy? I didn't know, but I was pretty sure my sea creature friend had it all sussed. The water skited up from its tail as it crashed back into the water. A dolphin maybe? Not that either.

I finished off my bar of chocolate and dropped the wrapper over the edge of the cliff. Maybe the seal would eat the paper and choke and die. That was me, though – always thinking of the consequences *after* I'd done the action. Madge used to say that all the time: 'No point crying now, Cari. You need to start thinking about stuff before you do it.'

Before you drink two litres of cider and throw up all over your new foster parents' bathroom. Think, Cari. Think.

Before you steal crisps from the school canteen (even if you're dead hungry and you know that there's no way anyone will lend you the money 'cause everyone knows they'll never get it back).

Think.

2

Before you try to dye your hair with lemon juice and a bottle of green food colouring and ruin your brand new (yawn) school uniform. (Well, how was I to know it was gonna rain on the way to school?)

Think.

Before you stay out all night and cause a village manhunt. (Why is it always a manhunt, by the way, even when you're not a man?)

Think. Think. Think.

Stop yourself from acting on impulse or having any fun. Think. Before you get chucked out of yet another foster home.

I watched the dark sea creature for a while and then it was gone again, and I waited for it to come up for almost another hour before giving up. *It is gone and doesn't exist any more,* I thought, like all the other moments and all the other hours and days and weeks and years. And I couldn't think of a moment I'd like to have had back. Not one. Except for maybe that seal-thing flipping up out of the water.

# Chapter 2

Here are some of the foster placements I've had:

### The O'Kanes *(three months)*

Not their fault really. I was thirteen and I didn't want a new home, so I was, quite deliberately, a little shit. I smoked in a classroom, and then I used the same lighter to set fire to my bedroom. Really bad stuff like that. I'm surprised they lasted as long as they did, to be honest. They had a lovely dog called Rufus and I cried when I had to leave him. I still miss you, Rufus Pooch.

### The McGibbons

The two-week drive-by don't-blink-or-you'll-miss-it puke-stained ship-in-the-night. Why the hell would you foster a kid if a bit of vom's gonna send you running? OK, so it was a self-inflicted illness involving the contents of their weird globe-shaped drinks trolley thing, and the stain will probably be on their hall stairs carpet for eternity, but still, two weeks? Amateurs!

### The McCunes *(one month)*
Punched my 'foster-brother' Jason McCune when I heard him calling me a refugee at school. I broke his nose and his parents totally freaked out. It was one hundred per cent worth it.

### The Whites *(almost a year!)*
They had stamina. And a guinea pig. I liked them. I was just starting to think that I'd pulled it off – actually found a 'family', but then Mr White died of a heart attack. For God's sake. And that was the end of that. He had always been the one who stuck up for me when I got in trouble, and to be fair to Mrs White I *was* a bit much to cope with when she was dealing with losing her husband, so it wasn't a big surprise when Madge told me she'd asked for me to be placed somewhere else.

Family doesn't exist, I told myself. Not for people like me, anyway.

I had other placements, and sometimes I lived in a 'home'. I had gotten away with loads of stuff – smoking blow, drinking, staying out. But now I was sixteen and by the time I was eighteen I'd have nobody. I kind of hoped that I'd pop off like Mr White some day: quickly, without a long illness, before life got too boring.

But then Dawn and Jacky happened.

I had been with them in Ballybaile for three months before Robin Merrow went missing. They were a good bit older than any of the foster carers I'd had before, and they had already fostered a few kids in the past, but none as old as me. Technically I didn't really need to be in care any more but my social worker,

Madge, thought it might be good for me to hang on for a year or two. I didn't have much choice. What else was I meant to do? It wasn't like I was going to go and rent a flat with my fabulous career as a serial foster-reject. You might wonder why an elderly couple would want to be bothered with someone like me. It's not as if they didn't know my history. Well, the answer was: God.

I found out pretty quickly – Dawn and Jacky were seasoned God-botherers. *Bingo*, I thought – a couple of naïve old dears who I could wrap around my wee finger and pretty much do as I pleased. But actually, as it turned out, they weren't going to be a pushover at all.

The first thing they did was set out One Hundred And One Rules For Naughty Care Kids. They literally had them written down and they read them out loud to me over breakfast.

1. We don't have a regular curfew – we'll work things out as they go. But when we say you have to be home, you have to be home. Or you don't get to go out the next time.
2. You do your homework or you don't go out.
3. You keep your room relatively tidy. Dirty laundry goes in the wash, dirty dishes go in the kitchen sink. We all pitch in in this house.
4. Nobody in this house smokes. If we smell cigarette smoke off your clothes we'll assume you've been smoking, and that'll be a strike against you.

'A strike? Like, "Three strikes and you're out"?'
'You'll not be getting rid of us that easily, love,' Dawn said,

smirking. She was enjoying this. 'It's more like *three strikes and you'll be spending Sundays volunteering with the Sunday School.*'

'Aw, what?!'

'Fair warning.' She smiled. 'Toe the line and you'll be grand.'

Church on Sunday wasn't a punishment (so they said) but it also wasn't optional. I'd never been to church in my life and it was just as boring as I might have expected, but I got used to it. I would use the hour to sit and daydream about the future I'd never have. I'd been doing this since I was a little kid. I used to make up stories in my head about having a great foster family who would eventually adopt me. They'd have a dog or at least some kind of pet. I'd have a nice bedroom all to myself with clean sheets. The house would be close to the shops.

When it got obvious that it was never going to happen I thought, screw it, why not dream bigger? The most outlandish, wildest dreams ever! Why not dream about heading off in a time machine to the year 3097 where people didn't have their own bodies any more – everyone's personality was just on a little microchip that you could insert into anything. You could be a class robot that never needed to sleep and could stay up all night partying, or you could be a bird flying around going wherever you wanted to. Because it's all a fantasy, isn't it? There is no actual 'happy ever after'. That's just for fairy tales and little kids. So, every Sunday morning, surrounded by people who thought that their sky wizard God was actually real, I'd sit there and make up a better story than the one they were selling. It passed the time.

As for friends, I had had one or two from previous placements. None that were actual, real friends, but that was how I liked it. Be nice to the majority of people and they won't bother you too much. Don't get too involved. Have a laugh but keep your distance. Dawn and Jacky wanted me to go to the church Youth Fellowship and make friends there. It wouldn't have been my first choice of venue to find friends, but I wasn't bothered – they'd do. I could always make other friends in school if I needed some variety. I found out very quickly that I was going to need the variety.

Jessica Crothers and her Holy Roller friends were obsessed with two things: God and gossip. They'd flit from discussions about what Jesus really meant in some parable or other to talking about their latest hot topic, which, right now, was Robin Merrow.

'Apparently Robin Merrow aced his history test last week.'

Jessica stirred her latte with a long spoon, raising an eyebrow as she spoke. I was dying to ask why getting a good test result would be newsworthy, but I didn't have to wait long to find out because everyone at the table leaned in and began talking. Jessica's statement was apparently all they needed to set them off. She flicked her gorgeous black hair from her forehead and smiled thinly as they gabbled.

'Oh my goodness! The best evidence yet!' said Martha, a small wiry kid with the neatest bob haircut I'd ever seen.

'There is *so* something going on.'

'Guuuuys, should we be gossiping about this?' said Alicia. 'Maybe we should pray for him at the break-time prayer meeting?'

Brief silence.

'Well,' said Martha, reddening, 'if we don't say *anything* about him, how will we know what to pray about?'

Another silence.

I sipped my Coke through a red straw. Dawn had thought it

was a good idea for me to spend time with them after school. Sometimes we just walked to our houses together, but sometimes we'd stop off at Jenny's café for a drink. I didn't mind them really. They were friendly and not bitchy in a really bullying way, despite the obsession with Robin Merrow, but I knew I'd never really be good friends with them. They really believed all the God stuff, and they kept trying to get me to believe it too. They called it 'witnessing' and they took every opportunity to 'spread the gospel' in my direction. Jessica noticed me and feigned an apologetic look.

'Oh my goodness, I'm sorry, Cari. You've literally no idea what we're talking about. How rude of us.'

The silence was broken and now the attention turned to me and the need to fill me in, for the sake of politeness, of course. I played along. I wanted to know the detail just as much as any of them.

'So,' I said. 'What? I'm guessing that he's banging the history teacher? Ms Trainor, right?'

An audible gasp.

'Oops. Sorry – I'm not used to minding my language.'

I was really making an effort when I was in public. I hoped that Dawn and Jacky would appreciate it. Martha giggled, and Jessica touched my arm lightly.

'Oh, don't worry – we take people as they come.' She flashed a wide, genuine smile. 'But yes, we're pretty sure, like, about eighty per cent sure, that they're having a fling.'

The group lit up with excitement to hear their suspicions verbalised by the demure Jessica who probably hadn't had a 'fling' in her entire life. Jesus. Had any of them? Is this what they did? Sat around talking about everyone else's love life so that they didn't have to have one of their own? I wasn't complaining, though, I wanted to hear more.

'Wow.' I leaned in too. 'So, how long has it been going on? And how do you know?'

A storm of conspiracy spun around them. They had it all sussed, naturally. The short skirts Ms Trainor wore 'only on the days when she had Robin's class'; the wink they'd seen Merrow giving her as he passed her in the corridor, followed by her blushes; the increasingly good grades he had achieved despite failing in every other subject; and, crucially, a rumour, 'which only might be true, but there's no smoke without fire', that Robin Merrow had had to leave his last school because of an incident which culminated in his name on the sex offenders' register for being a paedophile.

'Wait. What?' I set down my Coke.

'It's probably true, my mum says,' said Jessica, finishing off her latte.

Her mum was a lawyer and 'my mum says' was often the end of any conversation. Nobody else's mum was a lawyer, so what did they know?

'I can't believe . . .' I started. They all looked at me. 'I mean, I find that hard to believe . . . and how would that have anything to do with him having it off with a teacher?'

A chill had descended again. My fault this time. Jessica was putting on her coat and the other girls started to put on their coats too. Martha nudged me and half-whispered, 'Because. He's obviously a perv.'

I looked at Jessica and she shrugged her shoulders and flicked her hair again. 'Facts are facts,' she said. 'He's interesting, but you should stay away from him, Cari. For your own safety.'

What facts? I thought. But I didn't say anything, and we left the café and walked towards our houses quietly, led by Jessica.

# Chapter 3

Dawn and Jacky's TV was massive. I don't mean plasma wide-screen massive. More like you could hollow it out and house a family of five inside. The screen itself was a normal size. It sat in the corner of the living room and at night after dinner they'd sit, Dawn knitting on the sofa, and Jacky on his armchair, and tune in to the news, the big set sitting there like a giant dinosaur fossil. Sometimes, behind the headlines, you could hear it whirring as it struggled to light up the news presenter, grinding its gears like an old clapped out car.

The picture went fuzzy again and Jacky sighed, rising slowly from his seat to give it a bang on the side.

'We should just get a new set,' said Dawn.

'Nothing wrong with his one,' said Jacky. 'Not much, anyway. It would be a sin to get rid of it.' He sat back deeply in his chair. 'Besides, I wouldn't be able to lift the thing.'

Dawn smiled behind her knitting. They were so chilled. They never had arguments or got cross about things, even when the kids up the street threw eggs at their windows a while back; they just went out and cleaned them and got on with things. It wasn't as if they were feeble, though. They had opinions. Sometimes Jacky would chat back to the news presenter and explain why whichever politician they were interviewing was one hundred per cent wrong about everything they were saying. They'd say what they thought about stuff like that. They just didn't see the point of getting angry about anyone else's opinions.

The news was usually depressing: massive wars in faraway countries; stupid world leaders messing everything up; politicians, and their boring love-life scandals. Then after the main news it would be our turn in Northern Ireland. The local news was always crap too: someone who got their knees done at the back of Asda; a robbery at the Credit Union; a fire at an old person's house. Dawn would tut, and Jacky would shake his head. I wondered why they watched the news if it was always so terrible. But I kind of enjoyed the ritual because it happened every day and it meant that Dawn and Jacky's scheduled 'homework time' was over and it was nearly the end of the day, and I suppose it was a bit like doing the lottery – there was always the hope that one day something really interesting would happen. Maybe that's why Dawn and Jacky watched it too.

And then one day, something really interesting happened.

'Oh my goodness!' said Dawn. And instead of saying 'Sssh!' Jacky just sat there, his gob open, and I did too.

The news presenter read out the details: 'The massive luxury cruise liner has the capacity to hold over three thousand passengers. It is not yet clear if there are any casualties. Police are appealing for calm and asking locals not to visit the scene.'

And there they were – my cliffs, only now they were populated with cops, and the cops weren't watching dolphins. The ship had sort of crashed onto an awkward rock that you couldn't see properly if the weather was bad. Nobody knew yet how it had ended up there but the locals being interviewed were full of ideas.

'Well they must've gotten themselves rightly lost,' said one man in a flat cap, his white hair sticking out at all angles. 'I've said for years they need to clean that lighthouse more often. And this is the consequence. They'll keep it clean from now on, won't they!' He seemed almost happy.

'It's a big shock,' said another woman, somewhat younger. 'And Ballybaile's only wee. I don't know where they're all going to go.'

The close-up footage showed a huge ship, standing like a fortress, static in the water, its lights flashing as the sun went down, the choppy waves licking around its walls. The front of the ship was hidden by the rock it had run into. I couldn't imagine how it had happened, or how they'd ever be able to shift it. But I knew one thing. I'd be going back to my cliff as soon as I could.

# Chapter 4

'Stay away from him ... for your own safety.'

What was it to her, anyway? I walked up the hill, off the path, through the wet trees. Jessica was a weird one. On one hand it was impossible not to like her, because she never did anything nasty. She was perfectly pleasant to everyone, no matter what group they belonged to in school. She was friendly to the geeky kids, the popular kids, the goth kids, the gay kids, the bad kids. Everyone. In fact, I think that's why I was suspicious of her. She clearly enjoyed being the Queen of the Chrissos, letting all the Jesus freaks know exactly how they should behave at all times ('We should show Sandra some grace, it can't be easy when the whole school thinks you're a slut ...'. 'We should all volunteer for the environmental group to plant daffodils this weekend. After all, we are stewards of the planet as well as being concerned about the afterlife, right?') But it was all a bit ... controlling. For some reason the others hung on her every word, and I didn't mind going along with them most of the time – it kept Jacky and Dawn happy, and I just tuned out when they started going on about the Bible – but something was nipping my head as I walked up through the steep forest, slipping on the wet roots. That thing she'd said – the warning about Robin Merrow. She had started telling me how to behave, too. And I didn't like it.

Nearly at the top and the sun had almost gone. I was trying to make it to see the sun set but as I rounded the top of the hill I could see a blue police light flashing in the distance near my lookout. I turned off my usual route. Maybe I could get around the other side of them. Surely they wouldn't stay there all night.

But by the time I had got to a safe place where I could come out of the trees it was dark, and I'd also forgotten to lift a fag from underneath my secret hiding stone. So, there I was, at the top of the cliff, freezing my ass off in the dark, nothing to do with my hands but shove them in my pockets. I could see the police cordon, off to my left at the spot where I wanted to be. Stupid wee blue light flashing on and off, as if the emergency hadn't already happened. I'd get the fag on the way down, maybe. This spot would do. I settled myself on a boulder, drew my knees up to my chin underneath my black coat and wrapped my arms around them. Hood up. I looked out to sea. And there it was.

I'd never seen a cruise ship before. On the telly it had looked big, but now, in the dark, some of its lights still flickering, it looked like an alien spaceship. Far too big for our country. Completely still, as if it was ground into the bottom of the sea, it made the helicopter training its spotlight from overhead look like a tiny insect. The waves were black, and they beat high against the side of the ship like a shadow fire burning up and falling away. When I looked behind me at the forest and back again to the ship it felt like two universes had come together and I couldn't stop looking back and forth at everything that I knew and everything I had never known before.

The glow of the beam from the helicopter made me wish for warmth and I cursed myself for forgetting the cig. As I had the thought, I heard a noise, about ten feet away: the rasp of match on scratch. I saw the glow of a tiny light, the pulsing red of a sucked in flame.

'Who's there?' I hissed, before remembering that it was likely to be a cop.

I prepared to bolt, but there was no need. The light fell to the ground and disappeared, and I heard the swift retreat of a coat, or something like that, moving quickly. Whoever they were, they were gone. A tiny spark danced on the ground and I ran to it. I sucked hard on the cig, drawing in the warmth. I checked the tip; burning nicely again. Well, thank you, Mister Nobody. Thank you very much! Back on my rock, hugging my knees, puffing on my smoke, happy as a pig in poo, I watched that skyscraper in the sea until the fag was done and then for a few minutes more, and I thought about all those rich people and where they had gone, into a tiny country half the size of their spacecraft; weird alien people on a cold, wet planet.

None of them could have been as content as I was right then. Maybe I didn't have the best friends or any proper parents, but I had people I knew in a way – cops who lit up their presence so you could avoid them, religious do-gooders who expected people to be good so they'd never suspect it when you snuck off into the night; predictable people. That's what belonging meant, right? Knowing what moves other people were going to make. Belonging meant no surprises, except the odd stranger in the darkness who'd abandon their fag for you.

Shows how much I knew.

# Chapter 5

Jesus, it was boring trying to be good. Jessica's prayer meetings were equal parts hilarious and dull. We had special permission from the prissy English teacher to use her room, so we sat on the desks and closed our eyes. Well, the others closed their eyes. Sometimes I did too, because I don't know if you've ever sat in a room with your eyes open watching a bunch of other people, talking, with theirs closed, but it's weird.

'Dear Lord,' Jessica would begin, 'we just want to bring these things before you today, Lord. We just want to raise these things before you. We just hope you will hear our prayers.'

Whoever the Lord was, he really liked hearing the word 'just', because everyone used it way too often.

'Lord,' Martha would say, after an appropriate silence to make sure that Jessica was finished, 'we just want to raise Rebecca Sloan before you today. We just want to ask you to heal her from the burden of her eye infection. And, er, we just want to ask that nobody else gets it. Amen.'

'Amen,' we'd all say.

It was always stuff like that. Never mind babies getting bombed in Syria or people getting chucked in jail for protesting against the government. It was always, 'Please just let our exams go well,' or, 'Please just let the weather be good for the Scripture Union ramble next weekend.'

I never joined in the prayers, obviously, but I went along at break times because it meant I didn't have to go outside and wander around on my own, and also because Dawn and Jacky thought it was the best thing ever. It's the not the absence of things that people notice – it's the presence of things. I learned that at the last foster home with Mr and Mrs Green. You could literally bite your tongue to stop yourself telling the science teacher that his bullshit homework didn't matter to anyone on the planet, and you could take the long route back to stop yourself from punching Davy Stamford because you knew if you went the usual way you'd see him calling some kid gay or fat or flicking his floppy fringe at some girl he was harassing as if she should be grateful for his gross attention. Those kinds of things went unnoticed. But as soon as you got caught getting off with Cormac Kelly in the boys' toilets, then that's it: all beliefs about the Foster Girl confirmed. What harm does a bit of a feel do anyone for God's sake? They should've been rejoicing that I had normal teenage urges rather than wanting to have sex with donkeys or something. Or with a teacher. God, was he really having it off with Ms Trainor? I get it that she was good looking, but she *was* also a teacher . . .

I sat on the desk, swinging my legs, waiting for the rest of the God squad to arrive. Jessica was already here, of course, checking her watch and tutting. I felt like asking her why she was wasting precious time which she could have been spending talking to the Lord and filling him in on the latest gossip. Poor God, having to listen to this drivel every day. What would it be today, I thought? *Please just don't let anyone get food poisoning at the Sixth Form formal, the way they did last year?*

'What's so funny?' asked Jessica.

I didn't have to answer because Martha came in followed by a couple of the other Christians. Jessica smiled but not so broadly that they wouldn't know she was pissed off at their being late. They took the hint and got to work immediately. Everyone was sitting on top of a desk in a loose circle arrangement. Jessica began, as always.

'Lord. We just thank you today that we can spend time with you.'

Boke. I could just hear Jesus saying, 'Cut the crap, Jess. What is it you want?' She got to the point soon enough.

'We just want to pray for all those people who were ship-wrecked in Ballybaile last night. We just pray that all of them are safe and that, er, the ship won't cause any environmental damage with things like oil spills or whatever. And we thank you that nobody died in the accident.'

Yeah, *thanks so much for ramming a massive ship up against a huge rock. I bet the passengers are all deeply grateful for your goodness, oh Lord.*

Pause.

Martha began. 'Yes, Lord, we all want to thank you for your love in this difficult circumstance. Let us also remember those who are suffering difficulties in our school. Like Robin Merrow, for instance.'

You could almost see everyone's ears prick up at the mention of him.

'He is surely a troubled soul,' she continued, 'and we, uh, just want what's best for him –' (everyone nodded, prayerfully) '– and so we just pray that you will guide him along the path of righteousness, away from, er, Ms Trainor, and into your precious light.'

I bit my lip, but it was too late, a giggle had erupted. I tried to turn it into a cough. Jessica opened one eye and scowled at me.

'Help us, oh Lord,' she said, her eyes closed again, 'to take the troubles of our friends seriously, and to—'

The bell rang, and everyone said a swift 'Amen' before grabbing their bags and leaving.

The troubles of our friends? It wasn't as if Robin was a friend of any of them. I opened my locker and started looking for my maths books. And troubles? Ms Trainor was totally hot. Boo hoo, poor Robin Merrow, having regular sex (allegedly) with a smokin'-hot teacher on his lunch break. Hahaha!

'What are you smiling about?'

I hadn't noticed him until he spoke. When I turned around he wasn't looking at me, he was hoking through his own locker, a few doors up from mine. I didn't reply. Maybe it wasn't me he'd spoken to. We both closed our locker doors together. He looked over.

'Not speaking to me then?' His mouth turned up slightly at the corners. More amused than annoyed, I thought. I don't think I'd ever been that close to Robin Merrow before.

'I . . . no, I just didn't know if it was you who'd spoken.'

He looked around demonstrably. There wasn't another soul

in the corridor. Everyone was in class already. I could feel my face grow hot.

'Only messin',' he said, smiling. 'I've got fuckin' maths now.'

I shrugged. 'Yeah. Fuckin' maths. Hate it.' We began to walk down the corridor, side by side, but not close together.

'Probably beats prayer time, though, eh?'

Holy shit. He knew I went to prayer meetings? How did he know anything I did? I started wishing his maths room was closer. This was excruciating. It's not like I fancied him or anything, but he was clearly the most interesting person in the school, and right now I was looking like the *least* interesting person.

'I don't really ... I mean, I'm newish here so ... Jessica was nice to me and I'm just trying to be nice back ... I don't really believe ...'

'Hey, it's cool. I don't care what people are into.'

He wasn't looking at me, but his smile was broad. He wore his backpack with both straps, like he was going for a hike or something. Nobody did that except first years, and none of them did it after the first week, unless they had a death wish. But Robin Merrow clearly didn't give a shit. He must have been six foot at least and he had broad shoulders and big hands. Nobody was going to make fun of his backpack.

We walked from the old building to the new one without saying another word. *He thinks I'm a dick*, I thought. Shit. The price you have to pay to stay with the decent foster parents. How could I let him know that I wasn't like the Christians? We were at his maths room now, and the opportunity was gone.

'It was nice meeting you,' he said, as he walked towards the door.

'Um. Thanks. You too,' I said.

'Here,' he said, winking at me, still grinning, 'Mr Johnstone's raging with me. Say a wee prayer?'

If you'd told me yesterday that I'd soon be sharing a joke with Robin Merrow I'd have imagined it would be something to look forward to in a week full of boring bollocks about quadratic equations, news interviews with rich people having to get off their boat, emailed prayer requests from Martha about getting a C on her geography paper and, of course, the church sermon at the end of it all. I might've said that meeting the mysterious Robin Merrow would have been something of a highlight. But, as I sat in class and tried hard to pin down the words floating around the textbook, I felt like a sinking brick. The only thing worse than someone getting you all wrong is when they get you all wrong and think that you're the type of person who goes to prayer meetings during break time. And the only thing worse than that is *being* the type of person who goes to prayer meetings during break time. Urgh.

'Cariad?'

Who said that?

'Cariad? Are you listening?'

Shite, it was the teacher.

'Yes. Yes, sir.'

'Good. What answer did you get for number twelve?'

'Uhhhhh . . .'

He rolled his eyes and turned back to the whiteboard and started blahing on again. I looked at my blank page – as empty as the rest of the week, maybe my whole life, was going to be.

I felt the poke of a pen on my back and turned around. It was Stevie B., offering me a folded piece of paper. I glanced back at the teacher. Still waffling on with his back to the class. I took the note and opened it, using my bag for cover.

*Sesh at the well after school?*

God. What I wouldn't do for a can of cold cider right now. I was meant to be going to the café with Jessica and the Christians but surely they wouldn't miss me just this once. I could do without Stevie and his wandering hands but if there was going to be booze that meant that Brains Baxter would be there too, probably with some others, so it'd be OK. What would I tell Jacky and Dawn if they found out I hadn't gone to the café? I'd think about it later. Without turning around I signalled a thumbs-up to Stevie B. and smiled to myself, hoping that someone who knew Robin Merrow had witnessed the exchange and might tell him about it for some reason. I desperately needed some fun and I'd been good as gold. Surely the Lord himself wouldn't deny me that?

# Chapter 6

It was called the well. Nobody knew who'd come up with the name, but it wasn't really a well. It was essentially a big dip in the ground halfway up the hill. There was room in the pit for about five people, seven at a squeeze, and when you sat in it only your head could be seen. It was brilliant because it kept the breeze out and the trees overhead gave some shelter. When we went there you'd have to spend a few minutes clearing the rubbish out of the bottom of the pit where the last group had left it. Bottles and cans (mostly cans, though), crisp bags, fag ends, sometimes spliff ends, the odd condom (urgh). Nobody really minded, though, because when we were done we'd just leave all our cans there as well, and the next lot would clear it up. It was an unspoken rule – you can leave your own shit as long as you clear up whatever's there from the last time, so it doesn't get too piled up.

I hung back at the school library for a while just to make sure I wasn't the first one there. I didn't particularly want to be alone with auld octopus hands, although I felt like he was harmless enough. He usually backed off if you told him to fuck off, and to be fair sometimes I didn't tell him to fuck off, so I couldn't blame him for trying, I suppose. Still, it's always easier if there are more people around, and also, I wouldn't have any booze with me, so I was relying on the others to come up with the goods. Specifically, Brains, who could pass as twenty-four if he took off his school tie. Blokes are so lucky being able to grow a beard and just automatically look older or cooler. But Brains was also a good student – targeted for Oxford, sure to get a string of As in his A levels, president of the Physics Society. But he liked a drink as much as anyone, and everyone else was happy to let him use his 'unsuspectable' status to help them out.

By the time I got there Stevie B., Brains and his boyfriend Muff were there. I said hi and jumped into the pit. They had already started drinking. I was sitting opposite Stevie who chucked me a can of lager.

'Ta. What did I miss?'

Brains took a long draw of his cig.

'Only Stevie figuring out that you can still get an STD if you're gay.'

'I knew that!' said Stevie. 'I just . . . I just said, youse don't need to worry about condoms because – no babies.'

Muff snorted and slugged his beer.

'That talk about HIV go over your head last year did it?' smirked Brains.

'I know,' said Stevie, 'but at least if you got an STD that's not as bad as getting someone up the duff.'

'Oh, for God's sake!' I said.

'What? I'm just saying.'

'Firstly, some STDs are really serious,' I said. 'Secondly, you can't compare getting an STD to having a baby. They're different things entirely. And anyway, your chances of getting either are precisely nil.'

'*Burn!*' laughed Muff.

'Aye right, Cariad, yer ma wasn't saying that last night,' Stevie snapped back.

Everyone went quiet and looked at me.

'Ah shit,' said Stevie. 'Sorry, Cari . . . I'm a dick. I know you don't have a—'

'You are a dick,' I said, interrupting before he dug himself in any deeper. 'Givus one of them fags and I'll forgive you.'

He smiled and chucked me a fag. Brains lit the cig and changed the subject.

'So. I asked Robin Merrow if he wanted to join our little soirée this afternoon,' he said.

'Did you? Why'd you do that? He's really weird,' said Stevie.

'Because,' said Brains, stretching out his long legs, 'he's *really weird*. Aren't you interested in him?'

'Are *you* interested in him?' said Muff with a raised eyebrow.

'I only have eyes for you, Muff, darling,' Brains said, kissing him on the cheek.

'Christ. Get a room,' said Stevie, pretending to shield his eyes.

'If we got a room that'd leave you here all alone with our Cari, and we wouldn't do that to her.' Brains leant over and kissed my cheek too. 'Pass us another can of that fine-quality ale, lovely lady.'

He was dicking about, but I felt my face going red in spite of myself. You could tell that Brains was going to go to Oxford. He was smart enough to ace his exams, but he'd also have no problem with the interview. He could charm the pants off anyone. In fact, he'd probably do just that once he got there. It was a good thing he was well up on the benefits of condoms.

'So, what did Merrow say then?' I asked, trying to sound casual.

'He said he had –' there was a dramatic pause '– Other. Plans.'

'*Woooo hooooo!* Would they be *historical* plans I wonder?' laughed Stevie.

The chat turned to Robin and the sexy history teacher and speculation about how long their relationship would last, and whether or not they'd get found out, and if Ms Trainor got the sack who would be the new history teacher. I let them jabber on about it. I was enjoying their gossip and as they talked we all drank more. Empty cans and fag butts were piling up as the sun was going down. I knew I had stayed out too long and that Dawn would be putting dinner out for Jacky now and wondering where I was. I thought about the switched-off phone in my pocket and wondered if I should text her to say I was OK. And I wondered what Robin Merrow would think if he could see me here now, drinking cans and having the craic. Not so holy now, eh?

'You're not saying much, Cariad. Do you fancy him?' asked Brains.

'Who?'

'Merrow, obviously.'

I spluttered a spray of beer on my shirt. 'As if!'

The words came out slightly more slowly than I had intended. How much had I had to drink? Oops . . .

'Nah, Cari only fancies me. Isn't that right, Cari?' said Stevie B., ambling across the pit to sit beside me.

His eyelids were starting to droop. He put his arm around me and I couldn't be bothered moving. It was OK. Nothing more was said. He leaned in for a kiss and I didn't stop him. We lay back against the wall of the pit, continuing to kiss, and he put his hand up my shirt. It moved across my bra. I thought briefly about Brains and Muff but when I caught a glimpse of them they were getting off with each other as well. No more gossip. All you could hear now was the shuffle of clothes moving against clothes and the odd sigh.

We stayed like that for a while, kissing, pressing against one another, letting our drunk selves get lost in the pit. Then Muff sat up and said, 'Shit, it's eight p.m., I'm meant to be helping Dad at the garage tonight.' He stood up and zipped up his trousers. His hair was a mess and although it was getting dark I could tell he was in no state to be dealing with people's cars in his dad's garage. None of us were really in a fit state to go back. Time to write that text.

I pushed Stevie off me and sat up. I knew I would have loads of messages from Dawn. The phone exploded into life as soon as I turned it on. Six increasingly anxious messages. I had messed it up, big time. I texted Dawn back, trying my best not to sound drunk.

HI Dawn. It's fine. Am so sory I dint text back. Couldn't find my pone. Am with friends from school and Ill be back soon. Sory. Xxxxxxxx

And that is how I ended up spending the next few weekends teaching Sunday School to five-year-olds.

# Chapter 7

It wasn't just Sunday School either. I got a massive lecture about drinking and how disappointed they were in me. Not that I hadn't heard it all before, but Jacky actually looked really sad. I felt like I could almost see a tear in his eye. Jesus. They also said no more drink or fags, obviously, and no going out after dark for the foreseeable future. Flip sake! Lucky they didn't see what else I was getting up to or I'd probably have had to wear a chastity belt too.

Still, it could have been worse. They didn't even mention sending me back to the home. Most other foster parents at least used it as a threat. But no, Dawn was just disappointed and angry, and Jacky was just sad. They both said they'd pray for me. Like God really needed any more boring shit to listen to. What was he meant to do about it? Turn me into a nun? Fat chance. That would be a tall order, even for the Almighty. Did I regret the afternoon at the well? Nope. I really didn't. I had had a laugh, and that was all that I had wanted. Mission complete. And I was quite looking forward to the word getting around about what a slut I'd been. Hopefully Robin Merrow would hear about it, and then he'd know that I was more like him than I was like Jessica Crothers and the God squad.

But the following day in school came and went and I didn't see Robin Merrow. Nobody did. Nothing unusual there – he skipped school sometimes. But he wasn't in the next day either. By the following week Brains said that teachers were starting to look anxious when they called his name in class and nobody replied. Especially Ms Trainor. She was practically in tears by Wednesday. Everyone had noticed. Our little gathering in the well had been gossip for about twenty minutes, paling in comparison to the rumours going around about what had happened to Robin Merrow.

'I heard that that girl he was abusing at his last school showed up and they ran off together.'

'Bullshit! Where did you hear that?'

Brains shut his locker door and walked off without waiting to hear the eager Year 10's answer. The kid practically had to run after Brains, his long legs striding off down the corridor. I was having trouble keeping up myself.

'Nicky told me all about it. They used to be friends before he came here.'

'Utter bollocks,' said Brains, still not looking at the boy who was struggling to keep up. 'If that rumour was true you would have seen it on the local news by now. They're desperate for stories since the big shipwreck.'

'But that's just it!' said the boy.

'Just what?' Brains finally stopped and turned to face the boy who had to tilt his neck right back to see Brains's face.

'They're living on the ship. Him and that girl. Someone said—'

'Someone?' Brains rolled his eyes.

'*Someone* said they saw Robin Merrow swimming out to the wreck and—'

'Look.' Brains sighed. 'This gorgeous chick and I have a hot date at the library now.' He linked arms with me. 'So please do us both a favour and go sell your story to the local paper. I'm sure they'll give you a million quid for it.'

The boy shrugged his shoulders and walked off and Brains said, 'Shall we?' before ushering me through the library doors.

It was only one of the many rumours going around. There was a solid group of students who were convinced he was dead, so much so that they were already talking about him as if they'd been to his funeral weeks ago.

*'I can't believe he's gone! He was so nice!'* (He wasn't. Or rather, nobody knew if he was because he didn't exactly have a massive group of friends.)

*'He was so good looking, wasn't he?'* (Nobody really thought this. He wasn't ugly or anything, but he had a nose like one of those little squashed-up dogs. A pug, I think. He had cool hair, but hair's just hair, isn't it? Anyone can have hair; it just grows out of your head, doesn't it? It's not an actual achievement.)

*'Such a shame! What a waste!'*

Well firstly, way to write someone off when you don't actually know if they're dead. Like, maybe he had run off with a million-aire bloke and was living the life of Riley, sipping champagne and eating posh crisps, spread out on a fluffy rug in front of a massive telly in exchange for the odd blowjob. And secondly, how did they know it was a shame that he was gone? Nobody really knew him that well. Maybe he was a puppy-kicking Hitler-worshipping Justin Bieber fan. Maybe everyone should be praising the Lord that he'd popped off before he went on a rampage gunning down the entire school wearing nothing but the fluffy rug belonging to the pervy millionaire.

Urgh. People are so full of it. One thing was certain – nobody really knew where Robin Merrow was.

By the following week the police were in the school asking questions, but it was pointless. Robin didn't have any friends – only fascinated admirers who were only too glad to share their stories of how weird they thought he was. Someone must have blabbed their suspicions about Ms Trainor too because Jessica saw her coming out of the head's office with red eyes and heading straight to the staff loos.

I felt slightly guilty about loving the drama of it all, but life was so boring. After-school activities were now severely restricted, and Jacky and Dawn were taking it in turns to phone Jessica to make sure I had been with her after school if I hadn't appeared at their house straight away. Another day in the coffee shop with the God Squad and I was starting to lose the will to live.

'I think it's terrible that everyone's only talking about Robin Merrow this week. What about the shipwreck?' said Martha, sipping her Frappuccino.

'What about it?' I said. 'It's still there. All the rich Americans have gone home. What else is there to say about it?'

Martha looked slightly hurt. She was OK really. They all were. I'd just rather have been at the well, or up on top of my cliff, than sitting here listening to them.

'Cariad's right,' said Jessica. 'It will take them ages to deal with the ship, and everyone's safe now. We can't say the same for Robin Merrow, can we? What's wrong, Cariad?'

Oops. Had I rolled my eyes accidentally? Everyone was looking at me now. I took a gulp of hot tea and burnt my mouth. Ow!

'Sorry. I didn't mean to be rude ... I just think ... Like, maybe he's OK? Maybe he just moved on and he isn't in any real danger?'

'Moved on?' said Alicia, almost spilling her coffee. 'He's seventeen. We don't just *move on* at seventeen.'

Some people do, I thought. But what was the point in trying to explain it? I shrugged. I didn't know why I had said it anyway. I was as interested in Robin Merrow's whereabouts as any of them. It was certainly more interesting than trying to get a bunch of five-year-olds to colour in a picture of the Last Supper.

Desperate as always to avoid awkwardness, Jessica shifted the topic slightly.

'I was going to wait until Youth Fellowship Bible Study to bring this up, because we're talking about witchcraft and spiritual warfare on Saturday, but have you heard what Johnny Douglas is planning for this weekend?'

Everyone's wide eyes were on Jessica. This was clearly going to be prime gossip. A waitress came over to collect used cups. She thanked us for helping her pile everything on the trays but we only helped her because we wanted her to go away so we could hear about Johnny Douglas and his witchcraft-related activities.

Johnny was a metal-head; a member of the school's very tiny group of heavy metal enthusiasts. He wore a black leather dog collar studded with spikes around his neck when he could get away with it, and he had his own band, Death Noise Asylum, which played terrible music with guitar solos that seemed to go on for hours. None of the metal-heads spoke to anyone else. They had their own handshakes and sometimes in class they'd all start laughing together and nobody knew why. Some people laughed at them, but it was easy to see why the Christians were afraid of them.

'Well,' beamed Jessica, loving being the centre of attention, 'apparently, Johnny's irresponsible parents got him a Ouija board for his birthday.'

The collective gasp was audible, and it almost made me laugh out loud. A Ouija board? Someone in one of my old primary schools had one of those. They'd tried to contact the spirit of Kurt Cobain and freaked themselves out when 'Smells Like Teen Spirit' suddenly started playing in the next room. But it was only their sister dicking around. Hahaha!

'Oh my God!' said Martha, both hands on her mug as if it was her anchor. 'He's seriously not wise!'

Everyone nodded.

'You haven't heard it all,' continued Jessica. 'He's having a little party on Saturday night and I heard that they're going to try to contact the spirits to see if Robin Merrow's dead or not.'

'What?' said Alicia. 'That's ... that's just awful! We have to pray against this!'

'I know. That's why I was going to wait until Saturday night to tell you.'

Jesus. Saturday night. I was going to have to be at a meeting where we'd all be sitting in a sincere circle praying to Jehovah to ruin a party that I'd really like to be at. I wondered if there was a way I could sneak off and get to the seance ...

'You're very quiet, Cariad,' said Jessica. 'I hope I haven't freaked you out.'

'No. You haven't freaked me out,' I said, drinking some more tea to stop my mouth from saying what I felt like saying.

'Well, good. Because spiritual warfare is serious. Demons are real, and we have to protect Johnny and our classmates, even if they're being idiots.'

'That's right,' said Martha, still wide-eyed. 'There's no telling what they might be opening up if they go ahead with this crazy plan!'

'I can't believe his parents are letting him do it in their home,' sniffed Alicia.

'Oh, it's not in their home,' said Jessica. 'I heard they're going up to the temple to have it in there. And they're going to have a black mass as well.'

'A black mass!' echoed Alicia in horror.

Gabble, gabble. On they went. It was probably a load of bollocks. Who knows where Jessica was getting her information from, anyway. The waitress was eyeing us as she turned over chairs and set them on the tops of empty tables. We were overstaying our welcome, but I guess when you're plotting to save souls you don't have to take notice of closing time.

Mussenden Temple. It wasn't far from my lookout spot, right on the edge of the cliff. I had read the plaque on its door a few times. It was an old building from the eighteenth century. A small dome that people sometimes used for weddings. Cool place for a black mass, I thought. Maybe Johnny wasn't such a twat after all. I wondered who else was going to the devil party. I wondered how I could get there. I had been good for ages. Days

36

and days. I was *so* bored. Bored of TV, bored of church. Bored of this café.

I scraped my chair back. 'I have to go, guys. Dawn and Jacky need me back early.'

They smiled sympathetically as I got up. To their credit none of them had been nasty or judgemental to my face about the well incident, although they had all heard the embellished details, no doubt. I was sure they were secretly praying for my soul, but I didn't care, as long as they didn't feel the need to talk to me about it. I had probably done them a favour, providing them with some extra juicy gossip for when the Robin Merrow rumours got tired. If anyone could exhaust a rumour, it was this lot.

'OK, Cariad,' said Jessica, getting up to give me a weak hug, 'we'll see you tomorrow, and at Youth Fellowship on Saturday night? I think we need to be prepared for this one. Satan clearly has a hold on some of our classmates.'

I nodded, unable to think of an unsarcastic response, and walked back to Dawn and Jacky's.

# Chapter 8

It was Saturday night and I was changing my clothes to go to Youth Fellowship. But I wasn't going to go to Youth Fellowship. I had had enough. I had to be myself. Being good was driving me nuts. Maybe if you'd spent your whole life in prayer meetings, or maybe if you believed all the God stuff, maybe then it would seem normal to go and sit in a circle on a Saturday night and read the Bible and talk to Jesus. But that was not my kind of normal. It was more like torture for me. Even just the sitting down bit was hard enough. For God's sake, at least walk around a bit, people! I just couldn't cope with another one, not when I knew there were other people out there having a good laugh.

So, I pulled on my jeans, my heaviest jumper and my black coat and I left the house while Dawn was in the loo so she couldn't tell me to have a nice time with the Christians. I had no plan beyond going to the temple for the black mass, and I knew there'd be hell to pay, excuse the pun, but I'd think about that later. *Yes, yes*, I knew it was a strategy that hadn't always worked very well in the past. I could hear Madge's voice reminding me that people who always went by the motto 'you only live once' might not live as long as people who occasionally thought about the future. But, give me strength, surely Jacky and Dawn would give me some leeway? They could hardly expect me to be the perfect foster child overnight – not given my history, right? I knew that's exactly what they were expecting, really, but it was worth the risk.

As I began to walk up the steep pathway towards my cliff I could already hear the water's constant dull roar. I love the sea in the dark. You can't see it, but it won't stop telling you about itself. Black, vast, like a monster waiting for people to fall off the cliff so it can swallow them. I wondered how many kids had done just that. I loved leaving the town behind – the lights in the houses, everyone doing normal, everyday things. I loved entering the forest as the dusk was falling; as you walked past trees and rocks you were leaving behind things you could just about see, and when you returned they'd be completely invisible.

I strode up the hill. Smiled to myself going past the well. I looked over to see shadows moving near it. I could hear muffled whispers. Good luck to them, I thought. I zipped up my coat and stuck the hood up. I climbed. It was vaguely dark at the top. I paused for a few moments at my spot and looked out towards the outline of the vast boat. No cops here now. It was a giant ghost ship, waiting to be exorcised.

Half a mile on and the wind was picking up. The waves grew louder and I could see a light from the direction of the temple. A pair of hands closed around my eyes and I jolted.

'Didn't know you were going to be here,' a voice said.

I jolted again. It was Stevie B.

'Don't scare me like that, you dick!'

'Sorreeeeee . . .'

I punched him on the shoulder.

'Owww! I *said* sorry!'

I laughed. 'That'll learn you.'

He rubbed his arm. I was glad to see him really.

'I haven't been invited to the . . . party, thing,' I said. 'They won't mind, will they?'

We walked on together. My boots began to squelch underfoot. Sheep poo.

'Nah, they'll not care. I'm only here 'cause there's nothing better to do.'

'Me too,' I said, thinking of the girls at Youth Fellowship. They'd be in full-on preach mode by now, probably praying for our souls already.

Stevie and I didn't say anything else as we walked to the temple. We had nothing in common really. Well, maybe we did – who knows? We'd never really spoken to one another that much. I knew we both liked beer. He must have read my mind because as we reached the temple he took two cans, one out of each pocket, and stuck one in my hand. I hesitated. There was no way I could get into the state I was in at the well again. Being out at a black mass was one thing, but getting pissed again . . . I didn't know if Dawn would forgive me doing it twice. I tried not to think of Jacky's sad eyes.

'Go on, take it. The world might end tonight.' Stevie winked, and I took the can.

'Thanks, man.'

'No worries. I can't go drinking alone, can I?'

The temple was bigger than I had expected. The ones who were already there had forced open the door of the big dome and as we approached we could see that there were loads of candles lighting the inside. It was beautiful really. A couple of kids gave us funny looks when we came in but most of them said nothing. Someone was playing gothy-sounding music from their phone, but I reckoned the atmosphere would have been spookier without it because every so often it would be interrupted by their ring tone.

There was a large chalked pentagram on the ground and at the centre of it there was a small table with the Ouija board on top. There must have been about thirty kids in total – the metal-heads (of course) and a few curious randomers – but nobody I recognised. They were standing around, whispering and drinking from cans. Some were smoking. Pretty cool place for a meet-up, I thought. A bit more sheltered than our well. Stevie B. must have been thinking the same thing because I felt his arm go around my waist. I moved away slightly, and he dropped it. I wasn't really in the mood tonight.

To be honest I couldn't stop thinking about Dawn and Jacky. I really did want to be here. I really did *not* want to be at the Youth Fellowship prayer Bible group thing. But I also didn't want to hurt them. It was all so exhausting, trying to think of what the right thing to do was. Should I be myself and hurt people? Or do I wreck my own head for eternity pretending to be what all the other people want me to be? What if I kept on being like this and ruined their nice happy life? Then again, I didn't ask for them to foster me – it was entirely their own decision, wasn't it? And they could always get rid of me, just like my parents, just like everyone. *Cari*, Madge would say, *You keep winding yourself up like this. It's not good for you . . .*

Stevie had wandered off to talk to someone and I was standing on my own, looking around for a distraction. Thankfully, the music soon stopped and a guy cleared his throat and began to talk. It took me a minute or two to figure out that it was Johnny Douglas. He had a black cloak on and his face had been painted white with dark circles around his eyes. He looked like an absolute melter.

'Attention, gathered souls!' he said, dramatically raising both arms. 'We are here to attempt to contact the spirit of one who may be departed!' A few sniggers went around the room and Johnny cleared his throat again. He wasn't going to give up the role of the Dark Lord easily. He swept his cloaked arm towards the Ouija board. 'Using the board, we shall call upon the spirits of the underworld to usher us into a meeting with Robin Merrow. Should they look kindly upon us, we shall ask Robin some questions, and finally resolve the mystery of his disappearance! After the seance, there will be a black mass where we can give thanks to our Lord, Satan, for the communion of the dead and the living.'

How long had he practised that speech? I caught Stevie's eye and he pulled a scary face and made the sign of the cross over himself. I thought I was going to burst out laughing. My phone rang a jangly alert tone, incongruous in the solemn room. Johnny glared at me, his eyes goggling out from the black make up. I mouthed 'sorry' and I could hear Stevie giggle as I looked to see who the text was from. Jessica. I didn't read it. I put my phone on silent and tried to concentrate.

Johnny made us stand inside the five-pointed star, around the little table, and he asked for volunteers to put their hand on the upturned glass that was sitting on the Ouija board. I stepped forward. Why not? It might be the only time I got to do it in my life because if Dawn and Jacky found out they'd probably lock me in the church for the rest of my earthly days. A couple of other people also put their fingers on the glass. Johnny blabbered some more nonsense about Satan. I wondered if he might like the break-time prayer meetings because if you replace 'Satan' with 'God' it sounded pretty much the same as the stuff Jessica and Martha came out with. He told us not to move the glass, to let it move by itself, and then he put his finger on it too and told the room that we must have complete silence so the spirits could hear us. I looked around to find Stevie. He was grinning from ear to ear.

'Good spirits, hear us!' Johnny began. 'Is there anyone willing to help us tonight?'

Silence. Nothing. We all looked at our fingers on the top of the glass. Then we all looked at Johnny. He said it again.

'Good spirits, hear us! Will you help us tonight?'

More silence. My finger was starting to itch. I wondered if it would be OK to scratch it.

And then the glass began to move.

I could feel the kids on either side of me tense up and I looked at Stevie and he wasn't grinning any more. The glass moved to the word YES.

'Oh, thank you, kind spirit!' said Johnny. Maybe it was him moving the glass, but he did sound very relieved. 'Can you put us in touch with Robin Merrow, good spirit? For it is he that we seek!'

Seriously. Where was he getting this Lord of the Rings language? I wanted to laugh but then the glass moved again. This time to NO.

There was more silence. I think Johnny wasn't sure what to do. By that stage I was certain that it wasn't him moving the glass. Must have been another of the kids. Probably not the girl opposite me who had started crying, though. I tried to catch her eye and give her a comforting look, but she was quietly freaking out. Maybe this wasn't such a great idea . . .

'Spirit! Do not leave us!' said Johnny. 'Give us a sign. Tell us where Robin Merrow is!'

The glass began to move almost immediately, this time towards the letters around the edge of the Ouija board. It felt like it took for ever to move as it spelt out:

B.O.T.T.

Bott? What the frig does that mean? Then it started again.

O.M.O.F.

This was just random letters. I started freaking out myself because if one of our group was the glass pusher then surely they wouldn't just spell out random shit like this? It started again.

S.E.A.

Sea. That was a word.

'This is bollocks,' said the kid next to me, breaking the silence. 'Gemma's shitting herself – we need to stop it.' Everyone looked at the crying kid. 'And it was a load of crap anyway – there was no message, it was just random words.'

Someone put their arm around Gemma who sobbed quietly into their jacket.

Wait. Put it all together. Bott-Om of . . .

Bottom of Sea.

I looked at Johnny. He'd realised too.

'It said, "Bottom of Sea",' he whispered to the group. He had dropped the Dracula act.

Everyone looked at him.

'You moved it!' said the kid who had spoken before. 'That's not funny, Johnny.'

'I didn't,' said Johnny quietly. 'I honestly didn't.'

I knew he hadn't as well. But maybe someone had. We didn't know. The tension from before was gone, replaced now with a different kind of awkwardness. I guessed that the black mass wasn't going to happen.

Stevie broke the stillness, passing round cans from the cool box at the side of the room. 'Come on, everyone. Let's have a drink and a laugh while we're here. It was just meant to be a bit of craic, wasn't it?'

A few took him up on the offer and opened their tins and slowly people began chatting and then someone put on some more upbeat music (heavy metal, but still, at least it wasn't as depressing). Good old Stevie B. I guess he wasn't as much of a twat as I once thought. I was walking over to talk to him when I heard something underneath the music. A kind of chanting.

The room settled as other people heard it too and soon we could make out the words, and it was then that I knew what was happening. It was the Youth Fellowship. Singing songs about Jesus. Outside the temple where we were meant to be having a black mass.

Oh. Shit.

I wanted to hide but there was nowhere to hide. The temple

was literally just one room and there were no cupboards in it, no tables to duck under. Nothing! Johnny started towards the door.

'Wait!' I squeaked. He turned around and I pulled him to the side.

'Johnny. It's Jessica and the Christian group. They can't find out I'm in here – my foster folks will flip. Please don't let them in!'

'No worries. I'm going to tell them to fuck off,' he said, storming towards the door again.

I hung as far back from the door as I could, hoping nobody would see me in the candlelight. As the door opened light shone in. They must have had torches. The whole room was silent as we listened.

'Fuck off!' Johnny shouted, true to his word. 'Just. FUCK OFF.'

The singers sang to the end of their chorus before Jessica's defiant voice rang out. 'We heard that you were performing the black arts in this building, and we have been praying for you. Jesus told us to come and order you to stop your Satan worship!'

Oh bloody hell. Jesus 'told' them to come? Stevie B. laughed out loud and I gave him a hard stare. He giggled and covered his mouth with one hand, putting his other around my waist. God loves a trier, I thought. This time I let him. It was comforting to have him there in a way. I knew I was in deep shit in so many ways if the Youth Fellowship saw me.

'Well,' said Johnny, clearly gobsmacked by Jessica's audacity, 'you'll be glad to know that the Satan-worshipping part of the evening is over, and all we're doing now is getting pissed and off our faces on dope. That OK with Jesus?'

'Not really!' said Jessica.

'Well what are you going to do about it? Tell the teacher?'

'We . . . we're going to stand out here and pray for you. Loudly. And if you'd like to, then you can join us.' She raised her voice. 'And that goes for anyone else in there!' she shouted. 'Join the Youth Fellowship! Jesus loves you! We meet at break times and on Sund—'

Johnny closed the door and instructed his metal-head friends to crank up the music, but it was only playing on someone's phone so it couldn't completely drown out the fervent prayers of the youth group. I could hear Jessica, Martha and the others loudly saying, 'We just ask you . . . ' and listing their fears for the sinners inside. If they knew one of those sinners was me . . . Stevie B. started kissing my neck and I shrugged him off.

'Come on, Cari. We always get on OK, don't we?' he moaned.

Suddenly, the girl who had been upset at the seance got up and ran full pelt to the door. She flung it open and ran down the steps shouting, 'I repent! I'm really sorry and I want to give my life to Jesus!' As the Youth Fellowship girls embraced her, Johnny ran to shut the door, but it was too late: Jessica was standing at the top of the steps looking in, and she was looking right at me, with a beer in my hand and Stevie B. stuck to me like a bloody leech. I dropped the can.

'Jess. Please . . . '

'I can't believe you!' she shrieked, as if I'd personally hurt her feelings by being there.

Who did she think she was, my mother? I almost laughed. Jessica was as far away from my mother as it was possible to be. I felt something hot and angry rising inside me and it made me want to slap her stupid perfect face, but in that moment there was a bright light from behind her and four large men with huge flashlights pushed past her into the room.

'It's a fucking RAID!' yelled Johnny, and a bunch of kids tried to push past the cops, but they were too big and the doorway was too small. Jessica was crying, and the cops were yelling for people to calm down and sit on the floor.

Eventually everyone did just that.

'Who's in charge here?' said Cop 1.

'Nobody say a word! You don't have to!' yelled Johnny.

Cop 1 rolled his eyes. 'This isn't Miami Vice Squad, son. We're just trying to figure out why the hell you lot are all here.'

'Pretty obvious, I think,' Cop 2 chipped in, inspecting the Ouija board. 'Bit of devil worship, is it?'

'That's not why *we're* here!' blubbed Jessica. 'WE came here to stop them!'

'That's right, we did!' said Martha, who had her arm around Jessica. 'Are you going to tell our parents? Because it's honestly true – we were trying to stop them, and Jessica's mum's a lawyer, and we're CHRISTIANS!'

Cop 2 sighed and shook his head. 'Stop crying. There's no need to be dramatic. We're going to take all your names and phone numbers, and then we'll call all your parents and get them to pick you up. And before they get here, I suggest you pick up all this crap off the floor, OK?'

Martha started crying too, even harder.

'It's OK, Martha,' said Jessica, who had steadied herself. 'Our parents will understand that it was the Lord's will, especially when we tell them that we won a soul for Christ this evening.'

Cop 2 raised an eyebrow and the newly converted girl beamed towards Jessica.

Maybe it was going to be OK for them, but it wouldn't be OK for me. I was done for. Not only sneaking out. Not only skipping church. Not only drinking. Not only getting caught with a boy. Not only attending a Satanist ritual. But getting caught by the Youth Fellowship? I didn't have a leg to stand on – they'd seen the whole thing, and everyone knew they weren't liars. They might have been pains in the ass but they weren't liars.

Cop 1 started writing down Stevie's details. He didn't seem too bothered. His folks pretty much let him do whatever he liked. Then Cop 2 came over and asked my name. I told him.

'Nice name,' he said.

I tried to smile to show that I was a nice person as well. But I couldn't.

'And, what were you doing here this evening?' the cop said without looking at my face.

'I . . .'

'She was here with us,' said Jessica, appearing at his shoulder.

'What? I . . .'

Jessica stared at me. 'She was here with us. The Youth Fellowship group. We were praying at the church and—'

'Yes, yes,' the cop said, 'I know. Jesus told youse all to come here.'

'That's right. Isn't it, Cariad?' said Jessica.

The cop looked up at me wearily. He just wanted to finish his shift. I wanted to leave as well.

'Yes, that's right. I'm here because of Jesus,' I mumbled.

'OK.' He dotted the end of his sentence, flipped his notebook shut and turned to the next victim.

'Jessica ...' I said, unsure how I was going to finish the sentence.

'Cariad, don't you get it?'

'Get what?'

She took my arm. 'We're your friends. The Youth Group. I know you're not used to praying and everything. But you have to stop acting like this. We forgive you, but one day you'll get into a lot more trouble than this. Jesus,' she said, 'is the answer.'

The concern was almost too much to bear. The trouble was, I *believed* that she cared. The parallel lines on her forehead. The straight mouth pleading with me to be good, to be like them. And part of me wished I could run into their arms like the girl who had freaked out earlier. But I wasn't like them. They had settled lives and boring parents who cared about them and didn't want to give them away. They knew that this time next year they'd be living with the same people they were living with now. Me? I liked the things that they were afraid of. I had been excited when the glass started to move. I liked the buzz of cold beer in my throat. I liked the thrill of a guy's mouth on my neck, even if I wasn't that into him, maybe especially if I wasn't that into him ... My whole life was about movement and looking for things. I liked the search, and I didn't know if I *wanted* the answer.

So I did what I always did. Nothing. I shrugged and let Jess lead me towards the door to wait for her parents. Jesus might not have saved me that night, but she had. As I passed the window I saw a face looking in. A pale face in the night, just for a second, with wet hair, a split second. I thought it was Robin Merrow. But it must have been a reflection of someone else.

# Chapter 9

Nobody's parents were exactly happy about the seance/prayer meeting, but as predicted the Youth Fellowship's report was widely believed and for this reason Dawn and Jacky weren't that bothered about it. Dawn raised an eyebrow when Jessica's mum told her that I had merely been assisting the cause for Christ, but Jacky believed her completely and Dawn really had no choice but to go along with it since doubting the word of Jessica Crothers would have made her more anxious than thinking that I was up to my usual tricks. Besides, since I'd been grounded I had been really good up until that point, so I suppose she felt like giving me the benefit of the doubt.

The curfew still stood, however. I asked Dawn how long it was going to last. She stopped stirring the pancake mix and turned around to look at me.

'It's not that I don't want to answer that question,' she said, wiping gloop from her hands on her apron. 'What worries me is why you're asking.'

She turned back to her wooden spoon and the glass bowl,

and that was all she said on the matter. I slunk off to the living room, threw myself on the sofa and started channel hopping. It was so unfair. I was allowed to ask when the grounding was going to stop, but I was only allowed to ask whenever I didn't want to ask any more? How was I meant to figure that one out? I guess I wasn't. I was just supposed to practise being good until it became second nature and I actually *became* good. But what if badness is in you, like part of your DNA? And what if you actually enjoy it?

The channel flipped from crappy kids' cartoons to a nature documentary where a mountain goat was making its way down the sheer face of a high cliff. No chance, I thought. It's dead. But I watched on, because you never know. Some things just aren't fair. If you're a kid whose parents want you, like Jessica, then you get to have parents whether you're good or bad. If you're a foster kid you don't, because they can send you back, and they do. The goat stumbled and slipped a few feet. I turned the channel back to the kids' show.

Jacky came in and sat down in his chair, shuffled his newspaper and opened it to the sports section at the back. So this was it; as far as I could imagine – nights with Dawn and Jacky in the living room watching quiz shows and having cups of tea. Jesus. *And him too*, I thought – I'd be hanging out with Jesus too. I just couldn't do it.

'Jacky?' I said.

He peered over his paper. 'Yes, love?'

Lovely, gentle Jacky. He was the kind of man who'd always believe you, even if he caught you with your hand in someone else's handbag. I might as well try the honest approach with him. If anyone would feel some sympathy for my plight it would be him.

'Do you think that I could, like, just for a short while, go out for a walk?'

'A walk?'

'Yeah. I mean, just round the road. To get some exercise.'

He shook the creases from his paper and took his eyes away from mine. 'I don't know about that, love. You'd have to ask the boss.'

Urgh. No point in that considering the conversation I'd just had with her. But I needed to get out. Even if it really was just for a walk.

'Jacky?'

'Yes, love?' He looked up from his paper again.

'How about if you came with me?'

'Me?'

'Yeah. No big deal like, just a walk. I'm gonna go mad in here if I don't get out. Er, no offence.'

Jacky smiled and folded up his paper. He heaved himself out of the chair and walked towards the kitchen.

'I'll see what she says,' he mumbled as he walked past.

And ten minutes later we were out in the drizzle, Jacky with his heavy coat on and a shopping list, me trailing the tartan shopping trolley behind me. But it was better than staying in.

# Chapter 10

The rain had cleared by the time we'd got round Tesco with Dawn's massive list of highly specific items ('Bread: Ormo white, medium slice, if not Ormo then any pan loaf but medium slice and light crust if poss') and Jacky and I began the walk back.

'You OK?' I asked Jacky.

'Yes, love. A bit slower than usual today. Think I might be coming down with something.' He beamed at me and linked my arm. That was just like him. He never complained about anything and if you noticed anything wrong he'd immediately try to do something to make you feel good – as if he'd inconvenienced you by making you worry about him. I'd never be good the way that Dawn and Jacky were good. It went beyond the religion thing – it was like they actually enjoyed being nice, like it was part of them.

'You're a bit quiet, love,' he said. 'How about you? Are you OK?'

'Yeah.'

We walked past the chippy and the smell of vinegar soaking into hot chips made my stomach gurgle. Jacky must have noticed it too.

'Let's have a chippy tea tonight, shall we?' he asked, his eyes twinkling like a little kid's. It made me want to cry how kind he was.

In the chippy queue I tried to make small talk with Jacky so that he wouldn't be worried about me being quiet, but it was too difficult, and I gave up. I really had nothing in common with him and Dawn. I guessed they wouldn't want to know about the black mass or what I really thought about the Youth Fellowship. So, we stood in silence and I was relieved when the couple in front of us started having an interesting conversation that I could eavesdrop on.

'You know that child, Merrow, has been missing for quite a few days now,' the woman was saying to her partner. The two of them were middle-aged. Their raincoats were dripping wet and the woman's short curly hair was starting to frizz up in the heat of the chippy.

'Aye, I know. Frankie next door said he heard people talking about seeing him swimming out to the cruiser. Maybe he's living on it.'

The woman tutted. 'People will believe any nonsense. He couldn't make it out to that thing, not in the weather we've had lately. Sure, the police would have found him by now if that's what he was at.'

'Ach, I don't know,' said the man, not wanting to let the theory go. 'Who knows what kids will be up to?'

I wondered if it could be true. Maybe I had seen him that night at the temple after all. But why would anyone want to live on a wrecked cruise ship? As Jacky took our turn in the queue I found myself excited by the idea of having some gossip to bring to the Youth Fellowship prayer group. I tried to shake it off immediately. Was I actually becoming one of them? Urgh.

We left the chippy and walked out into the dull evening. A fifteen-minute walk back to Dawn and Jacky's. By the time we got there the chips would be still warm but only just. We passed the post office and the school with its rusty blue gates. I could see something on the big tree at the entrance to the forest. I couldn't take my eyes off it. It was an unfamiliar dark shape. Not the usual poster advertising someone's birthday or an event at the town hall. A kind of three-dimensional shadow.

'What the hell is that?'

Jacky looked at me, rather than the thing I was pointing at.

'Sorry. I mean, what *on earth* is . . . Jacky . . . what *is* that thing?'

It was nailed to the tree. It hadn't been there the last time I'd gone up into the forest and we'd missed it when we passed the tree earlier as it was on the side of the trunk facing us now. Jacky squinted at it and moved closer as I took a step back.

It looked like a little dried-up person. A head, a body, two legs. But the head came to a point and it had wings, and a tail. The wide mouth grinned like a clown in a horror story, and two large almond-shaped eyes looked out of its shrunken little face. For a second the Youth Fellowship flashed across my mind again: demons; angels. Jacky touched one of its little wings and I shrieked a bit. I hadn't meant to and he laughed, turning his face to mine.

'It's OK, Cari love. It's not alive. Not any more, anyway.'

What the hell? It not being alive wasn't the thing that was freaking me out. It looked *real*. A real alien. Or something.

'What do you mean "Not any more"?' I said.

The air of calm curiosity as he browsed the little body was too much to bear. It was like he'd met a long-lost friend or something. Finally he said, 'It's a Jenny Haniver, I think.'

'A what?'

'A Jenny Haniver. I haven't seen one since I was a boy.' He was grinning as if the tiny demon had returned some comforting memory.

'What the frig's that?'

His smile dropped slightly.

'Sorry,' I said, 'I mean, what's a Jenny Hannver?'

'Han-*i*-ver. Essentially, it's a dried skate.'

I had seen a skate. At the aquarium at Portaferry. It was on a school trip a few years ago. You could put your hand in the tank and feel it as it swam past. Jonty McGann tried to grab it by the tail and it went mental and scared the shit out of him. Funniest thing ever. And he got banned from the aquarium. Brilliant. But apart from its size this thing looked nothing like a skate.

'It's been altered,' said Jacky, seeing my confusion. 'They dry them, then they sort of shape them with knives and ...'

'Urgh. That's awful!'

'It is a bit horrible, I suppose. Fascinating, though.'

'Why would anyone even do that?' I asked him.

And why would they stick it up on a tree? People are bloody weird. I took a couple of pictures on my phone, but I didn't think I'd keep them for long.

'Well,' said Jacky, gazing on the freaky little alien, 'I reckon it's got to do with that shipwreck.'

'The cruiser?'

'Yes. Listen, let's walk on, the chips'll be getting cold. I'll tell you about it on the way home.'

So, we walked on and as we went Jacky sparkled with the story he was telling me. I swear he was walking faster too. He was obviously really pleased to have come across the Jenny Haniver and, I have to be honest, I loved listening to him talking about it.

He told me that years ago, when he was a kid, there were stories about mythical creatures, 'way out in the country,' he said, pointing off into the distance, as if *the country* was another planet and not just a couple of miles up the road. 'The children out there had banshees and they'd wail in the night. You'd hear stories of people who heard them. But out here it was mermaids.'

'Mermaids? Like Ariel from Disney?'

He rolled his eyes as if I knew nothing. 'Ariel from Disney isn't from Disney,' he said. 'They took that story from Hans Christian Andersen.'

'It's a Christian story?'

'No! Hans Christian Andersen. That's his name!'

'OK, don't laugh. I've never heard of him.'

'Sorry, sorry.' Jacky was trying not to crack up and I was trying not to scowl like a baby. I hated being laughed at.

'Anyway. No. Not mermaids like in Disney. These mermaids weren't pretty girls with flowing red hair and big blue eyes. These ones had scaly skin and sharp teeth. And they were murderers.'

He wasn't smiling any more.

'You sound like you believe all that stuff, Jacky,' I said.

He ignored me and went on. 'It was said that the mermaids would sit out on the rocks at night and sing the sweetest song you ever heard. An irresistible song which drew sailors in. They'd be helpless, you see, the sailors. They had to follow the tune.'

'Like the Pied Piper?'

'Sort of. I suppose so. But in the sea.'

'Obviously.'

'Anyway.' He blinked twice, trying to get back into the flow of his story. 'That's how shipwrecks happen, they say. The sailors would follow the deadly beautiful music of the mermaids and as they drew close the demon would duck under the waves and leave the ships crashing into the rocks in the dead of night.'

He said it all so matter-of-factly that I swore he was believing his own nutso story. Then again, he believed in God too. And he'd said 'demon' instead of 'mermaid', and they all legit believed in demons.

We were getting closer to the house now and I was starting to wonder why I was the one who found the dried skate spooky when I would never take a crazy mermaid story seriously, not for a second.

'So . . . were many boats shipwrecked then?'

'No. Not one.'

God. How could people be such idiots? I liked Jacky but surely he could see that a wild story like that would need a *tiny* bit of evidence before people started believing it? But not Jacky.

'No shipwrecks mean no mermaids,' I said.

He was smiling again. 'The Jenny Hanivers kept the mermaids away.'

I looked at him. Come. On. Did he seriously believe this? 'You can't be serious, Jacky?'

'That thing we found on the tree there. I used to see them all the time when I was wee. Every so often they'd stick one up in the town to scare away the mermaids you see, so's the mermaids would get to know what the people would do if they ever caught one.'

'Like a mermaidy scarecrow?'

'Exactly.'

'A mer-crow!' I giggled. 'Wouldn't it be better to have a mer-crow stuck in the sea, though? Like, how did the mermaids find out about them – did they grow legs and walk around the town at night or something?'

Jacky giggled too. 'Word gets around. We can laugh about it,' he said, 'but we never had a shipwreck. And that's a dangerous bit of water.'

'So,' I said, opening the garden gate, 'what happened to all of them?'

'What, sailors?'

'No. The mermaids and the banshees. Where'd they all go?'

'Oh they're still around,' said Jacky calmly. 'I expect that's why our little Jenny Haniver has popped up again. We took our eye off the ball and *bam*! Big shipwreck.'

'You can't seriously believe that!'

We were in the living room now.

Dawn saw the bag of chips. 'I've made a stew,' she said. 'But it'll keep till tomorrow. Believe in what?'

She began setting out knives and forks on the coffee table. A treat – dinner in front of the telly.

'Believe in mermaids, and banshees,' I said.

Dawn rolled her eyes. 'He's not the only one in this wee town who does.'

'Well . . . where'd they all go then? How come nobody hears a banshee screaming these days?'

Jacky reached out and tapped his finger against the dangling ear buds around my neck. 'Those things,' he said. 'And that thing.' He pointed to the telly. 'And all of your *social media* and video games. It's noise, noise, noise all the time now.' He waved his hands. 'Nobody pays attention to what's around them any more.'

We sat down to eat and the chips were still a bit warm and the vinegar had soaked through the paper and it made the living room smell warm and delicious, and I understood then, how finding a dried-up alien nailed to a tree might have made Jacky pleased, and I knew that the horrific thing that was meant to keep the monsters away would draw me back. Maybe this place wasn't as boring as I'd thought.

# Chapter 11

Whatever it was about that night, I found it easier to behave myself after that. Well, for a few days, anyway. Jacky and Dawn noticed it too. Not that I was doing anything differently really. When you're a prisoner there's very little you can get up to, even if you want to misbehave. I just found it easier, that's all.

'Something's different with you,' cooed Dawn as we did the dishes, her washing, me drying. No dishwasher, of course. It had really bugged me when I'd first arrived here – everything having to be washed by hand. Big pans having to be soaked overnight. If I ever have a house and it doesn't have a dishwasher, I thought, I'll just use paper plates and get takeaway food. But I got used to doing the dishes with Jacky and Dawn. They didn't talk too much, and you could just kind of zone out, and somehow it was nice, slowly making all the dirty things clean. Not that I was going to tell Dawn that I enjoyed it. She had me doing enough around the house as it was.

'What do you mean, different?' I said. Even though I knew what she meant.

'You seem a bit more, I don't know, content maybe?'

I nodded. It was true. Dawn smiled to herself. It wasn't as if I wasn't bored or didn't want to go out. I guess I'd just given in a bit since the night of the black mass. I'd had a lucky escape and I felt grateful to Jessica for helping me. Being good was dull, but it was OK. Evenings watching telly with Jacky. Back from school on time. Doing my homework and listening to a bit of music. Bed on time. Youth Fellowship on a Saturday night. The kids from Belfast would've pissed themselves laughing if they could see me now.

But it really was OK.

I was going through the motions. My grades were improving. The Youth Fellowship was boring me stupid with their tame gossip about who might be flirting with who. I literally fell asleep in one of their prayer meetings. Stevie B. asked me out to the well a few times, but he gave up after a while. I missed it a bit, but I had a feeling he'd still be up for it if I decided to see him again. I wasn't sure I would, though, because I didn't miss it all that much. I found myself surprised by how much 'boring' I could put up with. And yet ...

'What are you looking at?'

I stuck my phone in my pocket and snapped my head up to meet Ms Trainor's.

'Nothing! I mean ... I'm looking at my phone ... but it's OK, isn't it? We were packing up?'

She nodded. She'd been a lot more chilled lately. Happier. I wondered if she was a bit relieved that Robin Merrow hadn't come back.

'Don't worry,' she said. 'It's fine. I was just interested. You looked engrossed, whatever it was.'

I felt my face burn. I knew the whole class was looking at me. 'It's nothing. Just a text.'

Yeah right. Who sent me texts? Jessica and the others would see through that right away.

Ms Trainor smiled again, and the bell rang, and everyone started piling out.

I had been looking at the Jenny Haniver. Despite how things had changed lately there were two things I hadn't been able to shake off. Two things I thought about every day, sometimes several times a day.

One was the Jenny Haniver. It's little leathery demon body stuck up on that tree to keep the mermaids away.

And the other thing was Robin Merrow.

A person can change their life. Really change it. Act differently, look differently, talk differently. But changing your thoughts? That's a different matter. And it was my thoughts that were going to send me back to the cliffs. Back to danger. Like those mermaids singing their insane song. I couldn't resist them.

# Chapter 12

'Jacky?'

It was a quiet Saturday evening, just getting close to dusk. Not much traffic. The TV was burbling away as usual – some family show with a zany presenter making a middle-aged dad do a stupid dance in front of a laughing audience. The camera panned from the dad's awkward Beyoncé moves to the screeching audience members who couldn't control their hilarity, tears rolling down their cheeks.

Jacky was ignoring them, his face buried in his big paper. He liked the really large papers. He had a special way of folding them so that he could do the crossword and drink his tea at the same time.

I scrolled through my social media apps. Selfie. Selfie. Meme. Selfie. Someone's rant about the guy who dumped them. Meme. Selfie.

I googled 'Jenny Haniver'. There were a couple of pictures. One of them looked a bit like our Jenny Haniver on the tree. Someone had written a blog about them: 'In times gone by people might have thought that the Jenny Haniver was an angel, or even a devil or a demon.'

I thought back to Jessica's words: *Demons are real*. I wondered what she'd think of the Jenny Haniver.

I put my phone in my pocket.

'Jacky?' I said again, wondering if he'd nodded off beneath the tent of newsprint.

'Sorry. Yes, love?' Jacky flipped the top of his paper back so that he could see me, and he took off his glasses.

There was no harm in asking, I thought. They could only say no, and I'd be fine if they did. All the same, I asked Jacky first rather than Dawn, because he was a softer touch. Choose your words carefully, Cariad.

'Would it be OK if I . . . went out for a walk?'

'Good idea, love,' he said, folding his paper. 'I could do with a stretch of the auld legs myself.' He scanned the room, probably for his shoes.

'I . . . ' How could I put this? 'I sort of meant, could I go out by myself? Just for a walk, like.'

Jacky's face dropped slightly. 'Now?' he asked.

'Well, yes.'

'Hmmm. Let's see what Dawn says. You sit here for a second.'

He got up and shuffled into the kitchen. This was a good sign, I thought. He didn't say no. I wanted to go back and see if the Jenny Haniver was still there. I wasn't even sure why, I just wanted to look at it again in real life.

Jacky came back in with Dawn beside him, tea towel still in hand. She looked serious, not angry. Also a good sign.

'You want to go out?' she said. 'Just for a walk?'

'Yes, please,' I said.

Looking up at them like that – me on the sofa, them standing in front of me – it made me feel like a small child.

'Well,' said Dawn. 'This is *only* because you've been so good lately . . . '

My face broke into a stupid little-kid grin. I couldn't help it. I was getting out!

'I mean it,' Dawn continued. 'It's only because of your good behaviour, and we are trusting you not to get into any trouble. And . . . '

'Yes. Anything. Anything at all. I will totally behave.'

'And it's just for an hour. OK?'

'One hour. To begin with.'

I was pushing my luck, but what the hell.

'One hour. And *no* promises that it will increase. You have to understand that.'

'Yes. No probs! Thank you so much!'

I was on my feet and hugging them and I guess Dawn couldn't help herself either because I could feel her grinning against my cheek.

'It's one hour, from now,' she added as I broke the hug, 'so you'd better get moving. I want you back before dark. You have Youth Fellowship tonight.'

'Back before dark,' I repeated.

'Back in ONE HOUR,' chorused Dawn and Jacky together. The tone was gently humorous, but I knew they were serious underneath it.

And that was it. I was free for one hour. I only had one plan – one place to visit.

# Chapter 13

It was still there. I could see it as I approached. A grotesque little leg dangling from the side of the tree. I took a breath. I wasn't even sure why I had come, but I felt the need to continue. I sped up my pace.

It was undamaged by the days and untouched by the local kids or birds or whatever else might dare to disturb such a weird thing. Its horrible mouth grinned out a warning to mermaids and residents alike. Sometimes when I looked at the picture on my phone it seemed like a lonely figure – a crucified freak, at the mercy of whoever it was who had the hammer and nails. But now I imagined its little form with more malevolence, more control. Staring out at the town in defiance, daring people to come near.

*What are you?* I thought. *Who put you there? Why the hell do I care?*

My phone buzzed in my pocket. A text from Stevie B.

How comes you like that weird alien thing more than you like me?

I turned around and there he was, across the road. He shrugged his shoulders exaggeratedly, his palms raised. It was sweet, and I smiled, feeling the weight of the Jenny Haniver leave as he ran across the road.

'I can't hang out with you,' I told him. 'I've told Dawn I'm just going out for a walk.'

'That's cool. I can walk too.'

I started walking the long way back, Stevie beside me.

'I'm sorry I haven't been in touch,' I said, not looking at him.

'Temple too much for you?' I could hear the smile in his voice.

'No,' I said. 'But I was lucky that Dawn and Jacky didn't find out what I'd been doing there. I dunno. I'm just keeping things quiet for a bit I suppose.'

'The Hallelujah Chorus saved you then. Are you going Holy Roller on me?'

He nudged me, and I laughed.

'Fuck off!'

He laughed too. It was good to feel light again – to have a laugh over stupid stuff. I had missed it. Jesus, had I missed *him*? I looked at him then – hands stuffed in his bomber-jacket pockets, looking at the pavement. He was OK. And I *had* missed the craic. And I was glad he was here now. But I didn't know if I had really missed him in any other way.

We walked past the shops, stopping to get a drink, and then on back to the edge of the estate. Dawn and Jacky's was just a few doors away.

'You'd better leave me off here,' I said. 'I don't want them to think I've been ...'

'... off with some sexy stud?' he offered.

'Aye, whatever!'

We both laughed again.

'It was nice to see you, though,' I said.

'You too. Come up to the well tomorrow?'

'Ah ... I don't know ... I have to go to church ... '

'Praise be!' he said, waving his hands above his head.

'Heh. Not my favourite pastime, believe me.'

'Sure, come to the well then! Brains and Muff will be there too.'

'See what I can do,' I said, walking towards the house.

And that's how I found myself back at the well the next day. I wasn't going to bother going. I hadn't intended to. I really was trying to be good. But church was such a joy-killer. If it wasn't enough that they had to make those wooden seats so bum-numbingly uncomfortable, you had to sit there and listen to the Bible, and then you had to stand for the hymns with weird tunes in a key that nobody could sing in, and then you sat back down for a bit, and then it was 'stand for the prayers' and then sit back down again for the sermon. Bloody hell. It was a full-on workout.

The sermon would be something relating to the Bible verses, usually with a really crap 'real life' story tagged on – something from the news, or something which was obviously totally made up. They all had the same message: be good or else. But none of them ever told you *how* to be good. That's the thing I couldn't understand about it. They could tell you that smoking blow was a bad thing because God said so, in the Bible, or whatever. But they couldn't stop you sitting there wishing you had a spliff to make the time pass more quickly. Maybe if they didn't want people to do drugs they should've made their stories more interesting. Heh.

'Are not two sparrows sold for a penny?' read Pastor Ky from the giant Bible on his lectern. 'Yet not one of them will fall to the ground outside your Father's care. And even the very hairs of your head are all numbered. So don't be afraid; you are worth more than many sparrows.'

He was really called Pastor Kyle but he insisted that the young people called him *Pastor Ky*. Urgh. I wished God cared about my brain melting in this place more than he cared about how many hairs Pastor Ky had on his head.

On the walk back from church I had asked Dawn if I could walk over to the shop to get a drink. I'd only be twenty minutes behind her and Jacky, I had said. It was pushing my luck, but she agreed. I waited until she was out of sight and then ducked over to the entrance to the forest, passing the Jenny Haniver, and then up the hill towards the well. It felt a bit safer to be sneaking off to the well in the morning light, as if the daytime would remind me to behave. And Stevie B. was there waiting for me. I wondered how long he had waited.

We made ourselves as comfortable as you could on the dry dirt floor of the pit. Stevie had brought a blanket which helped to keep us warm, but it didn't make things much more comfortable really. I reminded myself that this really had to be quick. And as Stevie B. cracked open a can I reminded myself that under no circumstances could this turn into a drinking sesh. But man, that beer tasted nice on his mouth as I kissed him. Maybe just a sip, then. The church ones were allowed a slug of wine on a Sunday morning, so they couldn't complain that much, could they?

Half an hour later and a cough from above stopped us. I pulled down my T-shirt and turned to see who it was, my heart pounding. It was only Brains and Muff.

'Started without us?' Brains mused. His long legs made it awkward for him to get into the pit and he slid down on his bum part of the way.

'Sometimes it's nice to have a bit of privacy,' said Stevie, throwing him a can, and clearly not even slightly bothered about privacy as he hadn't put his shirt back on.

'Guys, sorry, but I have to go,' I said, getting up and trying to fix my hair.

'Awwwwwk. Don't be shy, it's only us!' Muff said.

I rolled my eyes. 'As if. Naw, if Dawn and Jacky suspect I was doing anything more interesting than reading the Bible I'll be grounded for the rest of eternity.'

'Well, givus a goodbye kiss then,' said Stevie, pulling me back down on top of him. He squeezed me against him tightly and I could tell he wanted more.

'We'll do it again some time,' I said, prising his hands off my waist.

He groaned and let me go.

'Hey,' he called as I climbed up the side of the pit. I turned around and gripped the grass to stop myself sliding down again. 'Halloween night.'

'What about it?'

'There's a big fireworks display in the town.'

'Yeah I know. The Jesus fandom's going. Beam me up . . .'

'Well, we're going too. Except we're going to camp out at the top of the forest. You coming?'

'Heh. Yeah – Dawn and Jacky will totally go for that idea.'

'Don't tell them. Say you're hanging with Jessica.'

'Nah, they all talk to each other in church. There's no way I'd get away with it. Sorry, Stevie, you'll just have to cuddle up to Brains and Muff.'

'Oooh, there's a first time for everything, Stevie!' cooed Brains. Muff thwacked him on the arm and everyone laughed.

'Well, think about it!' Stevie yelled to me as I left the pit. I could hear the sound of cans cracking open as I walked away.

# Chapter 14

The hall phone rang and everyone jumped. Nobody ever phoned me on a landline phone, and nobody ever phoned Dawn and Jacky full stop. If they needed to talk to someone they'd see them at church or in the bakery queue. But it was for Dawn. I started listening to her half of the conversation to see if I could guess what it was about.

I prayed it wasn't Madge checking up on me. She had visited last week to make sure everything was OK. Dawn and Jacky hadn't mentioned the well and the drinking. Not in front of me, anyway. I guessed that Madge had been satisfied that everything was OK because she'd smiled and said she'd call again in a month. But you never knew when she'd phone or call. She was nice but social workers are like ninjas – they can just show up or call out of the blue. I swear this was half the reason Dawn was so obsessed with cleaning and gardening all the time. Like she thought Madge might suddenly pop up from behind a hedge to judge her flowerbeds. Madge wasn't like that, though. She'd seen a lot of shit, I reckon. It would take more than the odd dandelion or a line of dust along the TV set to freak her out. Every time I spoke to her she'd end the conversation the same way:

'And you know where I am if you need me.'

And I'd say, 'Yep. In the pub with a G&T, slice of lime and not too much ice.'

And she'd laugh and say, 'But seriously. Call me any time, Cari.'

We could have a laugh, but it always had to end on a serious note, which reminded me that although Madge was nice, she was a social worker, not my best friend. She was good at her job, but it *was* her job. I liked to remind myself about it, because Madge basically knew more about me than anybody else, and that meant she had more power than anybody else. Not that I didn't trust her – she usually took my side – but I knew she didn't see me as an equal or anything like that.

Dawn smiled as she listened to whoever it was on the phone. 'Oooh yes, I'm sure that would be lovely!' she cooed. It wasn't Madge then. That was her talking-to-church-people voice. Bless. Maybe she'd been invited to a social event.

'Yes. Yes. I'll tell her now. Anything she needs to bring?'

Uh-oh. I did *not* like the sound of this.

'Hee hee! That's a lovely idea. Cariad will have such fun!'

Oh shit.

'OK. Yes, no problem. We'll see you then. And thank you, we're so pleased that Cariad is friends with Jessica.'

Holy crap. What now? Another prayer meeting? Please say it won't involve anything more holy than that.

'That was Jessica's mum!' trilled Dawn, entering the living room with a big grin on her face.

75

'So I heard.'

'Oh, don't look so worried! Jessica's a lovely girl. I know you two have different ... styles ... but you like her, don't you?'

Dawn was sitting perched on the arm of the sofa. Her face was willing me to be pleased. I didn't even know what I'd been invited to yet. Well, I say 'invited' but it was clearly a done deal, whatever it was. Nevertheless, I forced a smile. Play it cool, Cari. Everything is possible if you're in control.

'Yes, she's OK,' I said. 'So ... what's the craic then? Is she having a prayer meeting or something?'

Dawn giggled. 'Not everything has to be about church, you know!' she said. 'You can have teenage fun sometimes too!'

Oh, I really did not like where this was going. It was one thing hanging out with the Youth Fellowship and drinking coffee and gossiping about who they fancied now. But organised fun? This sounded serious.

'A party?'

'Even better!' said Dawn. 'A sleepover party!'

Kill me now. A Christian sleepover party. What are we going to do – get high on Jesus and stay awake all night reciting scripture?

'Yes! A Hallelujah party!'

'A what?'

*What the hell?* I thought.

'A Hallelujah party! They used to have them when I was a girl. It's on Halloween night. Instead of celebrating devils and frightening small children with masks and video nasties, you can have fun dressing as ... something else ... and have the fun without the horror!'

'What's a video nasty?' I said. *It sounds so completely awesome*, I didn't say.

'You know. One of those films about the devil and torture and things,' she replied.

Oh God. Literally: *God*. Did he have to ruin everything all the time? Flip sake. According to Pastor Ky, Jesus turned water into wine. And not crap wine either – good stuff. Even Jesus got to go to good parties! Dawn's smile had turned from gleeful to hopeful. I was obviously finding it hard to play it cool. *Come on, Cari, you can do this.*

'Thanks, Dawn,' I said. 'I'm sure the party will be fun.' Rictus grin. I was doing my best. *Hallelujah party?* Jesus Christ.

Dawn sat herself beside me on the sofa and put a hand on my arm. 'It *will* be fun,' she said firmly. It was almost like a command.

'Yes,' I said, still grinning insanely. And I'd make sure it was fun. Before Dawn had stood up and left for the kitchen I had started to make a plan. I had no idea how I was going to execute it, but I knew one thing for sure – I wasn't going to be living it up with Jesus at Jessica's house all night on Halloween.

I started working through the list of Positive Things About This Shitty Situation – a technique Madge had taught me to stop me from being so impulsive when I was reacting to bad news. (Imagine having to be taught a technique for how not to get angry at your shitty life? As if you should have to expect shitty things to happen 24/7. Huh!) Anyway. You were meant to write them down, but I couldn't risk Dawn finding them, so I just did it in my head:

*Positive Thing About This Shitty Situation #1* – I was going to be out all night, with Dawn and Jacky's permission;

*Positive Thing About This Shitty Situation #2 – . . .*

Hmmmm . . . this was going to be tricky . . . The obvious plan would be to sneak away to camp out with the guys. But how on earth could I pull that off? My phone buzzed. A text, from Jessica.

> So excited you're coming to the party! Don't be freaked out by the 'Hallelujah' thing. That's just what Mum's calling it. We'll have a good laugh. Martha might even be able to sneak us a few West Coast Coolers from her house!

I didn't know what 'West Coast Coolers' were but they sounded crap. Some kind of fake alcohol that Jessica and her friends would get fake-drunk on in about twenty seconds flat, I reckoned. I texted her back.

> Great! Looking forward to it. X

In my head it sounded sarcastic but on the text message it looked legit. The phone buzzed again.

> Yay! And we'll go and see the fireworks too so bring your coat.

OK, so: *Positive Thing About This Shitty Situation #2* – We'd be at the fireworks. Definitely potential for sneaking off for a short time at least! I texted her back:

> Great. Or should I say 'Hallelujah!' LOL

Buzz!

**LOL! Praise the Lord!**

Heh. Jessica wasn't all bad. She could take a joke sometimes. But I knew that her Halloween sleepover was going to be more 'Hallelujah' than 'Hellraising'. Still, at least I might be able to get away for a while.

# Chapter 15

Halloween. It was six p.m. and I was getting ready to go to Jessica's. Well, trying to. My phone kept beeping.

> Stevie B: **You coming out tonight or what? Big bag of cans. We're putting up the tent now, just up the hill a bit from the pit. Yeeeeooooooooo!**

> Brains: **Hope you're coming later on. Stevie will be lonely without you 😢 I'm bringing something special from the booze emporium chez la Brains**

> Jessica: **Squee! Can't wait for tonight! Are you wearing a costume?**

No, I'm not wearing a bloody costume, Jessica. What am I, eight years old? Besides, what costume could possibly pass the 'Hallelujah' test of non-video-nasty purity? A black cat? Too sexy, and a bit too witchy. How about just wearing a bed sheet and going as the Holy Spirit? Heh.

I ignored the texts for now and continued packing my bag. Torch. Chocolate. Mints (so I could get a drink and a smoke with the guys before returning to the Youth Fellowship). Money ... not much ... let's see ... five, six ... six pounds fifty. A half-empty plastic Coke bottle (so I could sneak some of Brains's parents' vodka back to the Hallelujah party to get me through the rest of the night). Something to wear in bed ... AC/DC T-shirt and black shorts ... it would be a talking point for the Christians at least.

A couple of hours later I was standing in the hall of the Crothers's pristine house. Jessica's room was actually a lot cooler than I had imagined. I had pictured pale pinks and blues, a My Little Pony aesthetic. Instead she had band posters, red and black decor and a guitar in the corner. Everything extremely neat of course – even the posters were remarkably straight and positioned at an equal distance one from the other. And, in my humble opinion, there were more Bibles on the shelf than was respectable for a teenager: a youth study Bible, a pink 'women's edition' Bible (Eh? What did they do, write God as a woman? I might check that out later ... ) and a huge black leather Bible that looked like it might belong to a Victorian vampire hunter or something. Anyway, I felt more relaxed in her room than I thought I would. She even liked some of the same bands as me.

There were four of us altogether. Jessica and Martha were both dressed as primary school angels, complete with tinsel and wire halos and white dresses made out of sheets under which they were wearing their jeans. They said it was ironic: primary school Christmas play angels at Halloween.

They were still talking about the night of the Ouija board seance and I was sure they thought of it as a victory – a successfully spoiled evening (even if the cops were the ones who really put a dampener on it) and a new convert for the Lord. The new convert was Gemma Bailey – Muff's younger sister, as it turned out – and she was here for the sleepover as well. She was dressed as a black cat and Jessica's mum raised an eyebrow when she saw it. I knew it wouldn't have been safe.

We weren't there for long. Just time to dump our stuff and get a look around the nice middle-class, semi-detached holy house. I was slightly disappointed at the lack of 'holy' items, actually. At one of the foster homes I'd been in, the two-week, puke-spectacular stint, there was a crucifix in almost every room (they weren't in favour of Jesus watching you having a poo, so there wasn't one in the bathroom). But Jessica's parents only had a rubbish embroidered picture in a frame by the coat stand which said 'Seven Days Without Prayer Makes One Weak', and that was all. Their house looked otherwise normal.

I don't know why I expected it to look like a holy grotto or something. It wasn't like Dawn and Jacky went in for religious decoration. I suppose that Jessica's family always seemed really concerned with how things looked to other people. They went out of their way on Sundays to greet newcomers and they sang the hymns loudly and with their eyes closed, sometimes with their hands raised.

Everything was so neat and tidy in their house. Newspapers folded and stacked in a special basket next to the spotless sofa. A kitchen that looked like they'd just installed it yesterday. A beige carpet on the landing that your shoes sank right into. The house that birthed the immaculate Jessica. It made me think of how Jesus was so holy his parents didn't even have to have sex to get him. I wondered if Jessica's folks ever did it. Urgh.

'What's wrong with you?' asked Jessica.

'Nothing!' I said, a little too quickly. I was glad she'd shaken me out of the horrifying image.

'Come on then, let's get out of here!' Jessica ushered me and the others out of her house and kissed her mum and dad goodbye, like someone out of an American sitcom, and we began to walk to the forest.

It was just getting dark and it wasn't raining, although the air felt damp. If it rained the fireworks would happen anyway. It normally did rain on Halloween night. The excited chatter of the Youth Fellowship girls was comforting in a way. It made me feel part of something, even if it wasn't something I wanted to belong to really, and the fact that they were glad to be together meant I also had a better chance of sneaking off. Maybe they were used to my moodiness by now, but nobody asked me why I wasn't talking much and that suited me fine.

Pulling our coats around us on Main Street, we passed the Jenny Haniver and the girls stopped to talk about it and guess at what it was. A plastic toy? A moulded demon stuck up for Halloween? I didn't correct them. To them it was a reminder of the malevolence of the holiday – a reason to pray. To me it felt like a special thing – something lonely watching the ordinary town; a thing that didn't belong anywhere; something people were afraid of; a warning.

The park was buzzing with families. Adults hopped from foot to foot to try to keep warm while their kids in skimpy supermarket ghost and witch costumes ran around shrieking and laughing at one another. We walked through the crowd and found a spot at the back where other groups of young people had gathered. None of them were in costume. I stood slightly apart from Jessica and the others.

'We don't have germs, Cariad!' joked Martha.

I looked around to see who was in the other groups. Nobody from our school, anyway. They were probably up in the forest having a laugh. You'd get a better view of the fireworks from up there as well. I wondered if Stevie B. was drunk yet and I felt a slight panic that he might finish off the cans before I got there. Chill out, Cariad, it's early yet.

'Oooh, toffee apples!' squealed Jessica. 'Who wants a toffee apple?'

I'd had a toffee apple once. I was being taken to a new foster family: the Hamiltons. I didn't want to go. It was Halloween and I was going to miss the party at the home. I cried.

'They might take you trick or treating if I ask. Would you like me to ask them, Cariad?' said Madge.

'I don't know them!' I wailed. I was in the passenger seat of her car. She had let me sit up front as a special treat. 'I don't want to go!'

'Don't you want your own bedroom? And they've got a really big TV, and a garden!'

I did want all that stuff. And I wanted adults to myself. People who were nice and didn't have too many kids, and I wanted toys of my own. But at that moment I felt lost in between two places – the empty space of going somewhere new. I hated it then. Nothing seemed like a possibility.

'You have to have good hopes,' said Madge. 'Stay positive!'

I was seven.

She bought me a toffee apple to stop me crying. The crack of the hard shell that stuck to the roof of your mouth. A sugar coating that made the acid white apple taste good and special.

'Do you want one, Cari?' shouted Jess and she walked off towards the stall.

'Nah, you're all right, thanks,' I called back.

She skipped off, a happy angel, glowing in the night, her tinsel crown bobbing from a wire over her head. Pop music, as sweet as the Halloween candy, jangled from giant speakers behind us. Kids sang along, and their parents tried to grab their hands to dance with them. The young people beside us laughed together. One was running away from another who was trying to spray her with a can of Coke. The first firework shot into the black sky and a peel of purple sparks burst over us to the sighs and screams of mums and dads and children. I thought about my parents. I wondered if they ever thought about me now. Did they ever wonder where I was? Well, I knew the answer to that, because it wouldn't have been hard for them to find me. I didn't belong here, standing with people at an event for families. It was time for me to get away.

# Chapter 16

I nearly tripped over them.

'Flip sake! Watch out! Oh it's you, Cari. Grab a can then.'

Stevie, Brains and Muff were lying flat on the ground on top of their coats beside their tents. The fireworks fizzed and spat rainbows in the night.

There was a Tesco bag of cider and lager cans and a bottle of whiskey in a fancy bottle that I assumed had come from Brains's house. I grabbed a cider and sat down beside the boys.

'What's the craic, Cari?' said Brains without sitting up.

'I'm meant to be with Jessica and the others,' I said, cracking open the can.

'Ah, my sister's with them,' said Muff, sitting up and grabbing a can from the bag.

'Wow, Halloween at the nunnery? Bet that's fun,' said Stevie. 'Pass us one of those, Muffter.'

Muff threw the can to Steve.

'They're at the park,' I said. 'We're staying at the nunnery tonight, though.'

Stevie snorted, cracking open the beer. 'You'll burn up on entry to that house,' he said.

'Actually I've been there already tonight, and it was OK. Jessica likes Green Day.'

'She does not!'

'She does.'

'Jessica the punk! Who'da thought!' said Brains. 'Maybe there's hope for your kid sister after all, Muff.'

Muff drank deeply from his can without responding.

'Jessica's OK,' I said, feeling a slight pang of guilt. She had been nice to me. And I hadn't forgotten how she totally saved my ass the night of the seance.

The boys went quiet. I had killed the joke.

'She's dressed as an angel tonight, though,' I added.

Stevie spat out a spray of beer. Joke successfully recovered.

It went on like that for a while, us chatting, us drinking, us watching the colourful sky-bombs cast their joyful shards over the town. I had told Jessica and the others that I'd left something important at Dawn and Jacky's and that I'd catch up with them later. I said the word 'important' in a whisper, so they'd think it was private — I hoped that they'd think I wanted to get tampons or medication. They didn't ask what it was, anyway. I think they knew I was spoofing, but they seemed OK with me wandering off.

'Just as long as we meet up with you again before we go home, OK?' said Jessica. 'My mum will go spare if one of us goes missing.'

And she would, too. She'd probably call the cops. She'd definitely call Dawn and Jacky.

'What time will we be going back?' I asked.

'Oooh, late,' said Jessica. 'Probably about midnight? We're going trick or treating on the way home.'

'Seriously?' I hadn't meant it to sound as sarcastic as it came out. 'I mean, isn't that a bit . . . Halloweeny?'

'I brought tracts,' said Martha.

'What?'

'For witnessing.'

She handed me a flyer. On the front was a picture of a cartoon pumpkin and it said: 'Christians are like pumpkins'.

*WTF?* I thought. Inside, the text said:

God picks you from the patch, washes all the dirt off, scoops out all the goo inside, removes the seeds of doubt, hate, greed and unforgiveness. Then he carves a new, smiling face and puts his light inside of you to shine for all the world to see. Are you letting your light shine? Be a Jack-o-lantern for Jesus!

Bloody hell. It made God sound like a total psychopath, apart from anything. I thought about a sci-fi series I'd seen on TV where the evil villain's superpower was that he could use a laser finger to slice open the top of someone's head and scoop out their brains.

'It was Gemma's idea!' said Jessica, beaming at Muff's sister, the newest convert, who shyly smiled back. 'We knock at the door, and instead of saying *trick or treat*, we give *them* a gift. The greatest gift of all!'

'Wow.'

I couldn't think of anything else to say, but I knew I wouldn't be re-joining them until they were finished 'treating' the local community to a taste of judgy Christian 'witnessing'. The locals would probably prefer to have their houses egged.

'Send me a text when you're done,' I said. 'I'll meet you at the Jenny Haniver.'

'At the what?'

'That creepy demon thing nailed to the tree at the entrance to the forest.'

'Oooh. OK. Yuck. But OK, see you then.'

I thought about them ooh-and-aaah-ing at the fireworks with their toffee apples and tracts. In some ways I wished I could be that innocent too. I wished that nice, good things made me feel cosy and safe, instead of sad. Stevie sat up and slipped an arm around my waist and I leant into him and sipped my cider. It was cold, and I felt the warmth of the alcohol starting to spread to my hands. Soon the jokes and the fireworks had ended, and we were kissing. Brains and Muff had disappeared into their tent. Stevie's hands pulled at my bra fastening. I stopped kissing him.

'It's freezing,' I said.

Stevie took my hands and pressed them together inside his own. He was being kind, but I knew what he was thinking and, tonight, I didn't want it to go there.

'It's late,' I said. 'I should probably be getting back to Jessica and the others.'

Stevie took out his phone. 'It's only ten-thirty!'

'I know, but I'm meant to be with them.'

He gave me this 'bullshit' look, and I couldn't blame him because he was right. It was bullshit. I didn't know how to explain it, though. I just didn't want to be with him in that way. Not tonight. Maybe you don't need an explanation, but it wasn't his fault I'd stopped, was it? He hadn't done anything wrong. How could I tell him that fireworks and toffee apples and kids in their hats and scarves were making me wish I was in my bed. On my own.

Stevie moved away from me and crossed his arms, looked up at the sky as if he was waiting for one final firework – a surprise for anyone left behind in the park. He looked like a six-year-old, huffing because he didn't get a lollipop. The cold silence between us was made all the more awkward by the faint sound of Brains and Muff in their tent.

'I'm sorry,' I said.

He turned around to face me. He looked angrier than I had expected. What *had* I expected? That he'd say, 'That's fine, Cari,' and smile sweetly like the boyfriend nobody has ever had? I knew he wasn't like that. Nobody was like that. At the same time I felt pissed off too. OK, so everyone knew I wasn't exactly a virgin, but that didn't mean I was obliged to get everyone off all the time, did it?

'That's fine, Cari,' he said. But his face said it wasn't fine at all.

'Look, I just ... I don't feel like it, OK?'

'I said it's fine?'

'Yeah, but it clearly isn't.' I thought about saying, 'It's not you, it's me,' but I thought *screw him*, why should I apologise for not wanting to have sex, just because *Brokeback Mountain* was replaying in the tent beside us? I'd done my best. I'd got to their camp, had a couple of drinks to try and make myself feel better, and it hadn't worked.

Silence.

'Fine,' I said.

'Where are you going?'

'Jessica's.'

Stevie snorted. 'Sounds right.'

'What's that meant to mean?'

I was standing up now, towering over him where he sat lighting a fag, a sneer on his face.

'Well. You're one of them now, right?' he said. 'Off you go, like a good little girl.'

He waved me off like he was a teacher dismissing some prissy little kid. I felt like kicking the fag out of his hand and smashing his face. He had no idea.

'Fuck you, Stevie,' I said, turning my back on him, and as I walked off he was shouting something in a drunken slur about not fancying me anyway and then I could hear Brains shouting at him to shut up and go to bed and then I was too far away to hear anything and I couldn't see their camp and the darkness had enclosed me.

# Chapter 17

It took me a minute to remember that I had a torch in my bag. I clicked it on and swung the beam around the forest. Hard to know where exactly I was with the thin beam lighting only a few branches and stones at a time, but I wasn't worried – I was walking further along the hill and once I got to my lookout point I could easily find the path back down by following the edge of the cliff round to the forest.

You'd think that having no light, or just a crappy light, at the top of a cliff would be dangerous, and I suppose it is really, but I could feel the edge somehow without being able to see it. There was an emptiness near me that was vast and moving in a way that made the ancient dead rocks beneath my feet seem even more solid. The sea's loud whisper broke against the sides of the cliff in a rhythm that made me feel safe and thrilled at the same time. This is where I should have come all along. I forgot about trying to find the path and started wondering how close I could get to the edge without falling off. I could just make out the water, undulating far below me, blacker than the silver-dotted sky, and I imagined the fish and the seals and whales and dolphins, curling and rolling silently beneath the surface. Whole families that nobody could see.

A light. A pinpoint of light, directly below where I stood as I looked across the water. But how was that possible? It was only the sea below, surely?

'Hello?' I said, feeling like an idiot, but not caring because nobody else was there.

The light went out.

Maybe it had been some kind of reflection. A shooting star lighting up the water for a second. I sat down. I'd stay here as long as I could. I had to be back for midnight so that gave me forty-five minutes at least. It was freezing but I didn't care. Finally, I was feeling like I belonged to this evening. I stuck my hand in my bag, looking for a fag, shining the tiny torch into its corners, my whole vision engrossed in the search for a little white stick, hoping that it hadn't disintegrated into paper and a little pile of tobacco. I suppose that's why I didn't notice him approaching. I suppose that's why I almost fell off the cliff when a tiny but bright orange light appeared right beside my face.

'Sorry! I didn't mean to frighten you.'

All I could see was the little light. Then the familiar smell of tobacco. It was a lit fag.

'You want this?'

I looked up. As he drew a breath in, sucking on his own cig, the tip glowed brighter. I took the fag with a shaking hand and shone my torch on his face. He squinted.

'Ow!'

I couldn't speak, and I couldn't let the beam drop.

'Do you mind?' he said, gently putting a hand on my wrist to lower the beam. 'That's better. Can I sit down?'

He sat, and I didn't know what to do. Should I run? Or stay? Should I ask what the hell he was thinking, letting everyone think he was dead, running off without telling anyone where he was? And where *had* he been? And why the hell was he sitting beside me now? On a cliff top on Halloween night? A thought made me catch my breath as I remembered the night of the seance, the face at the window.

'Everyone thinks you're dead,' I said.

'Heh. Good,' he replied.

We didn't speak for about five minutes. We passed the fag back and forth between us, looking out towards the dark sea.

# Chapter 18

After I'd come down the hill and met up with Jessica and everyone again we had gone back to her house. A couple of hours of
dissecting the evening (well, everyone else's evening, obviously,
not mine) and we were tucked up in sleeping bags and heavy
blankets, the others whispering in the dark like little children
about whether or not God would send Gandhi to hell when he
wasn't a Christian but seemed like an all-round good guy. I wondered if they'd send me to hell if they knew what I'd been up to
while they were out evangelising the town. I wasn't an *all-round
good guy*. Far from it. I lay in my sleeping bag looking up at the
glow-in-the-dark stars on Jessica's ceiling and thought about what
had happened earlier.

'Robin, isn't it?'

I had tried to sound laid back, as if I wasn't probably the
only person on the whole planet who knew for a fact that he
wasn't dead.

'Yeah,' he replied. 'And you're Cariad.'

He took a long draw on his cigarette, not looking at me but out, to the water.

'See that, over there?' he said, nodding at the cruise ship. 'I've been on it.'

So it was true what the people in the chippy were saying. But how the hell had he managed that? The waves lashed the length of it, spraying foam almost to its full height. It was totally inaccessible to anyone without a boat.

'How did you get over?'

'Swam.'

'Heh. No you didn't.'

He looked at me then, an eyebrow raised, a slight smirk on his face. The moonlight cast a dim glow on the water beneath us. 'Believe what you like.'

It was hard enough to believe I was sitting here having a random conversation with Robin Merrow. So much for him being at the bottom of the sea. I should tell people. But who was there to tell? Did he even have a family?

'Robin. Where are you staying? Like, won't your family be worried?'

He choked a bit on his cig. 'No. No, my family won't be worried.'

'Well then what's the craic? Why did you run off?'

'Don't tell me you were worried about me, Cari? That's so kind.'

He was being sarcastic, but he was right in a way – nobody was worried about him really. It had been a source of gossip for a while but nothing more really. Maybe the history teacher had seemed a bit upset but she seemed to have got over it.

'Is that why you ran off? Because you think nobody cares about you?'

'Oh, do me a favour!' He lit a new fag with the end of his last one and flicked the butt over the edge of the cliff. 'I don't give a shit what people think of me.'

'Yeah, I know the feeling.'

'I know you do, Cari. I think we're probably quite alike. Come and see this. I think I can trust you, right?'

'Sure.'

I followed him along the top of the cliff path. I didn't know if I was really like him. It was true that I wasn't really bothered what people thought of me, but if I had run off like him Jacky and Dawn would have been gutted. It was a weird thought. All these years of people pushing me out and here I was thinking that maybe someone might actually be sorry if I went.

Robin led me down some rocks on the edge of the cliff.

'Careful here,' he said. 'One wrong foot and that'd be the end of you.'

Far beneath us dark water crashed on black rocks. When I lifted my head again Robin was gone.

'Robin? Where are you?'

I was alone on the side of the cliff. I swung the pathetic light of my torch in a circle around me, but he was nowhere. I craned my neck behind me, wondering how safe it would be to turn my whole body around, thinking that maybe it might be better to go up the steps backwards the way I'd come.

'Cari! Down here!'

Robin's head suddenly popped out from the side of the cliff and I almost stumbled.

'You idiot!' I yelled.

He laughed, and an arm appeared as well and waved me down. I kept the torch on. As I stepped lower the rocks became smaller and more slippery and now all I could think of was how I was going to get back up again. As I got closer to him he reached with both arms and pulled me roughly into the side of the cliff. There was an opening, an alcove, no . . . I shone my torch into the dark . . . a cave.

'Here – turn that off,' said Robin. 'People will see it.'

'No chance. I'm in a bloody cave on the side of a cliff with someone I don't know. I'm not turning the lights off too.'

'OK. Here.'

He struck a match and started lighting a few candles which were dotted around the place. The cave was about the size of the bathroom at Dawn and Jacky's. Big enough to stand up in – at the entrance, at least. There was a sleeping bag, some blankets, a couple of mats, some cans of food, a couple of boxy-looking things, a couple of bags, some books and the remnants of a fire on the ground near the edge. Some of the candles he was lighting were in fancy holders, including a candelabra, like you'd find on top of a grand piano in an old film.

'Where the hell did you get that?'

'Told you,' he said, 'off the boat. Wait . . .'

He grabbed a dark blanket and hung it up on a number of nails that had been hammered into cracks at the edge of the rock. It made a kind of doorway. He shifted two large rocks to secure the bottom of it.

'What do you think?' He grinned. 'Pretty frickin' cool, eh? Have a seat!'

I sat down on one of the mats. He was right. It was pretty cool. And with the blanket up it wasn't too windy. It was still cold, though.

'I'll get the fire lit now. Here, take this.' He reached into one of the boxes and handed me a half-full bottle of brown liquid. 'That'll warm you up.'

I took a swig. It was whiskey. Or brandy. Something strong, anyway.

'Expensive one, that,' he said, lighting the scraps of kindling. 'Only the best for Mr and Mrs Posho Cruise.'

'Is this where you've been the whole time then?' I asked.

'Yep.'

'Why?'

'Long story. You got time?'

I looked at my phone. A text from Jessica, one from Dawn and one from Martha. Nobody panicking yet, but all wondering if everything was good and a reminder from Jessica of when we were meeting. 'Not really.'

'Shame.'

He was trying to sound casual.

Robin got up and took the bottle of booze. He took a swig. 'Sure you can't stay a bit longer?'

I wanted to. I wanted to hear his story. I thought about Stevie B. and it made me feel like staying here all night, with someone new. I thought about Jessica and how this would totally freak her out, Dawn and Jacky too. But this was what I lived for – new things, scary things, things I didn't know well enough, unpredictable things. God, I wanted to stay.

'Nah. Places to be.'

He shrugged. I wondered if I'd pulled off the cool-and-mysterious act. He probably just thought I had a curfew. Which was basically true.

'OK, then. Come back if you want to know the story. And no telling anyone, right?' His face grew dark. I couldn't tell if he was putting it on, or if there really was a hint of psychopath in his tone. Part of me thrilled to imagine that there was.

'Du-uh. As if I'd tell anyone. Nobody would believe me anyway. They think you're gone for good.'

'That's the way I like it.'

I was only five minutes late for Jessica and the others, but they were already starting to panic.

'Have you been drinking?' said Jessica, as if she'd never seen me with a can in my hand before.'

'Er, a little bit,' I said.

She rummaged in her bag. Oh God, was she going to call Dawn and Jacky?

'Here,' she said, pulling out a pack of gum. 'Chew that and maybe Mum won't notice. I'll make you some coffee when we get back.'

'I'm not drunk, Jess. I only had a couple of sips.'

'Well, we'll all be having hot drinks anyway, so you might as well.'

She smiled. It was impossible not to like Jessica sometimes. I mean, she was totally judgy about drinking and smoking, but at the same time you could tell she genuinely didn't want me to get into trouble.

'Thanks,' I said, taking the gum. We walked back to her house with them all chattering away about the events of the evening and me planning my next visit to the cave.

# Chapter 19

It wasn't unusual to find Brains in the library on a Monday morning. Not that I went there often myself, but sometimes when I was bored and couldn't be bothered going to the study room on my free period I'd hang out in the stacks and browse the titles or use the internet. Anyway, Brains was always there when he wasn't in class. I think he genuinely liked it, sitting around reading old books and making notes. But it was different today. When I entered the library he was sitting on one of the sofas staring into space. Not even reading. Just sitting there with his hands folded. He didn't even see me until I was right up close, waving a hand in front of his face.

'Oh, hi, Cariad.' He smiled but his tone was flat.

'What's up with you?' I said.

'Sssssh!' said Mr Morris.

Brains rolled his eyes. 'Fancy a walk?' he said.

We left the library and walked outside round the back of the school. Fifth and sixth years were meant to spend all but one of their free periods indoors, either in study or in the library. You weren't even meant to call them 'free periods'. 'It's *study hour*,' they'd say. But you were officially allowed one hour per week to have a wander around the school's grounds. You could get quite far from the school building in that time, and sometimes kids would slip over the fence and out to the shop for fags, but Brains and I just went and sat in the football shelter at the far end of the pitch.

He didn't wait for me to ask what was wrong again. 'Can I ask for your opinion on something? As a woman?'

I snorted with laughter and he rolled his eyes again. 'I mean you – you're the woman, not me.'

'I know, that's why I was laughing!'

He looked confused. Nobody had ever called me a woman before, though. Come to think of it I didn't think of myself as a 'woman' either. Or as anything, really.

'I'm not sure I can help you, Brains, but go ahead – I'm listening.'

'Well, I'd like your advice about relationships.'

'You going straight or something?'

'What? No! I don't mean like that, I just mean ...'

'Do you fancy me, Brains? I mean, I am hard to resist but I didn't realise I had the power to turn a gay guy straight.'

Brains tutted. He clearly wasn't in the mood for a joke. 'No. I'm not bloody straight!'

'OK, OK.' I shifted away from him on the bench, miming disgust. 'No hetero!'

He smiled then and took my hand. 'Don't be a dick. Look, it's a problem with Muff.'

He kept hold of my hand. I liked Brains. He was affectionate

102

like this sometimes – giving me a hug in the corridor or hanging an arm around my shoulder if we were standing talking to someone. I'd never met anyone like that before, where it felt nice, and safe, holding his hand. In fact I hadn't held hands with anyone before, ever. Not that I'd ever want to. The idea of a romantic relationship was something I hadn't really ever thought about. I tried to imagine Stevie B. holding my hand like this. Urgh. No. I wouldn't like it. I preferred it when I knew what a guy wanted, and he always wanted something else. But not Brains.

'What's up with him? Youse seemed OK the other night?' I raised an eyebrow and Brains knew exactly what I was talking about.

'I know. I mean that side of things is . . . well it's great, actually. But I mean in general. It's this thing with his sister.'

'Gemma?'

'Yeah. They've always been really close.'

'Does he think the Christians are stealing her away from him?'

'No . . . I mean, *I* think they are. But Muff and Gem are still as close as ever according to him.'

'OK, I'm confused. Nothing's wrong between you two, and nothing's wrong between Muff and Gemma. *So . . . ?*'

Brains sighed. Whatever it was, he was struggling to put it into words, which was so unlike him. 'You're part of that Christian group, right?' he said, finally.

'Woah. I wouldn't say that exactly.'

'But you know them. You hang out with them a lot.'

'I have to! Not my choice!'

'I know, I know. I'm not having a go, I just . . . I mean I wanted to ask, if it was a girl thing.'

'What?'

'Like, what's the attraction to it? Do they just like it because it's girls hanging out in a group? For like, gossip and stuff? Why do they do it?'

I hadn't thought of it like that before. All the coffees and milkshakes and prayer meetings and plotting to save souls. Maybe he was right. It was like one of those films with girl gangs in a way. Jessica as the leader; the others following her. And they had a kind of dress code: neat, expensive, skirts could be short but not slutty-short, push-up bras were acceptable at parties but not at school (because: slutty), hair straight and shiny, no flat shoes but only a very short heel (again: slut factor).

And they had a behaviour code too: always give the appearance of goodness. Sex could be spoken of, but only if you were referring to someone else's sex life. You weren't meant to do those things yourself. I thought back to the 'Hallelujah' sleepover and Jessica starting yet another conversation about whether or not Sarah Bradley was sleeping with her bus-driver boyfriend. As if she wasn't. The discussion was boring for me but for the rest of them there was a real spark – like maybe they could enjoy some of Sarah Bradley's exciting love life with the skinny driver of the number twenty-six just by talking about it.

'I suppose that's part of it,' I said, 'but they also really do believe all the God stuff. It's what makes it all make sense to them. And, I don't know, it's like it makes them feel totally safe all the time. So they can have a reason for everything they do or say – it's always about the big man upstairs.' I pointed to the sky and Brains looked up as if he was hoping to finally understand it.

'It's just . . . so weird the way Gemma's been sucked in. I mean, their granny's pretty religious, and I know they're both close to her. So maybe that's what it is. Flippin' religion. No offence.'

'None taken – I told you, it's totally not my thing.' I turned myself towards him so that he'd look me in the face. 'Brains. Please. Say you believe that it's not my thing.'

Brains laughed and nodded. 'Fine, I believe you!'

I slumped back on the bench again. I wondered how many people saw me with the Youth Fellowship and thought I was One Of Them. Loads probably. Jesus.

'Why are you concerned about Gemma, anyway? So what if she's a Christian now? Doesn't do any harm, does it?'

'Ah. Well, that's the point.' He looked up at the sky. 'It'll rain in a bit. You want to walk round the park?'

We got up, dropping hands, and walked towards the park. I could tell he was finding it hard to say whatever it was. I decided not to speak until he did. It was ages, though. A couple of minutes at least. Finally, at the entrance to the park, he let it out.

'It's not Gemma joining the God squad that's bothering me. It's Muff.'

'*What?*'

Oh. This was something else. Muff joining the Youth Fellowship?

'No. I mean, he hasn't actually done it yet. I just . . . I'm worried he's heading that way.'

'Oh come on. It's Muff. He's not going to turn Christian.'

Brains shrugged.

It couldn't be true, could it? I mean, Muff had always been the quiet sort, but he was happy, wasn't he? I mean, he was seeing Brains – clever, good-looking, funny Brains. And his family were cool, as far as we knew. He always looked OK. Why would anyone . . . ? I realised then that this was the question Brains had been trying to get me to answer. Why does anyone join the Youth Fellowship?

'Does he believe in God and everything then?' I asked.

'Yeah, I think so. I mean we haven't talked a lot about it or anything, but he goes quiet when people are slagging the Youth Fellowship, and I know he goes to church with his granny sometimes.'

'I didn't know that. But I can relate to that particular pain.'

'There's another thing, though. To do with him and me.'

'What do you mean?'

We walked down a small set of steps into a sunken garden. There were trees with small pink blossoms and roses framing the rectangle of grass. We walked to the other end of the garden and then turned to walk back before Brains spoke again.

'Well. Muff has always been a bit ashamed. Of us.'

'Really? I never got that impression from him.'

'That's because you only ever see us together when we're away from school and everyone else. That's all anyone ever sees.'

Oh God. Poor Brains. I had no idea. Now that I thought of it, though, I had overheard some first years giggling over a 'rumour' they'd heard that Brains might be gay. *How does everyone not know this*? I had thought. *Surely it's obvious. It's not like he's hiding it.*

And he wasn't hiding it. Muff was. It was my turn to take Brains's hand. We re-joined the path outside the sunken garden and turned to walk back towards the school.

'Do you think he feels like that because of God?' I said.

'Nope.' Brains's voice was low and quiet. 'I think he might be getting into God because he feels like that.'

'What do you mean?'

'I mean, that if you hate yourself and think you're wrong because you're gay, and then a bunch of people turn up and tell you that the reason you feel like that is because you *are* wrong, according to religion, and then they tell you that God can help you, you might be more likely to believe them.'

'Shit.'

'I know. Shit.'

'But why does he hate himself? I mean, you don't feel like that, do you?'

'No, but I didn't get bullied for being queer when I was in primary school, either.'

'Oh. That's horrible.'

'Yeah. For years, apparently. He was quiet and small for his age and I guess he just looked like a good target.' Brains sighed heavily, as if he had needed to pass all of this on to someone for ages. 'So,' he continued, 'you take some little primary-school dicks calling him a poof year after year, mix in a soupçon of his granny going on about God and AIDS, stir it up a little bit with the fact that he hates my online queer friends . . .'

'And you have a recipe for self-hatred?'

'Bingo. Primed for Jesus.'

God. It all seemed so hopeless. We continued walking and the closer we got to school the more relieved I felt because there was nothing I could really say to make it better. We passed a boy and girl so wrapped up in one another that they almost walked into us.

'But . . . it hasn't happened yet, has it? He hasn't said anything about becoming a Christian, has he?' I said, desperately trying to offer something positive.

'I think he's going to, Cari. I know him. He's been so quiet lately and even when we're alone he's been going a bit cold, especially if we're not drinking. At first I thought he was going to dump me, but then I saw him with Jessica and his sister and it just kind of clicked.'

'But, they're not homophobes, are they?'

I thought of Jessica and the others. They never talked about gay people. Ever. But I'd just assumed that they were cool with people going out with whoever they liked. They weren't horrible to Brains, or anyone. They were nice and kind to pretty much everyone. I just couldn't imagine them getting upset about two guys or two girls being together.

We were nearing the school gates now. I could see Stevie B. in the distance coming towards us. I wondered if he knew about all of this.

'They're not *openly* homophobic, no,' said Brains. 'But they're against it. That Youth Fellowship group you go to? They had a special event last year where they had a guy who came in from another church to talk about gay marriage and how they should all pray against it because it was a slippery slope and next thing you know people would be wanting to marry their horse and stuff.'

'What the hell?'

'Yep. Connor's mum made him go and he told me about it. They even had this clip from an American TV chat show from like two decades ago where some guy actually did want to marry his horse.'

I burst out laughing then. I couldn't help it. It was so absurd! But Brains wasn't laughing. I straightened my face. 'Jesus. I'm sorry, Brains. That is just so nuts, though.'

'Yep.'

He was looking at the ground and didn't see Stevie B.

'Hiya,' I said.

Brains looked up. Stevie didn't say anything. He hadn't spoken to me since Halloween night. He raised an eyebrow and looked at our hands. Brains snorted.

'No hetero,' he said, holding his hands up in surrender.

Stevie looked confused but shrugged his shoulders. 'Youse heading back?'

'Yep. Hour's up. Back to the grind,' said Brains.

We walked back to school together, none of us holding hands.

# Chapter 20

At the weekend Stevie texted.

> Everyone's going to the park later, Johnny's band's playing.
> Brains was asking if you were coming.

*Brains has my number*, I thought, *and I'd rather go out to the park with him than with you*. Still, I was glad, really. Stevie was obviously trying to make things better and although I hadn't really forgiven him, I didn't want us to fall out completely. Besides, when I thought of that night I wasn't thinking of him. I was thinking of Robin, and that thought made me feel good. Anyway, if the others were going out to the gig then it might be a good laugh. I asked Dawn about it. Jacky peered over his newspaper to hear her answer.

'That's fine, love. Are Jessica and the girls going?'

'Dunno.'

'Maybe you should invite them too? It might be nice, and they were very kind to include you in their Halloween plans.'

'OK,' I said, thinking, *Not in a million years.*

'Home by eleven p.m. please, and take your phone. And keep it switched on.'

'OK.'

God, she was so nervous about everything, it was exhausting sometimes. Jacky raised his paper again, clearly satisfied with Dawn's instructions.

I was meeting the guys at the Jenny Haniver and as I walked towards the hill I wondered what I would do if they suggested going to the well. It didn't seem exciting any more, especially after meeting Robin, but I felt like I should encourage Muff and Brains to get together as much as possible. I didn't want things to start up with Stevie again, though. I didn't mind being his friend, but he hadn't apologised for Halloween night.

Brains was at the Jenny Haniver already. He was inspecting it quite closely, lifting its little hands to look at the fingers.

'Boo!' I said, creeping up behind him.

He jumped slightly, which made me laugh. Sometimes Brains gets really caught up in something – a book or an idea – and he can get a bit lost.

'What *is* this thing?' he said.

'It's a Jenny Haniver. Something to do with evil mermaids and warning people away from the water.'

'It's friggin' creepy.'

'I know. It's class, isn't it?'

Brains was still checking out the tiny limbs when I saw Stevie at the end of the street.

'Muff's coming too, right?' I said.

Brains sighed and turned his back on the Jenny Haniver, resting himself against the tree.

'Yeah. I think he's bringing his little sis with him, though.'

'Oh, really? Didn't think heavy metal was her thing.'

'It's not.' He pursed his lips. 'They're inseparable these days.'

No *well* action for Brains tonight, then. Never mind.

'Maybe she'll get bored and go home later,' I suggested.

Brains didn't reply but I was pretty sure he didn't have high hopes for the evening. And here was Stevie now with a grumpy gob on him. You'd've thought we were heading to a funeral.

'Anyone brought any booze?' I asked.

Both of them smiled. Hallelujah. Brains opened his backpack to show us the various cans of lager and cider, and he had a quarter bottle of rum. He took a quick look up the street and passed it around.

'Rum? What are you? A pirate?' said Stevie, looking at the label.

'Yo ho ho!' said Brains, knocking it back.

'Who are you callin' a ho?' I said, making Brains splutter and choke.

'Your ma,' said Stevie.

Pause.

'I've done it again,' he said. 'I can't believe I've done it again . . . Cariad, I am so sorry . . . '

But I was cracking up. 'The look on your face!' I squeaked, in between giggles.

By the time Muff and Gemma arrived the ice was well and truly broken and it wasn't long before we were at the park. The gig was awful. Johnny's metal band, Death Noise Asylum, were taking themselves uber-seriously and at one point they had an onstage row about whether or not the drummer was speeding up. Then Johnny tried to stage dive and the crowd parted and let him face-plant onto the grass. When he got up he tried to pick a fight. With all of them. But people were laughing so hard that nobody retaliated.

We stood at the back and watched it all unfold. Me and Stevie were behind Muff, Brains and Gemma and I noticed Brains trying to take Muff's hand and Muff pulling away. Stevie noticed it too and he looked at me and shook his head.

'Look, I'm sorry about the other night,' he said.

'Took you long enough!'

'I know. I am sorry, though. I was drunk and being a dick.'

'You were.'

'So, do you forgive me?' He stuck out his hand.

I shook it. 'Sure.'

But it was weird because it meant a return to whatever-it-had-been-before and I didn't really know what it had been before. So now we were back there, but what even was it? And since when did I worry about stuff like this anyway? Sensing myself joining the realms of the uber-serious I pulled Stevie into the crowd.

''Mon to the mosh pit!' I yelled over the excruciating noise, and we got stuck in, right up at the front, head banging, jumping into people, letting people jump into us. Johnny had sorted himself out and was just letting rip at the microphone, and the whole crowd was up for it. A twenty-minute-solid battering of body against body, losing ourselves in song after song; the violence of guitar feedback and double-pedal bass drum. It was the most fun I'd had since I'd arrived at Dawn and Jacky's. When it was done we were both drenched with sweat and laughing our heads off.

As the crowd dispersed and we made our way to the back again I could see Brains standing against the park fence with his arms folded and Muff talking to his sister a few feet away from them. Brains was right – you could tell they were going to break up. It was horrible to see. And so weird: Gemma was really nice, and so was Brains. How come Muff had to choose? None of them hated anyone. I leant up against Brains and he put his arm around me.

'Knackered?' I asked.

'Yup. Wanna go for chips?'

'Sure.'

Maybe Stevie would be disappointed that I wasn't going to disappear off on my own with him, but he'd understand that Brains needed us now. And anyway, I was glad to have the excuse. Gemma and Muff went home because Gemma's curfew was earlier than his and I slipped my arms around both Stevie and Brains.

'Come on, lads, you're stuck with me. Let's eat.'

I was starving. Double veggie burger and a curry chip.

'How the frig can you put so much away?' said Brains.

'Practice,' I said.

We sat in the greasy chippy drowning our chips in vinegar and our sorrows in lemon Fanta, to which Brains added a sneaky slug of rum.

'Pure class,' I said.

'Only the best for you, madam,' said Brains, performing a theatrical bow.

It was nice to see him smiling – the first time all night since we'd met Muff. Maybe he'd be better off without him. Somehow, he knew what I was thinking.

'Muff's going to the Youth Fellowship special praise and worship night next week,' he said.

Stevie stopped eating mid burger bite.

Oh God. I was going to be there too – I had promised Dawn and Jacky. They were having some American speaker in and the Youth Fellowship were dead excited about it because they thought there'd be loads of converts. I was pretty sure they were hoping I'd be one of them.

'Well,' I said, after an awkward silence, 'look, I'm going to be there too. Maybe I could sit near Muff . . . and . . . I dunno, keep things light-hearted or something?'

Stevie snorted, chewing his burger once again. 'Come on, Cari. Did you see him tonight? If he'd smiled his face would've cracked. "Light-hearted" isn't exactly . . . '

'Shut up, you dick!' I said.

'Oh, sorry, Brains,' said Stevie.

Brains was staring into his chip container, trying to blink back tears.

'Nah. Stevie's right,' he sniffed. 'I'm losing him. Big time. And there's damn all I can do about it.'

He was right and we all knew it.

My phone buzzed and as I went to answer it the time caught my eye – 11.10 p.m.

'Oh shit, I'm late!'

I answered the call.

'Dawn. I'm so sorry. I'm in the chippy and I forgot the . . . yes, I should have set an alarm. Really sorry. I'm with Brains and Stevie and I'll be back in ten minutes.'

I swiped the call away. I didn't want to leave Brains staring at his chips. He looked so miserable. Outside the chippy the Jenny Haniver hung across the street, the little demon eyeing us as I stood up to go.

'I have to run. I'll call you tomorrow.'

I had said it to Brains but both of them said, 'OK'.

I gave them both a hug and left.

# Chapter 21

It had been a couple of weeks since Halloween and I hadn't gone back to the cave. I wanted to but somehow the longer I left it the more awkward it felt to think about it. You can't just casually drop by on someone who lives in a cave, can you? *I was passing along the edge of this massive cliff, so I thought I'd take the terrifying path down the side to see if you fancied a cuppa.* I wondered if Robin was thinking about me. Maybe he'd've moved on by now, regretting his disclosure. Maybe I should go back, just to let him know that I hadn't told anyone at least. I checked my phone to see if I had any messages.

'Put your phone in your bag please, Cari!'

Maths was so boring. Everything was boring. Tonight was the night of the Youth Fellowship special praise and worship event. Beam me up, Jesus. I'd rather have stayed in to do the maths, to be honest. Jessica and the girls had been especially excited about it at our after-school coffee meetings that week, to the point where I had started fantasising about ways to kill people with a latte spoon.

I put my head on the desk.

'Is something wrong?' asked Mr Johnstone, half annoyed, half concerned.

'Headache, sir,' I said, without raising my head.

Ten minutes to go until the bell. If you were a normal person you could leave, get the bus, grab a snack and sink into the sofa for a couple of hours of Netflix on a Friday night. But not me. Still, at least I wouldn't have to be in this classroom much longer.

The bell rang and everyone scraped their chairs back, ignoring Mr Johnstone's orders to write down their homework and leave in an orderly fashion.

'Have a good weekend, Cariad!' he chirped, clearly relieved to be shot of us all for a couple of days.

If only I could escape as well. As I walked to the café I imagined having a weekend break. Just leaving now; getting the wrong bus – a bus south, to Belfast maybe – visiting some old friends, crashing at theirs, having a laugh, not having to think about God . . .

Four hours later I was sitting at the back of the church trying to slink into a seat, hoping that nobody would notice me and that I could leave early, or at least before the excruciating and inevitable 'tea and coffee' after the service. No such luck.

'Cari! *Cari! CARIAD!*'

Jessica was waving madly from the front row. The. Front. Row. For God's sake. It was like arriving early for an exam or something. Did God really favour teachers' pets? Maybe he didn't, but the visiting speaker certainly did. As I was making my way up to the front, trying my best to look like the person they'd least want for a convert, the speaker was walking up and down the front row, beaming at the A*-grade Christians and shaking their hands.

'It's just so great to be here! And how wonderful to see you young folks out here for Jeeesus! The warriors of the next generation! You will surely see the coming of the Lord!'

Oh, for God's sake.

The speaker was an American woman, short and round, and so full of delight that you'd swear she'd just done a big line of coke in the loos. Maybe she had. Maybe that's how this whole thing worked. She started going on about the Holy Spirit.

'The spirit is sure going to move tonight! I can feel it!'

I looked down the line – Jessica, Martha, Alicia, Gemma and, next to Gemma – Muff. We made eye contact. I half-smiled, not really sure what he'd be feeling about all of this. Maybe he was thinking the same things as me and trying to sniff the breath of the speaker to see if she'd been drinking some of those 'holy' spirits herself. Muff half-smiled back. The seat next to him was free.

'Jessica,' I said, nudging her out of her beatific trance, 'I'm going to go and sit beside Muff. Speak to you after.'

At least if I had to be there I could try my best to do something for Brains.

'Hey,' I said, plopping down in the seat beside Muff, trying to ignore the grinning speaker who was doing her best to make eye contact with me.

'Hey,' he said.

'You been dragged here too, then?'

He shrugged. Jesus, this was worse than I'd thought.

'Look, it sucks, but maybe we can take off afterwards when people are having coffee? We could just go for a walk or something.'

'Can't. I have to walk Gem home.'

'We could come back for her.'

'Look,' he said, turning to me in his seat, 'just leave it, OK? I know what you're trying to do.'

Well, that's amazing, I thought, because I have no idea what I'm doing, beyond just trying to be a normal person in a sea of loved-up-stoned-on-the-spirit Christians.

'I'm just saying hi,' I said.

'You're not,' he replied. 'You're trying to make sure I'm going to stay one of youse, rather than joining them.'

'One of us? You *are* one of us, Muff.'

'Yeah, well, maybe I'm not.'

He had turned away again, eyes fixed on the speaker's lectern where the American woman was lowering the microphone and tapping it with two fingers to see if it was on.

'You *are* one of us!' I managed to whisper before she began.

'Welcome! In the name of the Lord!' the speaker boomed.

There was loud applause and a man with a guitar stepped up to the microphone. The praise and worship band started banging out a tune that clearly everyone knew because the whole congregation shrieked and jumped to their feet. Muff stood up too, and I stood up so I didn't look conspicuous, even though I didn't know the words or the tune. I tried to smile, conscious of the speaker's eyes on me. Forty-five minutes to go.

The band began to crank up the pace; they changed key and the gathered crowd whooped and a couple of people shouted 'Hallelujah!'. I looked behind me and saw a number of young people around my age with their hands in the air, swaying with the music, eyes closed. One was crying. I thought back to the mosh pit and the craic we had had pushing each other around, lifted by the bass and drums, bouncing in time, sweating. But we hadn't been contemplating anything or thinking about a higher being. We'd been putting ourselves and our bodies in the music; stamping, shouting, for no reason other than the fact that we were there, and it felt good.

Beside me, Muff was staring at the ground and he was biting his lip. Maybe he was in between places. I willed him to stay with me, not to give himself to something that he couldn't see for himself. Don't get me wrong, I'm not one of those atheists who give a shit if everyone else worships the Moon or whatever, but to look at him, wrestling with himself, fighting back tears, you could see that one way or another he was going to make a serious decision, and it was scaring him to death.

The band slowed, electric guitars become quieter, the drummer tapped on cymbals to make the music swoosh like the sea. The singer became quiet and started repeating a line over and over: *Come, Lord, Come now. Come, Lord, Come now.* The crowd began to sing it too, over and over, hands raised, eyes closed now, all except for mine. Gemma took her brother's hand. I saw a tear, blinked from his eye, falling towards the ground. He was lost now, wasn't he? Fuck the singer and his stupid whispery love song to Jesus. And where did all the guys in that band get off singing about how much they fancied Jesus when they wouldn't let Muff fancy Brains? I felt like storming the stage and letting them know how hypocritical they were. *Oh, Jesus, Jesus, 'come into me' and give me a big snog on the lips and deliver all the gays from their terrible sins!* Could they even hear themselves?

But instead of rushing the stage I sat down, the same as

everyone else, as the music stopped, and the speaker approached the mic, wiping the tears from her face.

It was a relief in some ways. It was easier to fake being engaged during a sermon. I'd had plenty of practice after all. All you had to do was to remember to look at the speaker from time to time, maybe even smile in encouragement. You didn't even have to listen to what they were saying. I drifted off into my daydream from earlier – escaping for a bit, getting the bus to Belfast, catching up with Christy and the others, maybe sneaking into a bar for a gig. I missed them a bit. Not loads, but a bit. Hanging out with Christy always ended with me getting a lift back to the foster home from the cops, but everything in the few hours that came before getting lifted was fun. Of course, I hadn't heard from him since I'd moved. That's how he was – if you were out with him and having a good time then it's like you were best mates, but if you weren't able to make it then basically you were dead to him. He didn't do social media and he couldn't be bothered to text. He never needed to because he always had someone to hang out with. I knew he wouldn't keep in touch when I left. He didn't even call to say goodbye. But I also knew that if I showed up out of the blue off the bus three months later he'd be glad to see me, and we'd start off again right back where we'd left off. He was cool like that.

The speaker was waving her arms around and saying how great it was to be a Christian and how free she was and then she said something that made me start to listen.

'And do you know why people resist this freedom? They need to bind those demons. Say it with me! *Bind those demons!*'

What the hell was this? She went on in a frenzy, addressing the invisible demons, pointing to nobody.

'Demon of lust, we bind you! Demon of unbelief, we bind you! Come on folks, say it with me! *WE BIND YOU!* Demon of lies!'

'*We bind you!*' replied the congregation.

*You must be joking,* I thought. I looked over to see if Jessica was similarly freaked out. But no, she had started to move her lips in time with the chant, and pretty soon she was shouting it too, and so were the others:

'*We bind you!*'

'Demon of addiction!' yelled the speaker.

'*We bind you!*'

'Demon of hatred!'

'*We bind you!*'

'Demon of laziness!'

There's a demon of laziness? Is there a demon of extra freaked-out-ness? I must be possessed, I thought . . .

'*We bind you!*'

'Demon of homosexuality!'

I looked at Muff and instantly regretted it because I could see that the whole youth group was looking at him. His sister grabbed his hand and they all chanted '*We bind you,*' and Muff looked at his feet and I didn't know what to do because I mostly wanted to bolt – to get out of that place and never come back. But I could see that Muff was rooted there like someone had planted him in concrete, and I wanted so much to drag him out with me, but I knew it wasn't going to happen.

'Muff,' I whispered.

No response.

'*Muff?*'

I tried to nudge him, but he was frozen. I got an evil glare from

Jessica as she repeated 'We bind you!' in response to the never-ending list of sins for which demons were apparently responsible. No doubt if I left it would be because of a demon too.

I moved right up close to his ear so that I knew he could hear me. 'Muff, I'm leaving. This is total bullshit. You should come with me. Please come with me. We're your friends and you don't have to stay.'

He had his eyes closed very tightly and his jaw was tense, like he was gritting his teeth.

The speaker looked at me sternly. 'Demon of disruption!'

'We bind you!'

Well, fuck this.

I eyeballed her back. People like that don't scare me. What scares me is how much I'd love to have punched her right in her judgy face. I stood up, gave her the middle finger, and walked out. Right up the middle aisle, not giving a shit who saw me. I knew Dawn would be raging but I didn't care.

# Chapter 22

It wasn't a long walk from the church to Dawn and Jacky's and I knew that I'd be in trouble for leaving, never mind flipping off the special guest speaker, so I needed to calm down and stay in control. I considered getting chips, but I was so wound up I wasn't sure I'd be able to eat. What I needed was a smoke. Or a drink. Or both. But I didn't have either on me. I looked at the phone. Nine p.m. Still early. That meeting would go on for another couple of hours if you included prayer, coffee and potential exorcisms.

The Jenny Haniver was lopsided, having fallen off its nail a bit. I wouldn't normally have wanted to touch it but at that moment I felt more on its side than anyone else's so I straightened it up and brushed a cobweb off its feet. Its skin was thin but tough, the little feet like cats' claws. Once it was straight again I made my way into the forest and up the hill towards the cliffs. To be honest I hadn't intended to go back to the cave but once I was at the top of the hill I didn't feel like stopping, so I just kept on going. The movement and the noise of the sea and the concentration that it took to get down the face of the cliff to the cave was helping to calm me down.

As I approached the cave, lighting my way with my phone, I could make out the outline of the curtain, a red fire glow. He was still there. The anticipation of him, and the warmth of the fire, made me shiver. I cleared my throat as I got closer. You couldn't knock on a curtain and I didn't want to surprise him. No response.

'Hello?' I called.

'Cari! Come in!'

He sounded happy to hear my voice.

The fire was too hot to sit next to. The cave was surprisingly cosy, despite only the dark curtain separating us from the sheer drop into the sea. Robin was lying back on a bundle of clothes. There was an open book, face down, on the floor next to him. He raised a fancy crystal glass toward me and smiled.

'Pull up a chair!' He indicated the cave floor.

'Like what you've done with the place,' I said, taking off my coat to sit on.

'Drink?' He was already pouring some golden liquid into another crystal glass. I took a sniff and it made my eyes water.

'Good Scotch, that,' he said, knocking his back.

I wondered how many he'd had. I took a sip. It burnt on the way down, but not in a bad way.

'So, where've you been, Cari?' he asked.

'Church.'

He spluttered. 'Seriously? You getting serious about the God stuff then?'

I downed the rest of my drink.

'Seriously pissed off with it, maybe.'

'So, why'd you go then?'

'I kind of have to. My foster parents think it'll keep me out of trouble.'

'Not exactly working, is it?' he smirked, and leant over to refill my drink.

I looked into the warm liquid and swirled it around, inhaling its heat. 'Nope.'

'Hey, cheer up. It could be worse. You could be living in a cave.'

'Heh. You don't seem too unhappy.'

'Well, yeah. It could be worse for me too. Sláinte.'

He held out his glass and I moved closer to him so I could clink it with mine. He smelled pretty nice for someone who had been living in an outdoor squat.

'So, what've you been up to then?' I asked him.

He sat up and leant over closer to the fire, arms dangling over his knees. 'Oh this and that. Reading. Walking around the dark hoping to bump into good-looking women in need of a smoke.' He looked at me with a smirk and I smirked back, pretending I thought he was being sarcastic, but his words made something bubble up inside me.

'And,' he went on, 'I've been back out to the ship for supplies.'

'Come on,' I said, rolling my eyes. 'Doubtful!'

He raised an eyebrow and his glass. 'Where the frig do you reckon I got these from?'

I had to admit, the crystal tumblers weren't exactly cave chic. But he couldn't have got out to the ship. Not without a boat of his own, anyway. The cops'd had enough trouble getting people off it with helicopters and lifeboats. How could one kid get there by himself?

'I dunno. But have you got a boat or something?'

'Nope. Swam.'

I remembered the gossip in the chippy. But it had to be bullshit. Maybe he'd heard it from someone in the town and decided to adopt it as a cool story. I looked over at him, staring into the fire, his glass dangling from his hand, the outline of his bicep underneath his shirt. He probably was a good swimmer. But nobody was *that* good. Both of us could hear the wind roaring into the sea outside. How could he think that I'd swallow something like that? How stupid was I to think that maybe he liked me when he was willing to feed me this crap, thinking I'd believe him like a little kid?

I got up to leave. 'I'm not a dick,' I said.

'What? I never said you were. Where are you going?'

'You obviously think I'm an idiot. Well I honestly can't be arsed with it. You didn't swim over to that ship. What did you do, carry the bottle of whiskey back in your pocket?'

'I did swim over.' He was smiling. So sure of himself. It made me hate him.

I walked towards the curtain.

'Suit yourself,' he said. 'But you have to admit, I'm more interesting than church.'

He was. That was very true. His cave was interesting. His whiskey was interesting. His upper arms were interesting.

'And you can come back whenever you like,' he continued. 'But I'm moving on soon so don't leave it so long next time. Just sayin'.'

Was there a hint of loneliness in his voice? It was hard to tell. *Whatever*, I thought. *There are too many assholes in my life*. Maybe I just needed to stay in the town for a bit. Stevie B. was an idiot but at least he wasn't a liar.

'And next time, if you like,' he said, 'I'll give you a kiss.'

Any hint of vulnerability disappeared as he narrowed his eyes and dramatically blew me a kiss. If he had been genuine before, he had recovered his macho confidence now. Urgh.

'In your dreams, mate,' I said.

I could hear him laughing as I slipped through the curtain and up the cliff path.

I was out into the freezing cold again, and shivering. I had no idea what time it was but I was looking forward to getting into my bed. I tried to think about the church service and remember how it had made me feel. I tried to work up the anger again, but it was all gone. I pulled my army coat around me and tasted the dried whiskey on my lips and wondered what it would taste like on Robin's. *In your dreams*, I had said – and how long had it taken me to start dreaming about it, too? Urgh. *You're pathetic, Cariad*. I tried to shake off the thought and I picked up my pace. I ran down the hillside, past the low moan of kids at the well and out onto the street. Soon I was at the estate and I could see the living room lights were on in the house. Dawn and Jacky had waited up for me.

# Chapter 23

Of course Dawn and Jacky had heard about my dramatic exit from the church service.

'It was rude, Cariad. I hope you understand that,' Dawn said. 'Even if you didn't like what was being said, you can't just ... you can't just be so *rude.*'

I stood there and let it wash all over me. I let them go on about politeness and the importance of respect and blah blah blah. I felt like letting them know how much I had put up with, and how polite I had actually been for weeks and weeks now, how it had all just boiled over, how I didn't care what people believed but that it was actually messing up Muff's life and Brains's life and how I couldn't just sit there and ignore it all ...

But I didn't. I stood there and let them preach at me. What difference would it have made? How on earth could I convince them, or anyone, that something bad was happening when everyone thought, everyone *knew*, that Jessica and Martha and all the others were kind and good and never did anything wrong? Even I found it hard to understand sometimes. They were the least threatening people you could ever meet. They tried *really hard, all the time* to be good. They really believed in goodness.

'And where have you been all this time?' continued Dawn.

'Eh?'

'It's half past eleven. If you weren't in church, where were you?'

I shrugged.

Dawn waved her hand as if words were failing her. 'Go to bed, Cari. We'll speak about this in the morning.'

I trudged up the stairs, wondering what my punishment was going to be this time. Another grounding, I supposed. God. Being super-holy was so dull. How did they all stick it? It wasn't like I wanted to go out robbing people's houses. I just wanted to do normal teenage things, like hanging out with people, maybe smoking a fag or having the odd drink. You'd think I was heading for the young offenders' centre the way they were getting on.

The thought brought me back to Robin. I lay back on my bed without taking off my coat. It was warm in the house; I just couldn't be bothered undressing. I thought about that freezing cave. I mean, it was a cool place to hang out, but it must've been crap trying to actually live there 24/7. I closed my eyes and tried to picture him right now, wrapped up in those blankets beside his bottles of booze and the crystal whiskey glasses. He couldn't have brought that stuff from the cruise ship on his own without a boat or something. But if he didn't get it from the boat then where the hell did he get it all from? Maybe *he* was robbing houses. But I hadn't heard about any break-ins recently. It annoyed me that he had been right – he was far and away the most interesting thing about this place. Nobody else had any mystery about them. The Christians were all going to pray their way to eternal virginity and drag poor Muff with them. Brains was going to be devastated but he'd go off to Oxford or something and shag a load of posho gay guys. Dawn and Jacky would shuffle around their lives going to church and making flower arrangements and reading the paper, and they'd die peacefully and happily. It was funny: I could imagine everyone's future really clearly except for my own. I could imagine Robin getting bored with his freezing cave life and then buggering off in the middle of the night to the next town where he could rob a few more places. But me? I could tell you what tomorrow might be like (a lecture from Dawn, finding out my punishment, staying in my room all day listening to music), but next year? Ten years from now? Nope. Not a clue. I could be anywhere, doing anything, with anybody. Part of me wished I had a plan. But fuck it, plans were boring too.

I turned over and pulled out my phone. Three texts. All from Jessica.

**Hi Cari. Hope you're OK. We're worried about you.**

**Hi Cari. You missed a good night. James became a Christian!**

Who the hell was James? Oh God, she couldn't mean . . .

**James is so happy. I wish you could have stayed for the altar call too. Next time stay . . . it's not scary really. Maybe you could bring Brains as well?**

Next time? She was having a laugh. They'd got him. Poor Muff. Poor Brains. Urgh.

I thought about taking off my boots. I switched off the phone and fell asleep.

# Chapter 24

The smell of coffee woke me up and for a moment I was almost happy. Then I remembered everything. Still, at least there was coffee. A violent cramp wrapped itself around my right leg and I tried not to scream. I pulled off my boots and stood up, leaning hard on the cramping leg, stretching out the muscle. It was a trick I learned in the last home before I came to Dawn and Jacky's. I always got a cramp when I slept with my boots on, but sometimes you needed to be ready to run first thing.

I took my coat off too and crept downstairs.

'Morning!' said Jacky from beneath his paper.

'Hi, Jacky,' I mumbled. The coffee was in the kitchen, but I knew that Dawn would be there too. I poked my head around the door.

'Can I have a mug of that?'

Dawn nodded, looking up from her crossword puzzle, stony faced. 'I made it for you,' she said with a disappointed smile. This was going to be tough.

I sat down opposite her at the small kitchen table and she

poured me a mug from the cafetière. I added milk from the small jug on the table. Why did she set out a jug of milk in her own home? Why not just pour it from the bottle? I thought that I had better be the first to speak. Sip of coffee first. God, it was good. Hot, though. Another sip.

'Dawn . . . I'm sorry about last night.'

'Which part?' she asked, not looking up.

'Em . . . what?'

She put the crossword book down and removed her reading glasses. 'Which part are you sorry for? Leaving the service? The rude gesture to the church's invited guest? Or for going off God-knows-where? *Or* for refusing to tell us where you went off to?'

'Em. All of it?'

'You don't sound too sure.'

I sighed. She wasn't in a forgiving mood, and I wasn't sorry for any of it really. I just didn't want to get grounded again. Tough luck, I guessed.

'I am. Sorry for all of it, I mean. What's my punishment?' I sipped more coffee.

'Cari . . .'

She seemed exasperated, like she had no idea how to respond. I hoped that she hadn't thought about it. Maybe she'd be more lenient this time. I didn't say anything. Seconds passed. I had finished my coffee. I wondered whether it would be a bad idea to pour another mug.

She spoke again. Her tone was more sad than angry. 'You don't seem to have any idea how to behave.'

'What do you mean? I know I shouldn't have given the finger to that American woman.'

135

'It's not just that, though. It's like you think you can do these things and get away with them as long as you take the punishment. It's like . . . it's like nothing really means anything to you.'

'That's not true!'

'Isn't it?'

There was a sharpness to her voice now, but if she was getting angry then I was too. How dare she think that nothing mattered to me? Just because I couldn't stick her boring life and boring friends.

'No, it's bloody not.'

A low, stern voice from the next room: '*Cariad!*'

'Sorry,' I muttered, staring into my empty coffee mug.

'You're not sorry, though, are you?'

Dawn had tears in her eyes. Jesus Christ.

I relaxed my voice as best I could. 'I'm sorry that I'm not like you,' I said. 'I'm sorry that I'm crap at being good, and I'm sorry that I didn't like that mental Christian woman.'

I thought I might have seen a tiny smirk at the edge of Dawn's mouth. I'd probably imagined it, though. The rest of her seemed completely cold. I went on.

'I know it's my fault, Dawn. I'm just . . . *not good*, though. I like Jessica and the others, but that woman was so, like, *pushy*, or something. And I knew they all wanted me to stay and become a Christian or something, but I just can't. I don't want to.'

Dawn's shoulders softened. She poured me another mug of coffee. 'OK,' she whispered. 'I won't pretend I'm not sad to hear you say that, Cari. But Jacky and I don't want you to give your life to the Lord until you're ready.'

'I don't think I'll ever be ready,' I said.

'Look at me,' she said.

I raised my head.

'That's OK. This is your home now. And we accept you, whether you're a Christian or not.'

Her words were so sincere that I felt myself welling up even though it was so patronising and I really should have been angry. I should have been ready to tell her to fuck off, but I couldn't. I couldn't say anything. I tried not to let tears spill over. I didn't want her to think that I cared that much about it.

'OK,' I whispered.

'I mean it,' she said. 'But ...'

Oh, here we go.

'But, you can't go giving rude gestures to visiting speakers. Even if you think they're a bit ... over-the-top. You do understand that that's rude, don't you?'

'Yeah.'

'And you understand that you can't just go walking around the town at night-time on your own, don't you?'

'Yeah.'

'Anything could happen. Just because this is a quiet town doesn't mean that bad things can't happen to people here.'

It was Dawn's turn to go quiet then. I nodded. We sat in silence, both of us looking at the table. Jacky appeared at the door.

'Let's take a day to cool off,' he said, as if he was interrupting a massive argument.

I wasn't complaining, though. Delayed punishment sounded good to me.

'Can I go and see Brains, then?'

He nodded. He stood behind Dawn with his hands on her shoulders.

'OK. You can go out after lunch. But back by five p.m., before it's dark. OK?'

'Yes. Definitely. I promise.'

'Don't let us down.'

Dawn looked up at me and smiled, putting a hand on one of Jacky's hands. I wondered if I'd ever be with anyone in that way.

'Five p.m., Cari. We'll see you then.'

# Chapter 25

I met Brains at the well. Just the two of us. I hadn't told Stevie B. about it, in case he got the wrong idea. Brains was already there when I arrived, leaning back on the dry soil slope, smoking a fag. He nodded.

'Did you get a text from Jessica this morning?' he said, as I shuffled my way down into the pit.

'Yep.'

He blew a cloud of smoke out into the air. 'You want one?' He stretched out the pack towards me.

'Sure.'

I took a fag and settled myself down beside him. Close enough so we could compare texts.

'Yep,' he said, 'that's it. Pretty much the same as mine.'

'Shit.'

'I know.'

He put his head on my shoulder and we sat there for a couple of minutes, blowing smoke clouds out into the cold until there was nothing left to blow.

'He's gonna dump me,' said Brains at last, his head still on my shoulder.

We both knew this was true, but I still said, 'Nah. He won't do that.'

'He will. Probably today, I reckon.'

There was nothing to say, really. It sucked so much. I slipped my arm through Brains's and squeezed. I could feel him shaking slightly and I knew he was crying. I squeezed harder, wishing I could make him feel better. But I couldn't even speak. What was there to say? If someone had come along to fill in the hole we were sitting in I think we'd both have just let them.

After a while Brains spoke. His voice slightly broken. 'Thing is, I'm not even worried about myself as much as I'm worried for him.'

'I know. He's going to waste his life.'

'It's not just that. I mean, the Christian group can be a pain and whatever, but it's dangerous for people like us.'

I sat up straight and Brains dug around in his pocket for a hanky. He blew his nose loudly.

'What do you mean, *dangerous*?'

'Think about it, Cari. Muff's gay. Really gay. Like, super gay. He's never fancied a girl. He's been seeing me for a year. It was hard for him, because of his past and his granny and everything, but he was starting to tell people. Not many people, and not people at school. But one or two kids, online, you know?'

I thought I understood. They were going to shove him back in the closet.

'You can't just suddenly start pretending to be something you're not, can you?' said Brains.

I thought back to my discussion with Dawn. *We accept you, whether you're a Christian or not.* 'No. You can't.'

'But he's going to try to. It's going to do his head in. And he's already on pills for depression.'

'Shit. I didn't know that.'

'Yeah, well nobody does really, so don't be sayin' anything.'

'Of course not.'

'Thing is, his sister will have told the Christian group about it, and they'll all think that it's because he's a homo, right?'

'Bloody hell. So they think they're curing his depression by making him become a Christian?'

'Right. He told me as much.'

'Why doesn't he tell them? That the depression isn't because he's gay?'

Brains shrugged and looked at me with a flat mouth. 'Because he believes it. He thinks that's why he's depressed, too. On some level he thinks it's his own fault.'

'Shit,' I said.

'I know.'

'What can we do about it? There must be something.'

'Nothing. Fuck all. I've tried to talk him out of it loads of times but he says it's like a voice inside him that he can't shake off.'

He lit another fag and offered it to me.

'It's sad,' I said. It was stating the obvious, but what else could I say?

'Yeah,' said Brains.

We sat there for a while longer.

'I'm going to try to talk to him again,' I said, dropping the end of my fag into the soil and covering it over. Brains was still smoking his.

'It won't do any good,' he said. 'He's lost to them.'

'But I'll try, anyway.'

I got out my phone and started messaging Muff: **Hi Muff. Hope you're OK.** I deleted it. I didn't want to seem patronising. **Hi Muff. I heard you became a Christian. Congratulations** ... And then what was I going to say? 'Too bad they're a bunch of homophobes'?

Brains stood up and wiped his eyes. 'I'm heading home.'

'Right,' I said, standing up too. 'What are you going to do?'

He shrugged. 'Wait for him to call? I might help Dad round the garden for a bit. Keep busy, I guess.'

'OK.'

Brains opened his arms and half-smiled. I hugged him.

'Thanks for listening, Cari. You're a good friend.'

He was being brave. It was heartbreaking.

'Any time. Will you text me, if he gets in touch?'

'Yeah. You free later? I might need a drinking partner.'

Five p.m. Jacky had said. But fuck it, Brains needed me, and I was in trouble already.

'Sure.'

My phoned buzzed and I stayed in the pit to read the text as Brains left. It was Jessica again.

**We're all going out for milkshakes to celebrate James's spiritual birthday at 3 p.m.! Come with us? We're just going to the café.**

I had nothing to do now for a while and it would be an opportunity to get talking to Muff, maybe. What the hell.

**OK,** I texted back, **See you there.**

# Chapter 26

The 'spiritual birthday' boy had seemed happy, I had to admit. Nobody mentioned my little protest at the praise evening and I was glad I didn't have to explain myself. I wasn't sure I'd be able to do that without going on a massive rant about how false it all was and how angry I was about Muff. I couldn't get close to him at the café. Everyone wanted to sit next to the new convert and make him feel thoroughly One Of Them. Urgh.

Jessica, of course, was the main welcomer. She couldn't take her eyes off Muff and I wondered if she was starting to see him as more than just a potential crusader in the cause for Jesus.

I tried making a loud comment to Alicia about having seen Brains that morning, but if Muff heard me he was ignoring it. I had no money with me so Alicia bought me a strawberry milkshake. I promised to pay her back. Why did good people always have to mess things up? I thought. They were so friendly and *kind*. I guessed that they genuinely didn't understand the harm they were doing. I thought of Brains, pulling weeds and trying not to let his dad see how he was feeling, dreading the phone call from Muff. How could they not *know* what they were doing was wrong, though? Maybe it wasn't Muff I needed to talk to.

Jessica squeezed out past Martha's chair. 'Gotta pee!'

'Oh, me too,' I said, scraping my chair back and following her.

I was in luck – it was just the two of us in the bathroom.

'Jessica. Can I talk to you for a second?'

'Of course!'

Her eyes gleamed. Did she think I was going to give my life to Jesus too? I looked into the sink as I washed my hands.

'It's about Muff.'

'James?'

'Yes. James.'

Flip sake, was he not even allowed his name any more?

'Look. I'm a bit ... worried, I suppose. About him.'

I had no idea what I was going to say but I knew I needed to say something.

'Why? He seems really happy, doesn't he?'

'Yes, but ... '

Jessica stopped applying her lip gloss and looked at me in the mirror as I tried to find the words.

'Jessica. He ... Muff, I mean James, he's gay. You know that, right? He's with Brains.'

She began touching up her blusher. 'Yes, we know that he had ... homosexual feelings ... for Brains.'

*Had?* I thought.

'Well,' I said, struggling to know how to put it. 'It's just that, it's OK to be gay, really, isn't it? And I'm just a bit worried that, the way he's become a Christian now and everything, like, maybe he's going to try to, y'know, be something that he isn't?'

144

Jessica applied mascara, her eyes wide and mouth open in the shape of a tight 'O'. She wasn't giving anything away. Finally, she finished, blinked a couple of times to check her look and slotted the mascara wand back into its holster with a *snap*. She turned her body towards me, her dark hair fanning across her shoulders, and she looked me in the face.

'Nobody's forcing James to do anything, Cariad. He has decided to be a Christian, and we have to respect that.'

By 'we' she meant me. Me and Brains. She wasn't finished talking.

'We don't judge anyone. The Bible says that it's wrong to have gay sex. But we're all sinners. Nobody's perfect. Jesus accepts us as we are.'

'*So*, he can keep on seeing Brains and Jesus will turn a blind eye?'

'He has to work it out for himself, as we all do. But God will help him towards a purer life.'

'*So*, he *can't* keep seeing Brains?'

She rolled her eyes. 'God accepts us as we are, Cari. All of us. If he called James to be a Christian then it was meant to be. It's called predestination. James was only opening himself to the call. But after God calls us, it's up to us to try to live holy lives. James has new priorities now. I hope you can understand that.'

I couldn't. Not if his *new priorities* meant trying to be straight. Jessica didn't wait for my answer, though. She was off, back to the table with a smooth flick of her hair. I watched her backside sashay down the café with a little more swing than usual. I didn't like to think badly of Jessica, she had been good to me. But I couldn't help feeling that this was all working out pretty nicely for her. I left through the fire exit so that I didn't have to talk to any of them on the way out. I was sick of their goodness, and I didn't want to think about what was next because I knew it meant heartbreak for Brains – probably by the end of the day if his predictions were right.

I had some time to kill. I pounded up the street towards the estate. As I got closer to the Jenny Haniver I felt the urge to turn up into the forest. *Why the hell not?* I thought. Why not get out of my head for a bit, right? It was exactly what I needed. A break from everything – Dawn, Jacky, Jessica, Brains. The cliff top was always where I'd gone to get away from it all. I remembered the days of smoking on my own, watching the seals. Now there was another distraction waiting for me up there, one with stolen booze and great upper arms. I hadn't meant to go back to him at all, but it was something nobody else knew about, away from everyone's judgement, away from sadness. It wasn't so much a temptation as a compulsion. A predestination. All I knew was that the Jenny Haniver no longer seemed like something ugly or frightening. I'd always been drawn to it, but it was no longer a freakish fascination. Now it was more like a signpost pointing up and out of the town, making me invisible and unreal, and free.

# Chapter 27

'Cari!'

He sounded pleased to see me. My face went hot remembering his parting words to me on my last visit: *Next time, if you like, I'll give you a kiss.* Well, that definitely wasn't happening. I had enough on my plate, and anyway, what about Stevie B.? It was true I hadn't really texted him for a while and I felt slightly guilty about having ignored some of his messages on social media. But it had been getting a bit full on with him. He kept asking me when we were going to go back to the well and he'd started signing his messages 'love, S x'. Still, it felt like it would have been a bit wrong to get off with someone else. Even if absolutely nobody knew that I was in a cave on the side of a cliff with him.

Ten minutes later we were kissing on a pile of soft blankets on the floor of the cave.

'Where'd you get these blankets from?' I asked, coming up for air.

'Never mind,' he said, kissing my neck, his hands sliding up my back under my hoody. 'You wouldn't believe me.'

'Ha. The boat I suppose?'

'Yep. But sssshhhhh.'

We kissed some more. He unhooked my bra. I sat up.

'Oops. Sorry,' he said.

'Nah, it's OK,' I said. But I fixed the clasp shut again. 'You got any drink?'

He sat up too and poured me a shot of something. It was sweet and thick and tasted like oranges. He poured one for himself too and we clinked glasses.

'You like the booze, don't you?' he said.

'You can talk.' I indicated the pile of empty bottles stacked neatly at the side of the cave.

'Fair point.' He grinned. 'So, now we've kissed.'

He raised his glass and I clinked mine against it again.

'Sorry about, you know, the bra thing. Carried away.'

I shrugged. It was hard not to like him. Nothing was serious here. Everything seemed easy.

'It's OK. It's what boys do.'

He shook his head. 'We shouldn't, though. I mean, not without asking, anyway.'

'It's seriously fine.'

I meant it. I was used to guys pushing their luck and not all of them were as nice as Robin if I knocked them back. I set my glass down and leant back into his body to show him that everything was OK.

'I'll have to go in a bit, anyway. Curfew,' I said.

'Oh dear. What did Cari do this time?' He smirked as he drank.

'I flipped off a preacher during a church service.'

Robin spluttered and laughed. 'Nice one!'

'Aye. They were being a dick, like.'

'Everyone's a dick.'

'Undeniable.'

We clinked glasses again and he refilled mine.

'So what's new with you?' I said.

'Like I said, Cari, you wouldn't believe me.'

I rolled my eyes. 'You're so cagey,' I said.

'Force of habit.'

'Well, why not try a new habit?'

'You think I should tell you all my secrets, Cari?'

He was joking around but I left the question in the air for a few seconds to see if he'd change the subject. He didn't. A seagull cawed loudly outside the cave and for a split second I had an image in my head of a bird falling out of the sky. It made me think of that thing Pastor Ky said about people being worth more than sparrows.

'Yeah. Why not?' I whispered.

He sat up, which meant I had to sit up too. The movement shook us out of the moment.

'Another drink?' he said, smiling, as if he hadn't heard my question.

'Nah, I really do have to go in a bit.'

'No probs.'

He poured himself another and I knew it was a signal to change the subject. Whatever his secrets were, he wasn't going to tell me today.

'They're gonna tow the boat pretty soon,' I said. 'You'd better get raiding the rest of the stuff soon as you can.'

He leant forward, suddenly growing serious. 'Where'd you hear that?

'The news. They figured out a way to shift it without wrecking it too much.'

There was silence for a minute. His face turned stormy. 'OK,' he said. 'Let's talk about something else.'

'Like what?'

'Dunno. Anything.'

'Really anything?'

He shrugged. I thought for a second. There was something I wanted to ask him, but it had never seemed like the right time, until now.

'OK. Did you shag the history teacher?'

He spat his drink out again and it made me giggle.

'You can't ask me that!'

'Why the hell not?'

'Cos she still works there. She could get struck off.'

'So you *did* shag the history teacher?'

'Jesus, Cari . . .'

He was smiling but I could tell he wasn't going to give me a straight answer. I felt so much younger than him then. It crossed my mind that I should've let him take my bra off. For what, though? So I could be on the level with him? Would it have made him trust me more? Or less? I shook myself to throw off the confusing thought.

'Fine, you don't have to tell me.'

'I will tell you,' he said calmly, 'But not now. Not here.'

'What do you mean? Where else is there?'

'C'mere.'

He got up and walked towards the curtain. I followed. He took the end of it off the hook and put an arm around my waist, pointing out with the other hand. The dark mass of water underneath us grumbled gently over the rocks, the quickly fading sunset lining its horizon. The outline of the cruise liner sat, out to sea, monolithic, the red glow at its edge making it appear to be on fire.

'Next time, I'm taking you out there.'

'Well good luck finding a speedboat then, because I'll not be swimming.'

He tightened his arm around me gently. 'I'll show you the way. You'll see.'

# Chapter 28

I made it back with five minutes to spare.

'You look happy,' said Jacky.

The thought surprised me. Maybe I *was* happy. I hadn't been thinking about it really. Maybe the walk down through the dark forest had cheered me up. The phone's buzz reminded me about Brains. I had forgotten all about him, my thoughts full of Robin and that ship and the chance of being able to actually get out there.

The buzz continued. It was a call, not a text.

I made my way upstairs.

'Not too long on the phone!' I heard Dawn calling. I closed the door behind me and sat down on the bed before answering.

'Hiya. Tell me everything,' I said.

And he did. He sounded half angry, half sad, sometimes there was a pause like he was trying to catch a breath. Muff had turned up at his house about an hour after he'd got home. He must have gone straight from the café to Brains's place. They had talked in Brains's room. They had cried. Muff had explained. Brains had pleaded. Basically, it was a mess. But definitely over. Muff had chosen to go out with Jesus instead. I wondered if I should tell Brains that Jessica was totally a rival for Jesus's attention as well, but I thought better of it. Nothing would come of it since even Jesus wasn't likely to be able to magic away Muff's gayness.

'You OK?' I asked, regretting the stupid question as soon as I'd asked it.

'Nope.'

'I know. Sorry.'

'It's not your fault. Thanks for listening, Cari. You've been brilliant.'

'Do you want to hang out?'

'Maybe tomorrow. I'm just going to go to bed now, I think. I'm done.'

I was glad really. Coming back on time today meant I stood a chance of getting out again tomorrow, especially if I swallowed my pride and went to church in the morning.

# Chapter 29

Dawn had made me apologise to Pastor Ky. It was fair enough really. I had made a scene in his place. I didn't regret it, though, so the apology was a lie, but apparently lying was the Christian thing to do in this circumstance. He was very kind and forgiving, which made it all feel ten times worse. It wasn't the most awful thing about the morning, though. The worst thing was seeing Muff sitting up front beside Jessica, who I swear had her shortest skirt on. She was giggling and chatting to him and every so often she'd put her hand lightly on his arm. Jesus, could she be any more obvious?

I sat up back with Dawn and Jacky. They had wanted me to join the rest of the young people at the front but settled for me doing the apology and promising not to storm out again. I couldn't avoid the Youth Fellowship for the whole service, however. Afterwards they practically ran to the back of the church to say hello to me.

'We're so glad you're here!' Jessica said, as if I'd just had major life saving surgery or something. It wasn't as if I'd really had a choice. 'Coming to the café with us for lunch?'

'No,' I said, looking at Muff, who was wearing a small gold cross on a thin chain around his neck. 'I'm going to meet Brains.'

Muff looked at his feet and Martha dragged him off to find tea and biscuits.

'No need to make him feel worse than he already does,' whispered Jessica.

'Well it's all right for Muff, isn't it?' I said.

'What do you mean?'

'He's got a new gang. And Jesus. And he's got you.'

Jessica went beetroot. I *knew* she was after him.

'Muff is a spiritual baby. He needs support. Look.' She sounded properly annoyed now. 'As I said before, we all need to respect his decisions, don't we?'

'I don't know,' I said.

And I didn't. I mean on the one hand people could believe whatever they wanted. But on the other he was really hurting people. Well, Brains specifically. And trying to be not-gay was probably going to mess him up too. How could I respect that?

'Well if that's how you feel ...' said Jessica, her smile darkening.

'I don't know how I feel. But I have to go now anyway.'

I knew she was pissed off, but I also knew that she'd forgive me the way that Pastor Ky had done. The thing was, I knew that if I lost Jessica I'd definitely lose Muff as well. Right now I was his only hope of getting out of this situation. It was me versus God. I didn't exactly fancy my chances but I had to try. I tried to smile at Jessica.

'I'm sure everything will be all right,' I said.

It was one of those stupid things people say that doesn't actually mean anything because, let's face it, nobody can actually be 'sure' that everything will be all right, and loads of times things won't be all right. But people like to hear it anyway.

Jessica smiled back. 'It totally will!'

She hugged me. Her hair was soft and it smelled of coconut. I always felt like I'd crawled out of the wheelie bin when I stood next to Jessica.

Dawn and Jacky were waiting at the church door, which was my excuse to break out of Jessica's embrace, thank God. As we walked to the house I congratulated myself on surviving. My phone buzzed. It was Brains.

Brains: **Fancy clubbing tonight?**

Me: **What club?! And it's Sunday?**

Brains: **Not here. Belfast. A gay club.**

I did fancy it. I'd never been to a gay club before. I wondered if Brains had. Maybe he had this whole other life I didn't know about. But how the hell could I persuade Dawn and Jacky? Maybe they didn't have to know exactly. But I couldn't say I was going to Youth Fellowship – they'd know that was a lie. Hmmmm. The phone buzzed again. Brains again.

**Say yes. I need this. I'm going mental.**

Poor Brains. He did deserve a bit of fun. But . . . what if he got off with someone and left me on my own? And how would we get back anyway? The last bus to Ballybaile was probably about nine p.m. from the city. Probably even earlier on a Sunday, I reckoned.

Me: **I'll see what I can do.**

Brains: **YES! Thankyouthankyouthankyou.**

Me: **I'll try my best. Is Stevie coming?**

Brains: **Do you want him to?**

I wasn't sure it would be his thing. And it would be massively awkward. A cool shiver moved across my back as I remembered the last encounter with Robin.

Me: **I dunno. Not sure he'd like it?**

Brains: **Me too. It's just us then.**

Me: **OK. How we getting back?**

Brains: **I'll check stuff out and see what I can come up with. Think some others from Instagram might be going. Chat again later.**

Me: **xx**

And that is how I found myself, eight hours later, sitting in between Brains and a girl with a shaved head called Suzanne, sharing a can of cider on the backseat of a Red Ford Fiesta, driven by Big Gay Dave from Tullycarnet.

# Chapter 30

Suzanne was loud and pierced. She had several studs and hoops on her face: eyebrows, nose, cheek and tongue. She had painted-on raised eyebrows which made everything she said seem like a question. I liked her. Big Gay Dave from Tullycarnet had no piercings. He was tall with long dark hair and a round face. He had an English accent and had apparently ended up in Tullycarnet estate in East Belfast after meeting his partner of several years (Wee Gay Dave from Tullycarnet) at the same nightclub we were all on our way to.

'Once I'd met him that was that,' he said, chatting amicably as the little Fiesta bumped over potholes on the road out of the small town. 'We just knew. We'd be the Gay Daves from the East, and it was meant to be.'

'Do you miss England?' I asked.

'Nah, not really. My mum doesn't know I'm gay. She's very religious since Dad died and she keeps waiting for me to tell them I'm engaged to some lovely Christian lady.'

Suzanne giggled. 'I'll be your beard if you like,' she said.

'I think they might sus you out, love.' He winked at Suzanne in the mirror.

'Beard?' I said.

'It's what it's called when someone pretends to be straight with someone so that nobody catches on that they're queer,' said Brains.

'Wow, I thought most people in England were cool with gayness.'

'I'm from a small town too,' said Dave. 'Most people vote for right-wing bigots. They don't like gays, or foreigners.'

I thought of Dawn and Jacky. Hyper-religious, small-town old people. I couldn't imagine them being rude to anyone, though. But I didn't really know what they thought about gays or foreigners. I had told them a half-truth this evening: that Brains had been a bit down because of 'relationship trouble' and that he'd asked me to go to a 'social event' with him in Belfast, and that we were getting a lift with someone called Dave who didn't drink. All of this was technically true . . . I told Brains to text me from the car when they arrived so that Dawn and Jacky wouldn't grill him on the doorstep, but they had come out to the car to meet the designated driver.

'I'm Dave!' beamed Big Gay Dave, leaning awkwardly out of the Ford Fiesta window to shake Jacky's hand. I saw Dawn looking at the length of his hair and trying not to stare at Suzanne and her silver face ornaments.

'Don't worry about a thing,' said Dave, who must have sensed her nervousness. 'I'm a teetotaller. Always have been. Dad was an alcoholic and it put me off for life.'

'Oh.' Dawn's face softened. 'I'm so sorry to hear that.'

'It's OK,' said Big Gay Dave, smiling. 'It was years ago now.'

'Oh, has he recovered then?'

'Dead, unfortunately.'

Dawn's face went white. 'Oh my goodness,' she said, 'I'm so sorry.'

Dave laughed. 'Honestly, it's fine!'

'Well, Dave, thank you very much for offering to drive this evening.'

'Happy to! What time do you need Cari back for?'

He was a real charmer. Dawn was actually, genuinely smiling now. Thank God he hadn't mentioned the gay club. He had clearly done this before.

'Midnight, please.'

I rolled my eyes. Suzanne smirked. It was so embarrassing.

'Midnight it is! And don't you worry, Mrs . . . ?'

'Oh, just call me Dawn!'

'Don't you worry, Dawn, I'll be keeping an eye on the young 'uns. Here's my number. You can call at any point.' He scribbled down his number on the back of an envelope and handed it to Dawn. Her shoulders relaxed.

'Thank you, Dave. And you all have a lovely evening!'

'You too! See you at midnight!'

Big Gay Dave winked at Dawn, shook Jacky's hand again, and we were off.

'Bloody hell,' I said, 'that was amazing!'

Brains leant forward and patted Dave on the back. 'That's our Dave,' he said. 'Looking after the queer babies of the North. He's our guardian angel.'

'I don't mind,' he said. 'I like driving. And if I can give you kids a chance to get out and play then it's good karma. Besides, our Brains needs a bit of cheering up.'

Brains smiled but there was a tinge of sadness to it.

'You'll get your reward someday, Dave,' said Suzanne. 'What would you like?'

'Ooooh, I dunno. A million quid? Massage from Harry Styles? I haven't decided yet.'

We went on like that. Everyone in a good mood. The little car slowing down up hills and speeding up down the other side. Dave told us about his childhood, the parents who would have 'totally freaked out' if they'd found out he was gay.

'Bummer,' I said.

'Ah, not really. If I hadn't moved here I'd never have met my lovely Dave.'

'And a background in homophobia was probably good preparation for moving to Belfast,' added Brains.

'I've been quite lucky,' said Dave. 'Most people here have been great. Although my next-door neighbours are a bit uptight about it.'

'Are they?' said Suzanne. 'How do you know? Did they say something?'

'Well, we suspect it was them who stole the pink unicorn gnomes from the garden.'

'What?? That's mad,' I said.

He laughed. 'Only joking. Wee Dave wouldn't be seen dead anywhere near a pink unicorn. You should meet him, he's the only man in the whole estate who goes around wearing a suit with a Vivienne Westwood tiepin.'

'Soooo,' I said, 'how do you know your neighbours are 'phobes?'

He shrugged. 'It's just a feeling you get. A look. A raised eyebrow when they see you holding hands. You know?'

Suzanne and Brains were both nodding.

'And one day I was out in the garden and I heard the wife say to the husband, "Don't forget to water the *pansies*, dear." Just like that.'

I laughed but nobody else did.

'No, that one really happened,' said Dave.

'Oh God. Sorry!'

'It's fine. As long as they're not throwing bricks through the window we can live with them. Everyone else in the estate's pretty cool. Almost there, kids!'

We'd been chatting for almost an hour. The scenery had changed from cows and sheep and narrow, mud-splattered roads to wide grey motorway, cars and lorries, and, as we drew closer to Belfast, taller buildings, blocks of flats and signs for the nearest McDonalds.

The club was called Bliss and although the entrance was dark you could hear the loud pop music thumping against the inner doors. Pretty soon Brains, Suzanne and I were sipping a bright red cocktail through straws directly from the jug. The woman on the door had eyed me up and down and for a second I thought she was going to refuse to let me go in because I was underage. Or because I was straight. I don't know how she might have known that, but I felt really straight. As if I was wearing a big flashing *HETEROSEXUAL* sign around my neck. I hoped it wasn't that obvious. I wondered if that's how Big Gay Dave had felt at home in his small town with his anxious parents. I wondered if Brains ever felt like that. But nobody asked me for ID or for my Gay

Card. As soon as the woman clocked eyes on Dave she grinned widely and stood up from behind the desk to give him a hug, and that was it – we were in. Dave had bought the jug of cocktail but warned us not to drink it too fast.

'I'm only getting two of these in, OK? And you,' he said, looking at me, 'your folks seem pretty nice, so don't go vomming up red sparkle juice all over the stair carpet, OK? Pace yourselves.'

My folks. It sounded so odd. They weren't really my folks. But they didn't seem like strangers any more, either. I would have taken offence at Dave's patronising tone, but he was impossible to dislike, and he *had* just got me into a nightclub and bought me booze. I nodded at him, mid-sip. My phone buzzed. A message from Stevie B.

> **Enjoying the gay club? At least I won't be worried about you getting off with anyone there.** 😉

Shit. Did he know about Robin? Nah, he couldn't. But anyway, I wasn't his girlfriend, was I? I put my phone on silent and back in my pocket without replying. Brains noticed.

'Stevie?'

'How'd you know?'

'He wanted to go out tonight so I had to tell him I was going out with you. Think he was a bit annoyed to be left out.'

'Ah.' I felt a little nip of guilt then.

'What's the craic with you two, anyway?' Brains asked.

'Em. Well, nothing really. We're just friends.'

'With benefits?'

'Heh. Sometimes. But not for a while.'

'Oh? You gone off him?'

'Em. I don't know if I was ever really *on* him.'

Brains was giggling like a wee kid.

'Shut up! You know what I meant!' I gave him a dig in the side.

'Ow!' he yelled, faking an injury. He calmed himself, then took a slug of the cocktail.

'Easy on that!' I said. 'Save a bit for the rest of us.'

'Plenty more where that came from,' he said, waving his fake ID. 'Anyway, look. You should talk to Stevie.'

I rolled my eyes.

'I'm serious,' Brains said. 'He likes you.'

I nodded, wishing he would change the subject. Suzanne saved the day by grabbing my arm.

'C'mon,' she said, 'I love this tune. Let's dance.'

She looked so brilliant. Shaved head turning all colours in the disco-ball light, dancing like a maniac, her small body lifting clean off the ground at times. Miniskirt, ripped fishnet tights. I wanted to be her. It was hard to keep up.

I felt a tap on my shoulder and turned around. It was another girl, slightly older. 'You want some?'

She was holding a tiny bottle and at first I thought it was alcohol, but then she took a sniff and I knew it was poppers. I shook my head. I was spinning a bit from the cocktail and I remembered what Dave had said about sparkle juice.

'What's up? You straight?' She laughed. It was a joke, but I shrugged and nodded.

'Awwwwww! That's so sweet!' she said. She gave me a big hug and danced off into the crowd. Suzanne was laughing hard.

'I don't think anyone's called me sweet before,' I shouted over the thumping bass.

'You enjoying the club?' she shouted back.

'Yeah, it's great!'

To be honest it wasn't my kind of music. I'd rather have been in the mosh pit with a bunch of sweaty metal-heads, but the mood was light and fun. I motioned to Suzanne that I was going to take a break and she joined me as I went back to our table. Facing out, I watched the congregation. Confident men with no shirts and six-packs kept jumping on to the stage or winding themselves around the pole in the middle of the dance floor; other people preferred to quietly sit with each other at the bar or dance with friends.

Then I saw him – Brains, in the other corner of the room, snogging the face off some guy. The guy he was kissing was wearing a string vest and he had tattoos all over his skinny arms. Even from a distance I could see he was much older than Brains. Well at least he's having some fun, I thought. Suzanne had noticed it too. She gave me a nudge and pointed.

'I know!' I shouted.

'Lucky sod!' she yelled back, indicating to ask me if I wanted another drink. But as she got up to head to the bar Dave appeared at the table with another cocktail jug, this time green. He sat down with us.

'Where's Boy Wonder?' he shouted.

Suzanne and I both pointed to the corner.

'Oof. He'll not be back for a minute. More Fat Frog for you two then!'

He handed us straws and, heads touching, we set to work.

The sticky liquid was cold and sweet. As we came up again the music changed to something slower and quieter. Couples paired up. Dave smiled politely and shook his head as a large man with a beard asked if he wanted to dance. Suzanne got up to dance with a pretty woman in a glittery mini-dress.

'Where's Wee Dave tonight then?' I asked.

'Home with the cat,' said Dave. 'She's about to have kittens.'

'Awwww!'

He beamed. 'What about you, Cari? No boyfriend?'

Out of the corner of my eye I could see Brains, still kissing the skinny tattoo guy, the two of them totally wrapped up in one another.

'Nobody special, really.'

It felt like a lie. But it wasn't a lie, really, was it? *Was* it? I didn't really know. 'It's good to get out of the town for a bit.'

That much was definitely true. Dave looked at his watch. 'Not for much longer, I'm afraid. Got to have you back before your ball gown turns to rags and my Ford Fiesta turns into a pumpkin.'

'How come you're doing this for us?' I asked him.

'Well, it's like I said ...' He took a long sip from his own drink. It looked like fizzy orange. 'I'm from a town like yours. It was crap growing up and I no idea if I'd ever meet another gay lad. I didn't get to go to a club until I was in my twenties and it was like coming home. Meeting other queers ... everything started making sense. And loads of them had parents like mine. Life sort of *started* for me then. By the time I'd met Dave and moved here the world was a different place.' He flicked his long dark hair over his left shoulder. 'Everyone was using social media to meet up with people. But I always felt bad for the ones who didn't live in the city and couldn't get out much. And then I met your Brains, and Suzanne, online. They talked about getting together and going to a club sometime. They were all desperate to get on the scene, but they were too young to drive and too broke to travel.'

'So you stepped in?'

'I did.'

Wow, so Brains *did* have a whole other life outside our town. He'd never mentioned it before. I wondered how long he'd been coming here. I felt a bit hurt that I hadn't known. And then Dave started talking again.

'He likes you a lot,' he said.

'Who?'

'Brains, you dope. Otherwise you'd not be here. You won't tell anyone about the club, will you?'

'Jesus, of course not,' I said.

Now, instead of hurt, I felt guilt. I hadn't told anyone about Robin and the cave and the plan to go on the boat. Nobody. I hadn't even considered it. And if I told Brains about it he might think I'd been taking the piss out of Stevie B. for leading him on, or something. Maybe I should tell him? But not yet. I mean, he didn't need anything else to think about right now, right? I looked back to where he and his kissing friend had sat down on a large pink sofa. They were lying back against the arm of it, still kissing, pressed together, their arms locked tightly around one another.

'Bloody hell, are they ever going to take a breath?'

Dave laughed. 'Just what he needed tonight, wouldn't you say?'

I nodded. I hoped he was right. But really I knew that tomorrow we'd wake up in the same town in the same country with the same friends, and that Brains would have the same feelings for Muff, and that Muff would have the same feelings for Jesus. Nothing would have really changed. Things don't really change. Getting a man, drinking yourself stupid, smoking until your eyes hurt. All fun things and good craic at the time. But they only last in the moment. And then you have to make another moment happen, and another. I used to live for those moments. When did it all start to seem so exhausting?

'Cheer up, Missis!' said Dave, giving me a nudge and handing me the straw. I smiled and took another sip.

'Drink up, now. I'm gonna round up the other two and we'll start making a move homewards.'

Pretty soon Suzanne was back at the table helping me finish up the Fat Frog. She showed me the Instagram name she'd got from her dancing partner. When we finished drinking I looked around for Brains and Dave. From across the room it looked as though they were having an argument. The skinny tat guy was standing up and pointing at Dave. Dave was backing off with his hands up, like he was trying to get him to calm down. Now the skinny tat guy was poking him in the chest. And poking him again. Then he pushed Dave. Brains stood up from the sofa and stumbled back down again. He tried to get up again. He looked drowsy and he tried to get in front of the skinny tat guy who was going for Dave, but he flumped back down in the seat, staring into the space ahead of him, completely wasted. Tat guy swung for Dave with his right fist and caught him on the side of the face. Dave stumbled and fell into the side of the bar. He got back up. Before he could lose his temper and hit tat guy back two huge bouncers had hold of them both and were hauling them out of the club. Suzanne and I ran over to Brains who was almost asleep on the sofa.

'Brains! *Brains!*' I was yelling into his face. Suzanne tried giving him a slap but I caught the eye of another bouncer and told her to stop. We grabbed one arm each and hauled him over our shoulders. God, he was so heavy, but we managed to drag him outside to where the angry bouncers were yelling at tat guy to get lost or they'd get the cops out. Dave was sitting on the step nursing the side of his head.

We set Brains down beside him and I let him lean up against me to keep him upright.

'Let me see it,' said Suzanne.

'No, no, it's fine,' sniffed Dave with a muffled voice, trying to stop tears.

'It's not fine. Let me see.' Suzanne sounded serious and calm. I was impressed. Clearly Dave was too because he dropped his hands from his head and let her take a look.

'It's bad, Dave,' she said. 'The wound's bleeding a fair bit. You might be concussed.'

'I'm not. I'm fine,' he said, trying to stand up. He stumbled lightly against one of the bouncers who set him back down on the step. 'OK, maybe not completely fine, but I'll be OK in a minute.'

'Even so,' said Suzanne, 'we should take you to A&E. You might need a stitch.'

'I don't, it's fine.'

'Look, I'm training to be a nurse, and if you don't come with me to A&E right now I'm going to count this as my first big nursing failure, OK? Don't do this to me, Dave. Don't make me a failure before my career's even started.'

She was trying to make him laugh, and it worked, but she had that tone – you knew she was serious too. Dave nodded.

'Can you call us a cab?' Suzanne asked the bouncer.

'Yep,' said the massive suited man. 'But you'll never get them to pick *him* up.' He nodded towards Brains.

Shit, he was right, I thought. I looked at my phone. We were going to be so late, but worse than that, we were stranded in the city in the middle of the night.

# Chapter 31

Sometimes there is no good option. Sometimes you have to think very carefully and then pick the least-worst thing. Or, like me, you could just totally panic and make everything worse by picking the first option that randomly comes into your head. For me that meant simply doing nothing. I was stuck on the steps of a nightclub with a drowsy drunken friend, who had started quietly weeping on my shoulder; our lift back to Ballybaile had gone to A&E with the only other person who I knew who could speak in sentences. Part of me knew that the right thing to do would have been to call Dawn and Jacky and explain what had happened. But instead I chose to just sit there. Not only did I not call them, but I also ignored *their* calls.

12.10 a.m.

12.20 a.m.

12.40 a.m.

01.00 a.m.

I knew they'd be worried. I was worried too. Where the hell was Suzanne? It was freezing now. People were starting to pile out of the club and look for taxis. I shuffled over to the side of the steps, dragging Brains with me, so that we didn't get stood on.

*What's the craic?* I texted Suzanne. No response. Brains began to snore on my shoulder. His head was heavy and my arm was going numb. And then a text from Suzanne:

1.15 a.m. It's taking forever. This place is crammed with drunk guys. We haven't even been seen yet.

And then another text, but not from Suzanne. From Jessica:

Hi Cari. Dawn's just off the phone. She wanted me to text you because she doesn't know how to do it herself. She said to say that she's very worried because you're not home and can you give her a call. She says she's going to call the police soon if you don't get in touch. Are you in trouble? Is there something I can do to help? Praying for you. J xxxx

Oh shit.

The phone rang again. Dawn. We were stuck. I had no choice. I answered.

'Hi. Yes, yes, we're fine. We're OK, seriously. No, I didn't realise you'd called so many times. Sorry. I was in the toilet and the reception was really bad. No, I haven't been drinking.' I took a deep breath. 'But . . .'

'But what?' said Dawn. Her voice was getting higher. She'd found out I was safe but it sounded like she was only just starting to panic.

'What? What is it?'

'Calm down. Everything's fine. Something did happen though ...'

'What is it, Cariad? Just tell us.'

'OK, well, you know Dave, who drove us here? Well, he had a bit of an accident.'

'Oh my goodness! A car accident? Are you all OK?!'

'Yes, we're fine. No, not a car accident. He ... he fell over and knocked his head against a wall, and he's had to go to hospital to get it checked out. He's *fine*. But he just needs to get it checked.'

'And where are you? And what about your friend? Where's he?'

I looked at Brains, now curled up on the step, his face on the cold concrete, his tongue hanging out.

'He's with me. Look, we're grand. I'm going to go over to the bus station and see if we can get a bus.'

'It's almost one-thirty in the morning, Cariad. There won't be any buses now.'

I knew that. I don't know why I had said it.

'OK, well, look, I'm sure Dave will be fine and he will drive us back when he's out of the hospital, OK?'

'Where exactly are you?'

'Um ... hang on ...'

I didn't really know where we were. I couldn't tell her we were at a gay bar called Bliss. I looked around and across the street. I covered the phone mouthpiece and stood up to talk to the bouncer.

'Here,' I whispered. He had to lean over. He was huge but he had an amused look on his face. 'What's that big clock over there?'

'Albert Clock, love,' he boomed. I almost told him to shush but I caught myself on.

'OK, thanks!' I removed my hand from the phone to speak to Dawn again.

'The Albert Clock. We're at the Albert Clock.'

Dawn let out a noise that sounded like a kind of anxious swoon, as if I'd told her some awful news.

'Cariad. That's where all the *prostitutes* work!'

I looked over at the clock. There didn't seem to be anyone except people coming out of bars and clubs. Then again, if Dawn could see how they were dressed she'd probably freak out. Her idea of getting dressed up for the night was putting on her dangly earrings and pearl necklace.

'There's nobody here but us.'

'You're on your *own*?!'

'No! I mean, yes. I mean ... look, there's no need to worry. We're fine.'

But we weren't fine, and Dawn knew it as well as I did. As the streets cleared we were almost alone, it was freezing and even the bouncers were starting to leave. Soon we'd be two kids sitting on the steps of a closed-up building in the city in the middle of the night. Dawn's tone of voice changed.

'OK, this is what I want you to do, Cariad. Are you listening?'

'Yes.'

'Can you get yourself and your friend – what's his name again?'

'Brains.'

'Can you get yourself and Brains along to the nearest police station? I think there's one close to that clock.'

I didn't fancy that. Dragging a drunk guy into the cop shop? I'd rather be as far away from the police as possible.

She went on. 'You go there, and you tell them that you're two minors on your own and that your guardian is coming to get you as soon as possible, OK?'

How were they going to manage that? Neither of them could drive. I couldn't imagine anything more embarrassing than having Dawn showing up at the police station to pick me up, like I was a little kid. And what would happen when she saw the state Brains was in?'

'I don't think that's necessary, Dawn. I think—'

'I don't care what you think, young lady.' This was a new tone. It was sharp and uninterruptable. 'You do as I say. Do you hear me?'

I nodded.

'Cariad? Do you hear me?'

'Yes. Yes I hear you,' I said.

'Good. Now I'm going to find someone to drive me down to Belfast to pick the two of you up, and when I get there I expect the policemen to tell me that you've been there since this call ended, and that you've been on your best behaviour. Do you understand?'

'I do.'

'Good. Now off you go and I will see you as soon as I can.'

And that was it. I had to accept that I was in the deepest shit possible. I gave Brains a shove.

'Wakey, wakey!'

'Urgh. Mum?'

'No, I'm not your mum. 'Sake. Wake up, you dick. It's me, Cari.'

Brains rubbed his eyes. 'Where am I? Where's Karl?'

'Who the hell's Karl?'

I remembered – the skinny tat guy. He'd run off ages ago, no doubt.

'Karl's gone,' I said, 'and we're in deep shit. Come on, we have to go over to the cop shop.'

I dragged Brains to his feet. He staggered and put his arms against the wall to steady himself.

'I feel sick. I think I'm gonna be . . .'

And then he was sick, all over the wall, and his shoes. Bright red sparkle juice. Nice.

'Urgh. Come on.' I dragged him towards the road.

'Wait!' he said, perking up. 'I actually feel loads better now! I think . . . I think I'm OK now! I'm grand, actually! Totally fine!'

He broke free from my grip and immediately fell into a couple of rubbish bins, knocking the contents all over the road.

'Oi!' shouted someone, hearing the clatter of bottles on the street. Shit. Better hurry up.

'Come *on*!' I said, pulling Brains up and heading again towards the road.

It felt like it took about twenty minutes crossing that bloody road. When we walked into the police station the woman at the desk looked at us, raised an eyebrow and then went back to making notes in her book. I felt like a complete tool standing there in front of her, holding up Brains. I cleared my throat gently. She looked up, obviously annoyed, and nodded silently towards a raggedy red sofa at the side of the counter. Glad to get a soft seat, I plopped Brains down and sat next to him. I was almost nodding off when a cop came out from behind the counter and approached us. He was massive. He had that kind of waddle that body builders have. I couldn't stop looking at his gun in its black pouch, strapped to his hip. I wondered if he'd ever shot anyone.

'How can I help you?' he said, sternly.

Brains looked at him with gormless red-ringed eyes.

'You all right, son?' the cop asked him.

Brains nodded.

'We got stuck in town,' I said. 'We were at a club … a social club, type thing, and there was a figh … an accident, and our friend had to go to hospital, and he was our lift, so we're stuck. My … guardian's coming to pick us up. She said to wait here.'

'I see.' The cop was still standing high above us. I wondered if I should stand up too. It felt so stupid having to crane my neck back to talk to him.

'And what was the name of this *social club*?' he asked.

'Uh … I'm not sure?'

He pursed his lips. 'And what age are you two?'

Oh crap.

'I'm eighteen. And Brains is nineteen. It was his birthday last week and …'

'I'm seventeen,' slurred Brains, 'and you're sixteen, Cari.'

Fuck sake.

Pursed lips *and* a raised eyebrow now.

'You're not in a great state, sunshine, are you?' the cop said.

Brains shook his head and started to cry.

The policeman tutted. 'Wait there.'

He disappeared.

I wondered how much trouble we were in. Underage drinking. Underage clubbing. Did 'drunk and disorderly' apply if you'd puked on someone's wall and knocked over some bins?

He was back in ten minutes, carrying two cups of black coffee.

'Two sugars,' he said, handing them to us. 'Drink those up and then I'll get youse another one before that *guardian* of yours appears, OK?'

We nodded and sipped the hot sweet liquid. I cupped the mug in my hands and let it burn me. We were going to be OK.

True to his word the cop did get us another coffee, and then another. Brains had stopped crying and was looking slightly more human. He was even speaking in sentences by the time Dawn opened the door. Jessica's mum was standing behind her.

# Chapter 32

Nobody had spoken much on the way back to Ballybaile. I had texted Suzanne and Dave to let them know we'd gone. It was two a.m. and they still hadn't been seen. I wondered how Suzanne was going to get home. She didn't seem too worried about being out so late. I knew I was probably grounded for life but in a really strange way I enjoyed the trip. The car was warm. It had started to rain outside. Brains dozed on the seat next to me. The radio was playing quietly, a song I didn't know about someone sending a message in a bottle out to sea and hoping that someone would find his note. We drove and drove until I knew we were in the countryside again because there were no more street lights. At some point I must have dropped off myself because the next thing I knew Jessica's mum's car was parked at our house and Dawn was thanking her so much and apologising for all the trouble. Brains wasn't in the car any more, so they must have dropped him off first. I wondered how his dad had greeted him. God, what a mess.

The next morning I woke up to the glare of dazzling sunlight.

Dawn had thrown open the curtains. She never usually came into my room without asking.

'Argh! Shit!' I said, sticking my head under the pillow.

'Language please!' said Dawn. 'Breakfast's ready. Have a shower and I'll see you downstairs in ten minutes.'

I looked at my phone. Seven a.m. Bloody hell. She wasn't actually going to make me go to school was she? My uniform was laid out on the chair. Oh my God. I'd only just got into bed. What a sadist.

The rest of the day was a blur. I could hardly keep my eyes open during class and took lunchtime to nap in the toilets, head on my knees.

'You look like hell,' said Stevie B. at break.

'Thanks, man.'

'Good night, then?' He grinned.

It *had* been a good night, up to the point where Big Gay Dave got punched. Brains wasn't in school, unsurprisingly. I imagined him waking up with the worst hangover ever. Been there, I thought. I hoped that someone was taking care of him, making him drink full-sugar Coke in small sips.

I looked over at Muff. He had his head down, pretending to read a book but not actually turning the pages. I wondered if he'd heard about our Big Night Out. He wouldn't have known about Brains kissing that guy, at least. Was there still a chance for him and Brains? Muff fingered the cross around his neck. He was sitting next to Jessica who smiled over at me sympathetically. God. Why did she have to be so bloody nice all the time? It was unbearable.

I turned back to Stevie B. 'It was a good night,' I said. 'Can I talk to you about something? Not in here, though.'

We left the canteen and my head was spinning but I knew I had to talk to him.

'I know what you're going to say,' he said as we reached the football shelter and sat down. *That's more than I do*, I thought. But he went on. 'You're dumping me, right?'

'Stevie,' I began.

'Nah, it's OK,' he said. 'I know we weren't properly going out or anything.'

Thank God for that.

'But I like you, though,' he said. 'I was gonna ask you out. Properly like. On a date.'

There was a kind of sad silence. I guessed he was hoping that I would say I'd like to go on a date with him. But I didn't want that. I didn't do 'dating' really. I was all about the casual. I guessed that I should have let him know that in advance, but I had assumed he was the same as me. Most boys were.

'I'm sorry,' I said. 'I wasn't trying to lead you on or anything. I just wasn't thinking, I suppose.'

He raised both eyebrows and shrugged. 'C'est la vie!' He smiled, then he said, 'You're a great kisser, you know.'

I laughed.

'I mean it. Snog of the century.'

'Shut up!'

'Awk, don't be embarrassed now, Cari. After all we've been through?' He was joking around, trying to cover up the awkwardness, and that was fine by me. 'How about one last kiss, to say goodbye?'

*Why not?* I thought. I felt like absolute hell. My head was banging like a thousand drums. My whole body wanted to lie down on that pitch and sleep for the rest of my life. A kiss might cheer me up a bit, knowing what was ahead.

And so we had our One Last Kiss, and then we had a hug where we patted one another on the shoulders and it made me feel like we were two business associates sealing a deal. Weirdest and best break-up ever. My first proper break-up really. Suddenly I felt something like a deep gratitude for Stevie B. being so nice about the whole thing and I grabbed him and pulled him in for a proper hug.

'I do want us to still be friends,' I said. 'Can we do that?'

'Yeah, not a prob,' he said, smiling. 'Come on, we'll be late back.'

The rest of the day was a tired blur. It was simply a matter of survival. I reckon I heard about ten per cent of what any teacher said to me. I couldn't remember actually writing anything at all.

By the time I got back to the estate Dawn had brightened up a bit. She actually smiled at me when I came in, which made me immediately suspicious.

'Let's have a chat in the kitchen,' she said.

Oh God.

Dawn poured the tea. She had a plate of muffins on the table. Was she trying to guilt-trip me? Or was this softening me up for a massive blow? Were they about to get rid of me? That was it. I was sure. We'd have our 'chat' and then Madge would turn up and that would be that. Shit. I'd really messed things up. Again. Shit shit shit.

'Are you OK?' Dawn asked. 'Have a muffin.'

I could feel myself starting to well up. Don't cry. Don't bloody cry now. 'I'm sorry, Dawn. I really am.' A couple of tears edged out and I wiped them away before they could fall.

'OK.'

*OK?* What did that mean? It clearly was *not* OK!

Dawn sipped her tea calmly and began peeling a muffin from its wrapper. They did look good, and I hadn't had lunch. She put it on the plate in front of me.

'Thanks,' I said, taking a bite. The sugar made my head zing and I realised how hungry I was. She let me finish the muffin before speaking again.

'So. I called Dave.'

Uh oh.

'He answered the phone and said, *Big Gay Dave?*'

There was no hint of a smile on Dawn's face. Oh, this was not good. I let her continue while my brain scrambled for anything I could say to make things better.

'So, *Dave* said he'd taken you to the *social club* and that there was alcohol being served. But, of course, I already knew that because of the state of your friend Brains.'

*Oh God, Dave. What else did you tell her?*

'He was very apologetic about that. He said he thought that the two of you were in final year of school.'

Thank God. I nodded.

'I asked him if he was all right after his "fall".' She did the air quotes. She knew. 'And he said he was fine, you'll be glad to know, but that he had had to get two stitches. Quite some *fall* he must have taken.'

I sipped my tea, hoping I could partially hide behind the dainty china cup. It was scalding and so good.

'Anyway. He was concerned for your welfare and I let him know that you and your friend were home safely.'

If she knew anything else she wasn't giving it away, which was almost worse. I didn't know what I was dealing with now. What was the right thing to say?

'I am sorry. I should have . . . ' Should have what? I didn't even know, really. 'I should have probably called you earlier.'

'Yes, you should.'

There was a silence. I had no idea what she was thinking. Was she angry about the drinking? Or was the gayness the worst thing? Or the fight? Or having to pick us up? Maybe it was everything. Someone had to speak, though, because silence was the worst thing of all.

'Whatever the punishment is, that's fine,' I said.

Dawn half-smiled. 'I think we'll have go back to that curfew,' she said.

I nodded. Was that it? A curfew?

'And . . . '

Oh crap.

'And I want you to tell me what's going on with your friend, Brains.'

'Eh?'

'He was in quite a state, Cariad. Did he have any drugs, at the "social club"?' Air quotes again.

'No! I mean, I wasn't with him all night, but I don't think so.'

'You weren't with him?'

'No. He was with . . . well, he was with other people.'

'What other people?'

'I don't know. Other . . . teenagers, like us.'

She raised an eyebrow. 'I'm being fair with you here, Cariad.

185

I need to know if there's anything that your friend's mum needs to know. If it's drugs, then—'

'It's *not* drugs!'

'Well? How does someone get into that state? The child was crying in the back seat of Mrs Crothers's car.'

Oh God.

'Right, OK. He had had a drink. Or two. But that's all, as far as I know. Brains doesn't do drugs. He's really smart.'

'He didn't look very smart last night.'

'He's going through a rough time at the minute, OK? He just, I dunno, let himself go a bit. He's fine, though. He's probably fine.'

'I phoned Mrs Baxter this morning. He *is* fine. But she's concerned about him.'

Another pause.

'I want to ask you something, Cariad. You don't have to answer but if you do answer I'd like the truth, please.'

'OK...'

'That *social club* you were in.' She was looking directly at me. 'Was it ... a homosexual club?'

It wasn't funny but the way she said 'homosexual' made me want to laugh. *Homo-seck-shual*. I bit the inside of my cheek and dropped my eyes to the empty plate. Eventually I was able to speak without smirking.

'Yes. But it's not like you think.'

'Oh? And what do I think?'

'I dunno. Maybe you think it was like some seedy place, or something. The way that some people talk about gay clubs, or even gay people, like they're weird or wrong or something. But it was just a club with people dancing and ...'

'And drinking and taking drugs?'

I thought back to the girl with the poppers. That didn't really count as drugs, did it? Then I thought about the jugs of colourful cocktail.

'Some people were drinking, but that's normal in a club. Nobody was doing anything wrong.'

'You're sixteen, Cariad!' Her voice was louder now.

'I know. I'm sorry. It's not Dave's fault. He did think we were eighteen.'

'Big *Gay* Dave?'

'Yes.'

It was my turn to start getting pissed off. They were all so backward. So what if he was gay?

'Big *Gay* Dave took us to the Big *Gay* Club for Big *Gay* Fun.'

Dawn's face was a storm. I'd really done it now. If she hadn't phoned Madge already then she was bound to do it now.

'Sorry,' I muttered into my teacup.

'Are *you* . . . gay, Cariad?'

I spluttered the tea. Not that the question was shocking in itself, but coming from Dawn? It was like someone asking if you slept in the nude or something.

'No. I'm not.'

'I'm not trying to embarrass you.' But she went on. 'Is Brains? Is he . . . a homo-sex-ual?'

Jesus. Was it OK to answer this? Maybe Brains didn't want everyone to know?

'You said I didn't have to answer the questions.'

'I did say that. That's fair, I suppose. I'm just worried about him, you know.'

'I know. But there's nothing bad about being gay. And you said yourself that he's fine.'

'He was so upset, though.'

I sighed. Maybe if I told her a little bit of truth she'd stop going on and on about it.

'OK, look. Brains was seeing someone. They were close. And he got dumped. It's only just happened and we went out with Dave to cheer him up. He got a bit drunk and he was upset because of the break-up. And that is *all* there is. OK?'

Dawn nodded. She probably knew there was a bit more to it than that, but really it was none of her business about Brains and Muff and she'd probably have been all delighted about Muff becoming a Christian and I couldn't have coped with it. If it wasn't for the church and Christians then they'd never have split up and Brains wouldn't have wanted to go out and I wouldn't be sitting here now contemplating another muffin and wondering if I was about to get sent away again. So actually it was partly her fault that this had all happened. And I was the one being punished! I wondered how long the grounding was going to last this time.

'Can I go now?' I asked.

'Yes. Dinner will be in an hour or so. Do your homework.'

Dawn got up and started clearing the table. I lifted anther muffin on my way out of the kitchen, trudged upstairs and fell, like a ton of bricks, onto the bed.

# Chapter 33

OK so, Dawn and Jacky hadn't called Madge, and that was good, and I should have been grateful. I *was* grateful. But I was also pissed off. Another curfew, to be heavily enforced, especially at weekends. For what? Trying to help a friend in need? Being responsible and letting Dave go to hospital when he needed to? As I dragged myself through the town towards school I felt like my brain was going to burst out of my head. Every time you tried to have a *tiny* bit of fun in this place there was someone ready to snap you back into the box. They were all *so* boring. And I was getting tired of being treated like some wild, feral animal that needed to be constantly watched. Tired of Jessica's niceness and attempts to 'include' me in a group that I had no desire whatsoever to be part of. They could all take a big leap off the cliff and get in the sea.

I passed the Jenny Haniver and thought about the cliffs and the cave and Robin. I'd far rather have been heading up that hill than getting on the bus to school. Urgh. I couldn't, though.

On the bus the only seat free was behind Jessica and Martha.

Their excited chatter stopped when they saw me, and I guessed I had been the subject of the conversation.

'Hiya!' said Jessica, brightly.

I managed a smile and a hello but I stuck my headphones in my ears so that they'd know I didn't want to talk. I sat down behind them. They'd probably rather be gossiping about me anyway, I thought. Sure enough, they resumed their chat as soon as the bus pulled away from the shelter. I lowered the volume on my phone so I could hear what they were saying. It wasn't me they were talking about. It was Brains and Muff. I stopped my music altogether, keeping my eyes down so they wouldn't suspect I was eavesdropping. They were whispering but I could just about make out their mutterings.

Martha: But do you really think James will go for it?

Jessica: He will if I ask him.

(giggles)

Martha: He mentioned you the other day . . .

Jessica: Oh my goodness, what did he say?

Martha: OK, well, you can't tell anyone I said this, right? I promised not to tell.

Jessica: Of *course* I won't tell!

Martha, leaning in closer: He said he really liked you, and that he didn't think it would be long before he . . . y'know . . . stopped liking boys . . . and then he might ask you out.

Jessica: Oh wow, that's amazing! I mean, it's amazing that he's already starting to like girls. That's so fast. It usually takes ages.

Martha: Yeah. I think sometimes it doesn't even work at all.

Jessica: Well, people really have to have faith, don't they? I think some people just don't give it a chance.

What *did* they mean '*it*'? Were they talking about Christianity?

Martha: When's Pastor Jeff coming to do it?

Jessica: After school today. I'm going to tell James later. It's best if he doesn't know much in advance, I think. Pastor Jeff's really brilliant, apparently. I read an article about him the other week. His results are amazing.

What the hell? What was Pastor Jeff, whoever he was, going to do with Muff? Prayer maybe. I hoped it was only prayer, anyway. It all sounded incredibly dodgy. I didn't get to hear any more because at the next stop Muff got on. Martha moved seats so that he could sit beside Jessica, and the conversation about '*it*' dried up.


Brains was back in school, at least. I found him in the library, face in a book about economics. He looked like hell. I sat beside him.

'Hiya,' he said. His voice was low, subdued.

'Hiya.' I smiled at him to let him know we were cool. He closed the book and looked around to make sure nobody was taking any notice of us.

'I'm so sorry about the other night.'

'It's OK. It really is.'

He shook his head. 'I made a real dick out of myself.'

'You didn't! You got pissed and got off with some fella. So what?'

Another furtive glance around the room. I lowered my voice to a whisper.

'We all got back safe, and Dave's totally fine. It's all good.'

He tried to smile. Poor Brains. His eyes were underlined with darkness. He looked like an old man.

'Hey,' I said, 'what about the skinny guy with the tattoos, then? Did you contact him?

'Nah. He sent me a few messages but I ignored them. I don't know what I was thinking.'

'Probably that you were sad and horny?'

He laughed.

'That's better,' I said. 'Come on, you're not the first person to get off your face after getting dumped.'

He winced. 'Sorry. Look, do you want to get out of here?'

'I really can't. I've got a test next period. I need to just focus on it and stop thinking about . . . about everything.'

'I understand. I'll leave you to it. Later, though?'

'Sure. And thanks.'

'What for?'

'For looking after me the other night. For not leaving me fast asleep at the feet of some scary bouncer in the middle of the city.'

'Duh, as if I would've done that.'

He smiled again and I moved my stuff to a different table. Jessica and Martha came in and sat opposite me. They unpacked their books. So neat, I thought. My files had torn pages hanging out and seemed to be half as full as theirs. Jessica's work was organised using pink and purple cardboard dividers and she had put every single page of notes into a little plastic cover. It must have taken her hours.

'Hi!' she whispered across the table.

I smiled at her and Martha as they opened up pencil cases stuffed with coloured gel pens and highlighters. I'd be lucky to find a leaky biro in my bag. Jessica took out a little book which had a wad of sticky notes inside. She wrote something and handed it to me.

*Sending notes as we're not meant to be talking, but also, it's a delicate matter. The Youth Fellowship are having a special meeting after school. Interested?*

Oh my God. Was she actually going to tell me what 'it' was?

*Yes.* I scribbled back. *What's it about?*

*It's about James. There's a special pastor who deals with relationship issues coming to speak to us. He's got this great idea about how we can help James.*

*Help him with what?* I wrote, knowing full well what she was talking about. I wanted her to say it, though.

*You know*, she wrote. *With his same-sex addiction.*

Addiction? That was a bit strong, wasn't it?

Jessica was scribbling another note. *He's doing so well. I think he just needs one final push before he can truly leave his past behind. I know this is all a bit weird for you, but hopefully you'll see why we're doing it later on. We just care about him. About you both. Xx*

I thought about sending a note back which said, 'Aye, you mostly care about getting into his pants.' Couldn't she see how obvious she was being? Then again, everyone else was getting involved too, and it was clear that almost everyone in this whole town thought that the world would be a better place if everyone was nice and neat and straight like the Youth Fellowship clones.

*OK*, I wrote. *I'll see you at the church after school then.*

I passed the note back and Jessica nodded at me. She showed the note to Martha who smiled at me and mouthed, 'Thank you', as if I was saying I agreed to whatever the hell it was that they were plotting.

# Chapter 34

Five-thirty p.m. and I was marching up the hill towards the cave with a fury I hadn't experienced in my whole life before. How dare they, I thought. How fucking *dare* they.

I had called Jacky and asked him if I could go to the church with the Youth Fellowship girls after school. He had said he'd have to ask Dawn but of course she was delighted by the idea. Maybe she even knew what was going to happen. Well, if I had known what was going to happen there's no way I would've gone. Or maybe I would have shown up just to torch the place. I was so angry stamping up that hill. I must have made it in double the usual time. I didn't even remember seeing the Jenny Haniver.

'It's me!' I called as I approached the cave, trying to slow myself so I didn't fall off the cliff.

'Come in!' he called back. 'Woah, are you OK? You look angry.'

'I'm really bloody angry,' I said. 'I'm gonna blow up. You got any drink?'

'Yeah sure. Here, sit down.'

'Don't tell me to calm down,' I said. 'If you tell me to calm down I might jump into the sea. And stop laughing, I'm not in the fuckin' mood.'

He bit his lip and handed me a glass. I downed it.

'Steady on. That's expensive stuff!'

'It wasn't expensive for you, was it, though?'

'Fair point.' He topped up my glass. His dark hair fell over his face. I could have kissed him right then, let all of the anger pass through me into his body and taken it back again from him. Instead I drank from the glass, let the harsh burn of the alcohol warm my throat and chest.

He poured another.

'So, what's up?' he said.

I felt slower. Able to speak. I told him what had happened. I told him all about Brains and Muff and the church and the night-club. And I told him about the after-school Youth Fellowship meeting. I told him how I had met them at the church. It was starting to get darker but the church was so quiet and black that I thought I'd got the wrong day, or that nobody else had shown up. But then I noticed a light at the side of the building. I walked towards it and went in through the side door.

'Jessica? Is anyone here?'

'Sssssh!'

Jessica appeared from the room with the light and took my arm, leading me in. 'They're just getting ready.'

'Ready for what? And why are we whispering?'

The people in the room were Jessica, Martha, Alicia and Gemma. Everyone sitting there on beanbags, in silence. Everyone looking solemn, like they were waiting for a vaccination.

'What's going on?' I said. 'Where's Muff?'

'James is with Pastor Jeff, in the other room.'

'Why? I thought someone was coming to give a talk to us? What's going on?'

'Sssssh!'

'And why the hell do I have to be quiet?'

'They're praying! And we're meant to be praying too. For James.'

I didn't like the quietness. The church was normally loud and busy, full of people jangling tambourines or making tea. Sitting in a dark room and wondering what was going on next door was giving me the creeps. Then Pastor Jeff came in. He was shorter than I had expected. The way Jessica had been talking about him earlier I'd imagined a six-foot muscle mountain, not some middle-aged balding bloke in a shabby suit.

'Ladies, your friend is ready now. Are you ready to support him?'

All of the *ladies* nodded. I looked at Jessica.

'Just go along with it,' she whispered. 'Try not to get freaked out. We're just going in to pray with James. It's to help him.'

Help him do what? I thought. Get straight? Get religious? Get *Jessica*? He didn't need any help with that one.

We filed into the dark room. Gemma gasped, giving voice to what I felt when I saw him. He was lying on a table in the middle of the room, his arms crossed over his chest, eyes closed, surrounded by candles, the only light in the room.

'Don't be alarmed,' the pastor said. 'James is fine. This is simply a spiritual illustration of what might be, should he continue on this path of unholiness.'

I can't believe I didn't walk out right then. I can't believe I didn't tell Pastor Jeff where he could shove his *spiritual illustration*. I could tell that the others hadn't been expecting this. Jessica's eyes were wide. But if we thought this was bad, the worst was yet to come.

'Now, ladies, as we imagine the departure of James due to unhealthy lifestyles, I'd like each of us in turn to imagine what we might say about him, if this was his real funeral.'

Gemma was crying now, her tears falling silently to the ground.

The pastor continued. 'It's upsetting, but this is the reality of the homosexual lifestyle, which so often leads people into drugs and disease. Let's take it in turns to let James hear what we might regret about this moment, if it were not simply an illustration of what might come. Let us speak out loud. Jessica?'

Jessica's face was stricken. She opened her mouth as if she was going to say something but she didn't speak.

Suddenly Gemma's crying became audible and she rushed forward, taking Muff's hand, and started pleading with him. 'Please don't be gay any more, Jamie. I don't want you to get AIDS and die!'

Muff's corpse also started to cry.

I wanted to switch on the lights and punch that stupid idiot pastor in his face. Something rooted me to the spot. I could feel the tension building in my chest and arms, like a knot of pure anger. *Say something*, I told myself, *just bloody say something*.

And then Jessica spoke. 'Pastor Jeff.' She cleared her throat and wiped her eyes. 'I think we've all understood the point now.'

'I haven't anointed James with oil yet,' he said. 'And then there are the prayers of exorcism.'

I lost it then.

'This is complete bullshit!' I yelled.

Everyone looked at me, including Muff, who sat up. I switched on the lights.

'How can you all fucking *do this*? It's warped! You all need a fucking head doctor – everyone except Muff who's just confused because you've all messed him up.'

I knew I was out of control at that point. I knew if I stayed there I'd start throwing things, or worse. Everyone was crying; everyone except for the pastor, who looked like he'd just seen someone streaking across the church car park. I knew I had to get out. I knew if I went to Dawn and Jacky's that I'd be in the worst trouble yet. Now I was really and truly in the shit. There was no getting out of it this time.

I ran out of the building, across the road, and I kept on running until I got to the cliffs. My mind was bursting with the injustice of it all. Yes, I had shouted at the pastor. Yes. I had sworn at him. But it wasn't fair. How come you had to be a homophobic prick if you wanted to stay in this town? How come not being like that was going to mean I had to leave yet another foster home? Madge used to tell me to remember – remember when you get angry that whatever it is, it's not the end of the world. Well that was easy for her to say, she had a world that stayed the same all the time. My world was always ending and then beginning and then ending. Nobody wanted me in their world, did they? Not really. Not actually.

'I do,' said Robin, after I'd finished ranting.

'What?' I was spitting fire. I'd been going on and on so much that I hadn't even stopped to drink more of the whiskey.

'I want you. In my world. I think you're class.'

I laughed and then choked a bit.

'Try to breathe,' he said. 'Woah, don't give me that look. I didn't say *calm down*, did I? You do literally need to breathe, though. It's kind of essential, for life and things.'

He was sitting beside me and he took my hand. I put my head on his shoulder and I breathed deeply. And pretty soon breathing turned to kissing. And kissing turned into lying down, so close to him. And lying down turned into . . . well, what it normally turns into. And it was different. It was warm and comfortable, and in that moment, I believed him, I believed that he did want me in his world, and I wanted him in mine. I forgot, for that moment, about Muff and Brains and Stevie B., and Jacky and Dawn and Madge, the Youth Fellowship and all their crappy pastors. There was just us, lying there together, not so much a *spiritual illustration* as a real, live something-good.

We fell asleep, covered by the cruise-ship blankets, and when we woke up nothing had changed. It was still dark. The fire was still burning. The sea was still outside, breaking on the rocks. Everything was calm. Everything was different.

We lay, wrapped in one another, for a long time.

'Are you OK?' he said.

'Yes,' I said. And I meant it.

The peace was broken by my phone ringing. The first thing I noticed was the time. 12.45 a.m. The next thing I noticed was that it was Dawn who had called. No doubt she had heard everything from Jessica by now. Well, I wasn't going back, not tonight, anyway. I left my phone and lay down again.

'You should send them a message,' Robin said. 'They'll be worried.'

199

'Fuck me, whose side are you on?'

'Yours.' He kissed my neck lightly. 'But there's no harm in letting them know you're safe and that you'll go home tomorrow, is there? You're lucky that someone gives a shit about you, really.'

Maybe he was right, but I hadn't wanted to break the spell. I wanted to forget about them all for as long as possible. It was all broken now anyway. I sighed and got up again to text Dawn.

**I'm fine. I'm staying out tonight. I'm with a friend. I'll see you in the morning.**

I switched off the phone. I wanted to try to get back to forgetting about them all. I needed another distraction; we couldn't just sit here in the cave all night.

'So. Are you taking me out to this cruise ship then, or what?'

# Chapter 35

'I knew you hadn't swum it!'

I swung my leg into the boat and hopped to get the other one in. Robin gave it a shove and jumped in before the whole thing was in the water. It was a canoe – a big one, but tiny in comparison to the massive ship we were headed for.

Robin handed me a plastic paddle. It seemed like a long way off and the water was dark, but it was still, like a mirror.

'I don't know how to use this thing,' I said.

'It's easy. Like this.'

Robin dipped the paddle and pulled. It did look easy but when I tried it I almost dropped the thing. He didn't laugh at me.

'Grip it here. Tightly. That's it. Now pull.'

'Shit. It's not easy!'

'We'll be grand once we get going.'

And soon we were coasting. I could feel the strength of Robin's pull and wondered if he was thinking about how weak I was, gripping the paddle for dear life, determined not to drop it.

It was freezing and the water made a glooping sound as we

passed over the surface. I tried not to think about falling in, or how the hell we were ever going to get from our tiny boat onto the ship, which loomed like a giant wall of metal as we got closer.

'Here!' Robin yelled, his breath working hard. He nodded to the piece of land to our left, not far from where the mighty ship had ended its journey. We paddled over and Robin jumped out of the boat, soaking his jeans to the knees. He trailed the boat in and offered me a hand.

'Leave the paddles. Help me pull this in.'

We shoved the canoe underneath a huge thorny bush. Not that anyone would have randomly come across it. We were at the bottom of a very steep cliff with only a couple of metres of shore – a slim path that wound around the edge of the sea. The boat's great bow almost tipped the cliff face a few metres away.

'Where'd you get the canoe?' I asked.

'That's what you want to know? Where I got the canoe?'

I shrugged.

'I nicked it. Some lads had been dicking around with it and they went for lunch. I dragged it for a bit, hid it, went back to the cave. It was easy.' He nodded towards the enormous ship in front of us. 'Any other questions?' he smirked.

'OK, smartarse. How are we getting onto this thing?'

'So glad you asked! Follow me.'

He led me around the path of sand.

'Mind the rocks.'

We clambered over the grey stones, slippery with seaweed and shining in the moonlight. 'I had a think about it,' he said. 'If all those rich people – families, kids, maybe disabled people too – if they were all able to get off this thing, then there must be a way to get onto it. Look.' Robin was pointing up to something on the side of the ship, but I couldn't see it. 'Here, help me with this.'

I followed him towards the bushes. He started to tug something out and I grabbed hold to help him pull. It was a ladder.

'Where the hell did you get this?' I said.

'They left it here when they were doing the rescue. I found it and hid it in the hedge.'

When it was free from the tangle of thorns he extended the length of it and set it up against the side of the ship. The rungs glittered with the movement of moonlight on the water. When he reached the top I saw what he'd been pointing at. A crack in the side of the ship which he was now heaving open. A little hatch. A balcony. Robin flipped himself over the rails and called down to me, 'Your turn now!'

I didn't want him to know I was scared but, climbing up that ladder in the dark, I felt the weakness in my arms and legs. I was tired from rowing but I couldn't go back now.

'Careful,' he said.

I could see the movement in the water below me, feel the breeze nudge the ladder softly.

'I know! Flip sake.'

'I just mean watch the ladder when you're climbing over. If we lose it we're stuck here.'

My heart pounding at the top, I clambered over the little fence and let him steady me as I looked down. We were less than halfway up the ship but it was still as high as my bedroom from the street.

'Now what?' I said.

# Chapter 36

Lit only by Robin's torch, the inside of the ship was dark and silent, like a haunted hotel. Large carpeted corridors led on to restaurants where the smell of rotting food filled the ornate rooms. There were other rooms with casino tables – abandoned dice and cards on the tables, and bars with half-drunk drinks on the counter, a huge glass chandelier with shards of crystal hung from the middle of the ceiling, dropping through several floors which darkened into black as we leaned over the balcony to peer down.

'This is class,' I whispered.

'Wait till you see this,' Robin said, taking my hand and leading me to the staircase.

We walked up and up in the shadows, holding the handrail, until we were at the top.

'Come on. This way.'

The electric doors had been prised open. One was at a weird angle, clearly broken. They led out to an eerie deck where rows and rows of loungers faced a swimming pool. There were towels and books all over the deck, flip-flops and bottles of beer. A lonely inflatable crocodile floated on the pool.

'Fancy a swim?' said Robin, taking off his shoes.

'You're joking,' I said. 'It'll be freezing.'

Nah,' he said, taking off his trousers and top, 'it's a luxury cruise. Heated pool.'

'Very funny.'

He was laughing, standing in his boxers.

'Oh come on, since when were you afraid of anything?'

Well, fuck it, I thought, there were bound to be dry towels in the rooms, weren't there? And when was I ever going to get a chance to do this again?'

I started taking off my jeans.

'Yeo! Good on you. I knew you weren't a wuss.'

'Oh aye? And how brave are *you*?' I said.

'What do you mean?'

I took off my top, and then quickly took off my bra and pants and jumped into the pool. The icy water stabbed my chest like a dagger and I came up screaming.

'Shiiiiiiite, it's cold!'

Robin was killing himself laughing.

'Your turn, oh brave one!' I yelled.

He pulled off his shorts and jumped in, holding his nose. Seconds later, he emerged with a wailing noise. 'Arrghhhhhh! Holy shit!'

'I know! Come on.'

We started to swim like mad to the other end of the pool, racing one another, Robin far ahead of me. I was laughing and trying not to swallow water at the same time. We raced around the deck pushing one another into the water, coursing down the huge tube slides and ducking under the surface trying to grab one another's feet. I thought about all the people who had been on the boat. All the little kids doing these things and having the time of their lives. This is what it's like to go on holiday, I thought. To be somewhere and doing things just for how good it feels and for long enough that you forget all about the real world and all the actual shit that you have to face up to. I didn't want it to end. But it was really cold, and even with all the running around our teeth were starting to chatter. Robin found a stack of towels in a store cupboard by the side of the pool and we wrapped ourselves up and headed down the stairs to the bars, leaving our clothes on the deck.

'Wait, sit here,' said Robin, patting his hand on one of the bar stools. 'I've always wanted to do this.'

He disappeared behind the bar and popped up, pushing his wet fringe out of his eyes, the water dripping down onto his bare chest. He adopted a broad Belfast accent.

'Right there, luv? What'll it be?'

'Ummm, pint of . . . I dunno, some beer or other?'

He shook his head sadly. 'Sorry, luv, Some Beer Or Other's off th'night. Taps are all bust. What about a wee shot, of –' he turned around to survey the shelves and lifted a bottle of green liquid '– a wee shot of apple sours?'

'Sounds like a plan.'

He lined up six shot glasses and dragged the neck of the bottle across them like we were in a cowboy saloon. He lifted one. 'Sláinte!'

'Aye. Cheers.'

The thick green drink was sharp bitter apple. We both pulled faces and had another shot. And then another.

'Urgh. Why the frig are we drinking this?' I said.

He shrugged. 'Let's see what else we can find.'

Fifteen minutes later we were in a passenger cabin, on a massive bed with a load of pillows, two heavy duvets over us, three bottles of fizzy pink wine and seven bags of crisps.

'OK, so,' I said, drinking straight from the bottle, 'this is class craic, and it does rather beg the question ...'

'Why am I living in a cave?'

'Exactly.'

'Well,' he said, opening a bag of salt and vinegar, 'it'd be more obvious if I was here during the day. There are people who go out with binoculars looking for dolphins and stuff. If they saw me sunning myself on the deck they might tout, or worse.'

'Worse?'

'Yeah, they might want in on it. Right now I've got this whole place to myself, and it won't last for ever, so I'm just kissing the joy as it flies.'

'What?'

'It's a poem. By William Blake.' He cleared his throat dramatically:

> *He who binds to himself a joy*
> *Does the winged life destroy*
> *But he who kisses the joy as it flies*
> *Lives in eternity's sunrise.*

I nodded. 'Live for the moment,' I said. 'I'll drink to that.'
We clinked wine bottles and took a drink.

'Exactly. But you don't want the joy to fly off sooner than it has to.'

I knew what he meant. You had to be prepared for good things to end, because they always did, but you don't have to chase them off on purpose. It made me think about Dawn and Jacky and I started wondering how badly I'd messed things up for myself. But thinking about it would ruin *this* moment.

'What's up?'

'Nothing,' I said. 'OK, look, I'm getting pissed here. I'm well on my way. And I'm gonna wake up in the morning and think, *Oh shit, I'm on a cruise ship and I'm in deep trouble.* So you have to distract me.'

'Well, no problem,' he said, leaving the bottle on the ground and reaching under the duvet to put his hand across my stomach.

'No, I don't mean that.'

He removed his hand and I put it back.

'It's fine. But, remember your promise?'

'Em, nope.'

'You said you'd tell me, on the boat, about you and Ms Trainor.'

'Oh aye. You really want to know about that?'

'Yeah. Please.'

Robin sat up, leaned over to pick the wine bottle up from the floor again. I leaned in against his chest and he told me everything.

'OK, yes, I did shag the history teacher. But it's not the whole story. It's not my whole story. I'm a bit drunk too, Cariad, so I'm gonna tell you the whole thing, and then when I'm done you can tell me if you believe it or not.'

# Chapter 37

This is what Robin told me in the cabin of the cruise ship.

'My folks divorced when I was little. Probably age five or something, I can't remember. My mum took it hard. She was working long hours at the Spar and not really making enough to pay the rent so we ended up getting kicked out and we lived with my aunt for a while, and then she wanted us out too, so we went in a hostel for a bit, and then we got a council house. It was pretty good. I made friends on the estate. My mum made some friends too. Everything was really OK until I was about thirteen.

'My mum got a new boyfriend: Richard. Then she got pregnant, and that's when stuff started going wrong. He was a dick. He wasn't violent or anything, but he really was an asshole to me. It was obvious he didn't want me around spoiling his nice new life. He'd send me to the shop at night knowing I hadn't taken my key and then lock me out till the morning, and then he'd have a go at me the next day for not taking my key. Stuff like that. My mum used to stick up for me and tell him not to be such a cruel bastard, but then she had the baby and she didn't have time to worry about other stuff any more. She didn't have time for *me*, really. And I guess I was getting older, I could look after myself. I started mitching off school, smoking dope in the park, generally just being an idiot.'

I tightened my arm around him. He continued.

'Then I met Ciara. She was so cool. I was sixteen, bored, *boring*. And she was this wild, red-haired girl who was good at stuff. Good at school, good at sports. That's how I met her, actually; she was in the park on the running track after school, just running round and round, training for something. Anyway, to cut a long story short, me and Ciara got along great. She even got me going back to school again. She was at a different one to me – the Catholic girls' school over the road, so I didn't know about her ... Anyway, she was great, and suddenly it felt like there was a point to everything. We even talked about going to college together, maybe even getting a place. All a big stupid fantasy, of course. A load of bollocks. What happened in the end was that I got her pregnant, her dad hit the fucking roof, and it transpired that good, honest, brilliant Ciara was actually only thirteen years old.

'Obviously, nobody believed me that I hadn't known. Her dad came over to our house and broke my nose. My mum's fella took a baseball bat to him and both of them ended up at the police station. It was wild. The two of them screaming blue murder at each other as the cops dragged them off, my mum holding my little brother, him wailing, Ciara phoning me in tears telling me she was so, so sorry. In the end Ciara's folks let it drop and the cops weren't that worried about the whole thing. Unfortunately, someone saw us in the police station and the rumour went round that I'd been arrested, and that was it. I was the town paedo. Women with little kids started crossing the street and someone spray-painted 'pervert' on our house. My mum was crying all the time, her boyfriend hated me more than ever, nobody in school wanted to hang out with me any more. I knew that once I left school I'd never get a job because everyone was totally convinced I'd been with a little kid. I passed my exams, but it didn't matter. Nothing mattered. Richard wanted me out, my mum was too depressed to want anything, and I didn't want to bump into Ciara ever again.'

Robin's voice shook slightly.

'So, I moved. Richard had a cousin who set me up in an apartment he owned while he was trying to rent it out. I enrolled at your school. It was OK for a while. I liked living on my own. Didn't like school but it was something to do and I had the Education Allowance money. I reckoned I was giving myself time to figure out what to do, and it was great being away from all the shit. Mum and Richard just dropped me off – never visited, never called. Richard's cousin never called in, either. I doubt any of them are bothered I've run off. Weight off their shoulders, really.'

He went quiet then. We lay in silence.

There were so many things I wanted to ask. Finally I said: 'Weren't you lonely? On your own in the apartment, I mean?'

He shrugged. 'Better than living in a cave. It was OK. There were people at school.'

I thought about Ms Trainor. We'd get to her soon enough, though.

'What about the baby?' I said. 'I mean, have you got a kid now?'

'Oh. Ciara's dad made her get an abortion. Best thing, probably.'

Jesus.

'So, why did you run off then?' I said. 'I mean, after moving here and getting a place to stay and everything?'

'Well, that's where the history teacher comes in.'

'Hang on,' I said.

I reached to the side table and grabbed another bag of crisps. I hadn't eaten anything since the end of school and I was starving. I wondered what time it was, how long until sunrise. Robin offered me the pink wine bottle and I shook my head. If I drank any more I wouldn't be able to get down that ladder again. I hoped he'd be able to manage it.

'So,' I said, 'Ms Trainor. What's the craic?'

'Well, first you have to promise not to pass this shit on. She really would lose her job.'

'No probs.'

I thought about how much Jessica would love to know the real story – all her suspicions come true. The Youth Fellowship would have prayer and gossip material for months. But I meant my promise. I mean, I might have a word with Ms Trainor, let her know that I knew – after all, if she had been a male teacher who'd shagged a female student it would be different, wouldn't it? But he must've been almost eighteen. I mean other kids his age were already married with babies, not still wearing school uniforms and worrying about homework. Still. She was a teacher. It wasn't right. Robin was lying with his head back on the pillows, a mess of hair swept over his face, eyes closed, hand still gripping the wine bottle. I put my hand on his chest and pushed slightly to see if he was still awake. He seemed really young in that moment. Like a little kid, almost.

Robin shook himself alert and carried on. 'It's hard to say how it started. I had asked for help with an assignment or something and somehow the after-school help went from an hour one day to an hour every week and then twice a week . . . It was obvious she liked me. She started wearing shorter skirts and more make-up. Started giving me little compliments, touching my arm a little bit when we talked.'

He smirked as he remembered it. I took my hand from his chest and his smile dropped.

'Hey. It was a while back. Don't be jealous.'

'Fancy yourself, don't you?' I said, trying to sound detached and cool.

'Yeah, and you fancy me too.' He winked, looking more like his brash, confident self, and I rolled my eyes. 'Come on, I'm only messin'. If you want to know the truth I've only done it with two people, three now . . .' He nudged me. 'And you're the best one.'

I wondered if he meant it.

'Better than a teacher and a twelve-year-old?' I said. 'Oh great!'

He picked up the humour in my tone. 'Thirteen!'

'Big difference, stud.'

'Ha! Well, it is actually. I might've ended up on the paedo register for real if she'd been twelve.'

'Shiiiiiit.'

'I know. Lesson learned.'

'Right. I can see how shagging your teacher would be safer.'

'Yeah. Safer for me, anyway.'

'So what happened? Youse started doing it. Like, where? In

213

the history store? Ewwwwww, I was in there last week getting a notebook.'

He laughed and put my hand back on his chest. 'It's *all* history now. Better to leave it in the history store, I think.'

'Very funny. But seriously, though. Why did it finish? Come on – you said you'd tell me.'

He sighed. 'OK then. We were meeting up for a few weeks. It was fun. It was something to do. I honestly didn't think it was a serious thing. And then –' he took another drink of wine '– well, then it started getting serious.'

'What do you mean?'

Part of me didn't want to know. Did he fall in love with her? Is that why he'd run off? What did it matter to me anyway?

'She started talking about leaving her husband.'

'Holy shit! She has a husband?'

'Yep. Big bastard, too.'

'Oh my God. So what happened?'

He stretched his arms out, sweeping them round the room. 'This.'

'Eh?'

'That's when I took off. She was gonna blow the whole thing up. She had this mad idea about us running off together. To be honest, I was tempted for half a second. She's really all right, like. But nah. I didn't want to do it really – settle down and everything. Not after Ciara and all that trouble. So when I said I didn't want to . . . '

'She got upset?'

'Yeah. I really think she might've announced it to the world or something.'

'Jesus.'

'Yeah, I know. I felt bad about it really – like I should have realised it was going to happen. But I didn't. And it wasn't totally her fault, she was just carried away with the whole thing.'

'Robin. She was your *teacher*. It *was* totally her fault.'

He shrugged. 'It was probably time for me to move on, anyway. She's not a bad person. I know she shouldn't have done it. But I knew it was wrong too. And she wasn't that much older than us, really.'

I knew that feeling: the feeling that you had to take responsibility for everything that happened to you. But watching someone else feeling it made it seem different. He was so cool on the outside, so controlled and strong. Maybe that's how people saw me, too. It's what I tried to convince them of, what I tried to convince myself of. Maybe it was the drink, but his eyes glistened slightly and it made me wonder what age we were when we started thinking that the things adults did to us were partly our fault?

There was a time of silence.

'Cariad?' said Robin.

'Uh huh?'

'Can I ask you something?'

I turned in towards him, and our faces were almost touching. 'OK.'

'I'm gonna have to leave here soon. You were right about them trying to tow the ship. There was a bunch of official-looking people with clipboards and stuff on the cliffs the other day and I could hear them talking about it. It's time for me to move on.'

'Can't you just go back to your place? Say you had, like, I dunno, a mental breakdown or something for a bit?'

He shook his head. 'Nah. I don't want to go back, and it's risky, you know.'

'Because of Ms Trainor?'

'Yeah, but also 'cause I've been robbing the ship and stuff. If they found out . . .'

'Damn.'

He pulled me closer to him. 'I know. I'll miss the free booze.' He smiled. 'But what I'll really miss is you.'

I felt sick then. He was deadly serious, and the worst thing was that I felt the same way. I tried to say something but nothing would come out. I knotted myself up with the thought of him leaving. I was sure he could feel the heat from my face, hear the thud in my chest, like maybe when you can't speak with your mouth your body steps in and says it anyway. We held one another in silence for what seemed like ages, both wanting to speak and not-speak.

Eventually he said, 'The thing I wanted to ask is, will you come with me when I take off?'

All of me wanted to say yes. Yes, with words. Yes, with kisses. Everything.

But I didn't say yes.

'I don't know,' I said.

'OK,' he replied, and it was like he snapped shut in some way. The seriousness was gone, a manhole cover wedged over everything that had just happened between us. 'Well, I suppose it's a big decision,' he said sharply. 'Think about it.'

I tried to imagine a note of disappointment in his tone. I wanted to reverse everything and go back to five minutes ago when he'd made me terrified to speak in case I said something

I'd never said before, something about feeling something new and frightening and brilliant. But now the silence had no electric charge. It was just empty. We fell asleep and woke as the sun began creeping past the cabin curtain.

# Chapter 38

I turned on my phone at around lunchtime. Angry texts from Dawn. Upset texts from Jessica. A couple from Brains just asking what I was up to. One from Stevie B. asking if I knew when the English assignment had to be in. I texted Dawn:

> Hi. Sorry about last night. I'm not at school. I'm coming
> back now and I'll tell you everything.

It was a lie. I wasn't going to tell anyone about Robin or the cruise ship. But there was no point in trying to hide anything about the church. She'd find out soon enough and, anyway, I'd had enough of apologising for getting angry about it all. I hadn't been sorry before and I wasn't sorry now. I knew I'd be getting sent on to another foster home, or just to a hostel or council flat if I was lucky. Or maybe I'd take Robin up on his offer. Either way, I had nothing to lose by telling the truth. That was a lie too. I thought about Brains. And the cliffs. There was always something to lose. But I was used to this, wasn't I? It wasn't like

I'd never had to start again before. The only thing to think about now is which way I wanted to start again.

I didn't rush back to the estate. I wanted a shower and to brush my teeth so badly but my head was pounding and I was starving. I stopped at the Mace and got myself a sausage roll and a tin of Coke. I wondered if I could text again and ask Dawn to put the water on so I could get a shower when I got back. I decided against it.

An hour later I was clean and sitting at the kitchen table in front of a bowl of lentil soup and a stony-faced Dawn and Jacky. It was obvious that Jacky had been forced to be there. He shifted around in his seat, trying not to look at me. But Dawn's face was focused. Her mouth was ready to speak. She'd probably been up all night thinking of what she was going to say. The soup was boiling. I blew on the spoon and sipped. It was rich and salty. I wanted to say *thank you* but the atmosphere was so tense it felt like whoever spoke first would be tossing a grenade right into the middle of the table. In the end it was Dawn, of course, who spoke.

'I'm angry, Cariad.'

No shit, Sherlock. I tried not to make a face. She continued.

'We have not asked much of you. Just that you stick to our small number of rules and give people a chance. But you've continually just done as you have pleased, and I cannot for the life of me fathom your continued rudeness to the Youth Fellowship and visitors to our church.'

Her voice had wobbled slightly on *visitors*. Jesus, it really meant a lot to her to be nice to those knobheads. I wanted to tell her that they deserved it, but I kept my head low. Being reminded of what happened at the church yesterday made me want to *be* the grenade. I wasn't sure I could hold myself back if I started trying to explain.

It was Jacky's turn to speak then. Dawn must have prepped him for it because there was no way he would've chipped in by himself. God. Had they been up all night discussing good cop/bad cop tactics? Just tell me when I'm getting picked up by Madge, for God's sake. No need for the lectures. His tone was softer.

'Cariad, we have to do something.'

Oh, here it comes. Finally.

'We've been thinking,' he said, quietly, 'that maybe it would be best if you moved—'

I stood up to leave.

'Where do you think you're going, young lady?' snapped Dawn.

'To pack?' I said. 'I get it. Just let me know what time Madge will be here. I don't have much to clear up.'

'Sit *down*. We are not finished!'

Well, I owed her the right to have a rant, didn't I? I could give her that. I sat down and started eating the soup again. It was so good. And it meant I didn't have to look at them.

'You've got it wrong, Cariad,' said Jacky. 'We don't want you to move out.'

I looked up at him. 'You literally just said . . .'

'Oh, for God's sake, won't you *listen* for a change!' said Dawn.

I dropped the spoon. Dawn *never* said *God* or *Jesus*, or any swears. She had my attention now.

Jacky looked uncomfortable. He put his hand over Dawn's and she dropped her shoulders. He shook his head.

'Cariad. This is your home,' he said. 'When are you going to realise that?'

Home. The word, coming from him, and said so kindly, made me want to throw up. I bit my top lip.

He continued. 'I just meant that maybe you'd like to move to the garage. We're thinking of converting it into a little apartment. You could have a key. We'd still be keeping an eye on you, and there'd still be a curfew and things, but, well, maybe it's time for us to trust you a bit more . . . let you decide who your friends are.'

'What?' I couldn't believe it. Dawn's face was still fierce. Did she agree with this? It didn't make any sense. 'But, I stayed out all night. I told that hokey pastor to fuck off. I don't understand . . .'

Dawn spoke, her voice calmer now. 'We spoke with Madge. We wanted her advice. We haven't been the parents of an older teenager before, Cariad. We were worried that maybe it was our fault that you were acting like this.'

'It's not!' I surprised myself by the force of the words.

Just yesterday if you'd asked me whose fault this all was I would've said all of them, for sure – Dawn, Jacky, everyone. Now I was defending them as they accused themselves.

'It's me!' I said. 'I told you before, I'm not a good person, Dawn. But, the thing is, I've decided. I've decided that actually I'm OK with that. I don't like the church, I really do think they're all homophobes. They're being total shits to Muff. And I know that you hate swearing, but if I'm honest I really love it. I love saying shit. And fuck. And Jesus. And I can't change! I just can't, and I don't want to. I don't want to, even though this soup is so nice, and you're so nice and . . .'

I was crying then, because it was all true. I would never have guessed that them being kind would be the thing that was hardest to deal with. But here I was, bawling my eyes out in front of them and all because I noticed how Jacky had winced when I'd said 'Jesus'. Why did I have to be so hurtful all the time? But at my very core I knew that that was just who I was.

'Sssssh, ssssshhhhh,' said Dawn, who had got up from her seat and now crouched beside me, pulling my head to her shoulder. 'You *are* a good person, Cariad. You do some really silly and dangerous things sometimes, but you are good, really.'

'I'm not. I'm not,' I blubbed. I felt like a seven-year-old.

'Why else would what's happening with your friend upset you so much? You're angry because you're afraid for him. And I have to say, I'm worried about him myself.'

I looked up and wiped my eyes. 'You are?'

'Yes. Jessica came over last night. She was very upset, and she told us what had happened at the church.'

I bet she did, I thought. She'd have told them all about how rude I was. How I interrupted their emotional take-down of Muff's entire personality. Maybe I had caused a row between her and Muff too. That would've upset her, wouldn't it?

'It was awful,' I said. 'They're trying to make him straight. Did she tell you they made us all pretend he was dead? It was fuckin' sick.'

Jacky winced again.

'Sorry, Jacky. But it was.'

Jacky nodded.

'She did tell us that, yes,' said Dawn, standing now, with her hand on my shoulder. 'And maybe you don't realise it, but Jessica thought they had gone too far as well.'

'Too far? He asked us to say *what we missed about Muff*. And then he said that being gay would kill him and we'd all be crying for real if he didn't give it up!'

Dawn frowned. 'That's horrible,' she said.

'Yeah, it is. But it's also horrible to even want him to be straight. It's stupid and wrong and I don't regret what I did, Dawn. I just don't.'

I needed her to know that I wasn't going to apologise again. That they couldn't bribe me with the promise of my own space. I was never going back to that church. Ever.

Dawn returned to her seat. 'What does James feel about all of this?' she asked.

'Well, that's a good question, because I don't know. He won't talk to me, or any of his old friends. But I doubt he's enjoying himself very much.'

She nodded. 'OK. Well, I want to think about all of that. But the main thing, Cariad, is that you realise that if we are angry with you it's because we are worried about you. When you don't come home, we are *worried*.'

'I texted.'

'Yes, and I'm glad you did. But we still don't know where you were all night.'

'I was at the cliffs.'

'The cliffs?'

'Yeah. I just stayed out. Because I didn't want to come back here. And I was angry. I wanted to think about everything.'

'OK.'

I looked up. How could it be *OK*?

'I mean. I'm still ... annoyed ... that you stayed out,'

explained Dawn. 'But I'm also sad that you didn't feel you could come and talk to us.'

Her lip started to tremble. Jacky put his hand on top of hers again. He leaned forward, a sincere look in his eyes.

'That's why we called Madge, love. We wanted some advice. Thought it was maybe our fault that you didn't come back.'

'It wasn't. Not really,' I said, suddenly feeling the exhaustion of the hangover underneath the heaviness of the conversation.

Jacky noticed. 'Why don't you go and have a wee lie down?'

I stood up to go.

'I'm sorry, though,' I said. 'I mean, I'm not really sorry about the stuff I said ... or about what I did, either. But I don't want you to be upset about it. I'm sorry for that.'

As I walked past Dawn, she grabbed my hand and gave it a squeeze. I knew that she had already forgiven me.

# Chapter 39

I tried to avoid Jessica and the others in school the next day. I could feel her looking at me across the canteen and I left before she could work up the nerve to come over. She was sitting with Muff and Gemma. They all looked depressed, to be honest, but that was their own fault, wasn't it? I was all out of ideas on how to rescue Muff. Maybe if this is what he wanted then there was nothing I could do. I walked to the library and the other misery was there, his face in a book as usual.

'Hey,' said Brains, looking up.

'Hey,' I whispered back, noticing the librarian's pinched face looking over. 'Did you hear about the church thing?'

'Yeah.'

That's all he said. I could see tears starting to line his eyes. I opened my bag and took out some work. How would he feel if he knew I had been thinking about Robin's offer to run off with him on top of everything? The thought of our last night in the cave and then being on the boat made my heart thump against my chest. It was the best secret. But it had to be a secret. And if

I left I wouldn't be able to tell anyone. I thought of Dawn and Jacky holding one another's hands at the kitchen table, and the lentil soup, and what they'd said about trying to be good parents. I wondered if I would ever hold anyone's hand in a kitchen like that. Whatever I chose to do, I'd be hurting someone, maybe I'd be hurting myself most of all. But how could I stay and watch Brains get pounded to bits like this? There was nothing I could do for him, anyway. I just wanted to get away from it – from this puzzle that didn't have a solution.

'I didn't mean to upset you,' said Brains quietly, blinking hard.

'Sssshhh, you haven't, I'm fine.'

I tried to smile and we both just got on with our work then, a relief from having to think about everything.

When I got back after school I headed straight for the kitchen. I had had a slight headache all day, still bruised from the cabin wine. It was the worst hangover ever, but it had been worth it. My head was still a bit fuzzy, so it took me a second to register that someone else was sitting at the kitchen table with Dawn, and that it wasn't Jacky. I almost dropped the orange juice when I saw who it was.

'Afternoon, Cari!' beamed Big Gay Dave, no doubt amused by the look on my face. He was sipping tea from Dawn's best china – the stuff with the roses on it. His long black hair was tied back so I could clearly see the fading bruise on his cheek and the stitches on his forehead.

'Dave! Are you . . . I mean, *how are you?*'

'Still livin'!'

Dawn invited me to join them and I sat down. A plate of

fresh scones sat on a plate on the best tablecloth. This hadn't been a casual 'dropping by' kind of visit. Dawn smirked at my confusion.

'Dave and I have been chatting,' she said.

'Really?'

'Yes. Don't look so surprised, Cariad. Old people can use the phone as well, you know.'

'I just meant—'

Dave cut in. 'Dawn phoned me. She wanted to talk about Brains.'

'And to see how you were, dear,' said Dawn, offering Big Gay Dave another scone.

'Yes,' he said. 'She's very kind.'

He smiled at Dawn like they were in some kind of mutual appreciation club. It was surreal.

'Anyway, Dawn told me something had happened, with Muff, at the church?'

Dawn interrupted. 'Yes, I called Dave to ask for his advice. I thought maybe he might know how to help your friends, Cariad.'

I tried to imagine the conversation where Dawn had explained things to Dave about my *homo-seck-shual* friends and asked for his advice. I wanted to sink under the table. But Dave didn't look bothered in the slightest.

'Incredible scones, Dawn,' he said. 'You must give me the recipe. When I make scones they're always ... I dunno, a bit *squeaky* or something?'

'Oof. Well there's an easy remedy for that. Next time you come we'll bake them together.'

What. The. Actual. Hell. Was. Going. On? It was like I wasn't there. What was Dave going to do in return? Teach Dawn about the gay scene in Belfast? They were chuckling together like they'd known one another for months.

'So . . . why are you here, Dave?' I asked.

Dawn answered. 'I want you to tell Dave, and me, what exactly is happening with your young friend.'

'Muff?'

'Yes. Tell us what you know,' she said. 'You were so upset about it, and Jessica was too. I really think we can't ignore what's happening, and maybe we can help.'

So I did. I told them the whole thing about Brains and Muff being boyfriends, and about Gemma being a Christian and Muff getting involved in the church, and about Muff trying not to be gay and the crazy pastor getting us all to pretend we were at his funeral. At different points Dawn looked shocked, but Dave didn't. By the end of the story he did look sad, though.

'I don't know what to tell you,' he said, when I had stopped talking. 'This all sounds very familiar.'

'Really? Even the fake death thing?'

'Well, sort of. I've had friends go through lots of things like that. So-called "therapy" that was meant to make them straight, exorcisms—'

'*Exorcisms?*' said Dawn.

'Yeah. More common that you'd think,' said Dave.

'All this is quite shocking,' said Dawn. She poured everyone a fresh cup of tea. 'I mean, I understand that some people think the Bible condemns homosexuality, but . . . '

'Do you not think that, too?' I asked her.

She put down the teapot and glanced at Dave.

'I hadn't really given it much thought,' she said, 'but I don't see why anyone would want to change another person if they're not harming anyone. God is love, after all. Don't look so surprised, Cariad. I might be old but they did have gay people in my day too, you know.'

Dave giggled and Dawn smiled at him.

'This is not your excuse to go gallivanting off and underage drinking, mind you,' she went on, looking at me. 'There's time enough for nightclubs when you're older.'

Why did I feel like the silly little kid in the room, all of a sudden? And how was she blaming me for the nightclub thing when it was her new BFF, Dave, who had taken me there?

'Don't scowl, Cariad. Let's talk about how we can help your friend, Muff,' she said.

It was the first time she'd said his name and I grinned in spite of myself. Dave caught my eye and I had to bite my lip to keep myself from bursting out laughing.

We hatched a plan until it was too late to make dinner, and Dawn sent Jacky out for chips for us all. It was nice having Dave there. Even with his black, torn T-shirt and the stitches you could see he was a kind soul. He helped Dawn wash the dishes and chatted gently with her about the garden and baking. I wondered if this was what it was like to have an older brother or a cousin or something. Someone else to be there taking the focus off you once in a while. Jacky came back with the chips and no more was said about the plan that evening, but as we waved Dave off it was clear that the mood had lifted and all of us were feeling more hopeful, like maybe Muff had a chance. We'd find out soon enough.

# Chapter 40

## Cruise liner to be towed

The newspaper on the doorstep had been folded so that only the headline was visible, and as I lifted it to bring in to Jacky I felt the urge to leave it folded, but I knew I had to find out more. Unrolling the story, I read the first few lines.

> Eight weeks after the 3000-capacity cruise liner was grounded off the coast of Ballybaile, authorities say they finally have plans to have the ship towed. The nature of the damage to the ship has meant that it has been stuck on our scenic coast for two months while experts researched a way to remove the ship without causing more damage. Finally work will begin to move the luxury boat which boasts 500 cabins, and fifteen decks. The starting date for the huge operation is Monday 3 December. Residents should be advised that the installation of equipment could disrupt local beauty spots for a number of days.

I looked at my phone. Third of December. That was just over a week away.

'Is my paper there, Cari?' called Jacky from the living room.

'Coming now, Jacky.'

I could hardly speak for the knot of panic forming in my throat. A week. A week to decide if I was going to say goodbye to Robin for ever. Or perhaps he'd leave earlier than that? Oh God, what if he got wind of the news today and decided to leave now?

'Jacky,' I said, trying to sound calm and breezy as I handed him the paper.

'Yes, love?'

'Em, can I get you a cup of tea?'

Jacky looked amused. 'OK. That would be nice,' he said. 'What are ye after?'

There was no point pretending, and it was urgent.

'I need to go out later. I mean, I want to go out later. To see a friend. Can I? I won't be out late, I promise.'

'Yes, that's fine,' he said.

'Really?'

'Yes.'

'But. The other night? Am I not grounded?'

He folded his paper closed.

'We haven't really decided about all that yet, Cari. We need to sit down and have a chat about it. All of us. A family discussion – that's what Madge suggested. We'll do it soon, though, OK?'

'OK.'

I went off to get the tea before he changed his mind. A *family discussion*. But I couldn't think about it now. I had to find out what was happening with Robin, if he was still there.

# Chapter 41

The next morning Madge had called. It was her usual check-in with me. She wanted to make sure I didn't feel that she'd been going behind my back talking to Dawn and Jacky. She was good like that. You could trust her with most things. I sat on the top step talking to her. Dawn and Jacky were out for a walk so I knew I could say anything at all, but obviously there were some things I didn't want to tell her.

'So, how's everything now?' she said. 'Now' meant 'after you stayed out all night and scared your foster carers half to death'.

'OK,' I said.

'*Really* OK? Or *I don't want to talk about it* OK?' She knew me pretty well.

'Really OK,' I said. 'Thanks for talking to Dawn. We had a good chat about everything.' Well, I thought, not about *everything*.

'OK, good. I'm proud of you, Cari.'

'What? Why?'

'Because you came back.'

'What do you mean?'

'You were angry, you stormed off, you stayed out all night. All stuff you've done before. But this time you came back. By yourself, I mean.'

She was talking about all the other times I'd run away from homes or foster placements and the cops had brought me back. It hadn't occurred to me before, but she was right – I'd never returned through my own choice in the past.

'You're really making an effort,' she said.

The funny thing was I hadn't even thought about it. It hadn't been an 'effort' at all. I knew I would go back – that time, at least. It was automatic. I hadn't even felt like staying out. I didn't tell Madge all of this, mainly because the thought of running away with Robin was still on my mind. *What I'll really miss is you.* His words had been going round and round in my head since he'd said them. I thought about everyone caring about each other – Dawn caring about Jacky, Jacky caring about Dawn, Brains caring about Muff. Maybe this was my chance to be like that – to care about someone properly, someone who cared about me too.

'So,' continued Madge in a breezy tone, 'what are you up to today then?'

I was going to go and see Robin.

'Dunno,' I lied. 'Might go for a walk, see some friends, maybe.'

'Sounds good,' she said. 'Anything else you want to talk about?'

'No, everything's cool.'

'Well, I think you're doing really well, Cariad. And I know you're sixteen now, but if you want to talk through anything then you know my number. I'm here for you, OK?'

'Thanks, Madge.'

I meant it and I knew she meant it too. She'd been with me for years now. Closest thing I'd had to a real family. Maybe that's all a real family is – people who stick with you for years. We said goodbye. I hung up the phone, got changed and went straight out.

Robin was at the cave. He had heard the news about the ship getting moved, and he was going to be moving on, for definite. We spent the afternoon doing everything that you can do in a cave to avoid talking about whether or not I would be going with him, but as the time came for me to go back to Dawn and Jacky's, I had to ask him.

'Do me a favour, Robin?'

'What's that?' He lay back on the rolled-up blankets, stretched out like a cat, one arm below his head, making his jumper ride up over his stomach.

'Don't leave without letting me know. OK?'

'Here, you. C'mere.' He beckoned me back to the ground and put his free arm around me. 'I can't just leave like that, can I? I'd have to have one last go at persuading you to come with me.'

'I might do,' I said.

If only I could have made myself forget about things like *family discussions*, or Big Gay Dave doing the dishes with Dawn, or Brains trying not to cry in the library. Everyone trying to cope, everyone needing other people. Who did I need the most? What if we managed to save Muff after all? Wouldn't that be something to stay for?

'I know you won't come with me,' said Robin.

His tone felt harsh and mocking but maybe it was just sad.

It was hard to tell. I decided to ignore it. I kissed him goodbye and walked off, hoping that he'd keep his promise and give me more time to think.

I let thoughts of him crowd my head for the rest of the evening and I stayed up as late as I could so that my body was more tired than my brain by the time I went to bed.

I woke up what seemed like just a few hours later and lay in bed until I couldn't stand the smell of fried bacon any longer. Today was the day of the plan to help Muff. I had to stop thinking about Robin and focus on what we were going to do this afternoon.

'Morning!' said Dawn brightly. She was looking forward to it and it made me feel stronger. Maybe everything would be OK.

While Dawn and Jacky were at church I let Big Gay Dave and Brains into the house. They both seemed nervous. I made a pot of tea, the same way Dawn made it – in the big pot and then putting it on the stove. Dave and Brains eventually got chatting and seemed to relax a bit. They talked about the night of the nightclub. It was the first time they'd seen one another since then. Brains asked Dave about Suzanne and Dave said she was good and had been asking about us too. Then the door went again and we all looked at one another.

'It's him,' I said.

'Want me to answer it?' said Dave.

'No, it's OK, I should do it, it's my house.'

The man at the door looked like he was in his thirties. He had curly brown hair and glasses and he was wearing jeans and a hoody. He grinned widely and stuck out his hand.

'I'm Danny.'

I shook it. 'Cari. Come in. Dave's here.'

Dave and Danny hugged and Danny sat down next to him.

'Tea?' I asked. 'I can do coffee too if you want.'

'Tea would be great, thanks,' said Danny.

I was glad he seemed so confident because I knew that the next time the door opened it was going to be Dawn and Jacky and that they'd have Muff with them, and I was starting to wonder if this had all been a giant mistake.

'Don't look so nervous, Cari,' said Dave. 'It's going to be fine.'

'I'm glad you think so,' I said, sitting opposite him on Jacky's armchair.

'The worst that can happen is that he's annoyed that we've all ganged up on him.'

It was Brains's turn to look worried then.

Dave nudged him. 'Only kidding. It's not like we're staging an intervention or anything.'

'It's exactly like we're staging an intervention,' said Brains. 'Only he's addicted to Jesus, not heroin.'

'There's nothing wrong with a bit of Jesus,' said Danny with a wink.

'Sorry,' said Brains, 'I didn't mean it badly. It's just . . . '

'Ah don't worry, I know exactly what you mean.'

He was smiling so kindly that it was obvious he wasn't offended. Still, I hoped that church would finish soon and that we could get this over with. Dawn and Jacky had spoken to Muff's mum and asked her if Muff could come over for lunch and she had agreed. And it wasn't a lie – we would be having lunch – but we had another agenda too, and not one of us knew which way things would go.

Ten minutes later the locked clicked and I started to lift the tea things to bring them to the kitchen, not wanting it to look as though we'd all been sitting around anxiously, waiting on their return.

'Now, you young ones have a chat, and I'll get to work on the soup,' said Dawn, shuffling Muff into the room.

'Oh, eh, hi Brains,' he said awkwardly.

So, Dawn hadn't told him Brains was coming then. Brains waved hello with a half-smile and I showed Muff to a seat.

'Muff, this is Big Gay ... I mean, Dave, and this is Danny. They're friends of ours.'

'Hi' said Muff, grabbing a cushion to hold to his chest like a shield.

'I'm going to go and help Dawn in the kitchen,' said Jacky.

We didn't speak for the next five minutes. I was trying really hard to think of something to say. But what?

*How's church?*

*How's Jessica?*

*Why are you letting people do mad things to you like making you pretend to be dead?*

It was excruciating.

Finally, Dave spoke. 'Muff. Cari says you're planning to be a mechanic?'

Muff nodded.

'Well I've got this problem with my car, garage says it's gonna be three hundred quid to fix it, and I'm thinking *no way mate*.'

Muff immediately perked up. 'What's the problem?'

'Well, I *think* it has to do with the carburettor.'

'Hmm. OK. Is that your car outside?'

I could've hugged Dave. The two of them headed out to the street to look at his car and Brains gave me a hard stare.

'This is awful,' he said.

'Soup will be ready soon. And Dawn will help – she's good at getting things going.'

'I flippin' hope so.'

But he needn't have worried. Sitting at the table after Jacky said grace, the conversation soon came around to the real reason we were all there, and it was Dawn who started it. Somehow being old meant that nobody minded if she was totally blunt about everything, and her breezy conversation cut through the tension easily.

'James,' she said, passing him the basket of bread rolls, 'I invited Danny here especially to meet you. Danny's a Christian, and he's also gay.'

Muff dropped the bread roll into his soup with a splash. He fished it out, burning his fingers.

Danny laughed. 'That's how most people react. Either they're gay and they freak out when they hear I'm a Christian, or they're Christian and they freak out when I tell them I'm gay.'

'I'm not freaking out,' said Muff, blushing. He didn't look angry, at least. 'How can you be both, though? I mean, you can't be. Can you?'

'I know lots of people think that you can't be both,' said Danny. 'And, believe me, I spent years believing them. What a giant waste of time *that* was.'

'When did you stop believing them?' I asked, imagining Danny at his own intervention, his gay friends trying to persuade him to see the light.

He shrugged. 'It just got too difficult. I tried really hard to be straight. I saw therapists. I got prayer. I even tried to like playing football at school because one of my best friends thought it might help me be *more of a man*. I prayed and prayed. And nothing worked. In the end I thought that one of two things had to be true: either there was no God, and everything I believed was a total load of crap, or there *was* a God and he wasn't making me straight because actually there isn't anything wrong with being gay.'

'But the Bible says there is,' said Muff.

'Yeah, I know,' said Danny. 'And I'm not a Bible student or anything. But at the end of the day I just thought I'm a Christian – I'm meant to be following Jesus, not this ancient book. And Jesus never said anything about being gay. So maybe he didn't think it was that bad, right? In the end I was just so exhausted that I thought I either have to give in and accept myself this way, or I can just go to pieces and lose my faith. The thing I knew for sure was that I couldn't change. You know?'

Muff stared at his soup. I hoped that he did know. I was willing him to know. I could see that Brains was too.

'Don't let your soup get cold now,' said Dawn with a gentle smile, and everyone started eating again.

'How do you and Dave know each other then?' asked Brains, speaking to Danny.

'He used to give me a lift to the New Hope church.'

'You went to church?' said Brains to Dave.

'Nope,' said Dave, dunking his bread in the soup, 'I just gave this Holy Roller a lift.' He grinned at Danny. 'He was a friend of a friend and the church was miles away, and I don't do much on a Sunday morning so it wasn't a bother.'

'He's being modest,' said Danny. 'This guy's a lifesaver. My mate Karla told him I was in a bad way and that she'd heard of some church up the country that had an LGBT service once a month, and the next thing you know I'm getting a lift with a complete stranger to a church where I knew nobody.'

'Were you scared?' I asked.

'Totally bricking it.' He laughed. 'But it was cool. Very friendly, and the LGBT service was a bit cheesy, but it was amazing to hear the word *gay* in church without it being followed by *hell* or *abomination*. I'd found my people.'

I could see that Muff looked as though he was about to cry. Brains noticed and excused himself to go to the toilet. When he came back his eyes were red.

'Let's go into the living room for some cake,' said Dawn.

She got up and started setting a tray with teacups and a large cream sponge that she had made specially the day before.

'Oh, Dawn!' gasped Dave. 'That is magnificent!'

Dawn beamed. 'Thank you. I hope it tastes all right.'

'It's a work of art! And I'm adding it to my list of things you can help me with when I come around to talk about the scones.'

'Lovely!' said Dawn.

How does he do it? I thought. He's totally not putting it on, and he's not pretending to be anyone else, but he's got her eating out of the palm of his hand.

We all settled in the living room with more tea and giant pieces of cake. Muff was quiet, but he didn't look so upset any more. Dave and Danny entertained everyone with stories about their friends and their childhoods. It became an easy afternoon and when it was time to go nobody seemed desperate to leave.

'James. Thanks for the help with the car, mate,' said Dave.

'No problem at all,' said Muff. 'Oh, I should look up the number of that breaker's yard for you.' He fumbled in his backpack for his phone.

'Don't worry,' said Dave. 'Here's my number. Give me a call when you find it. I might get you to come out with me to the yard if you're free?'

'Yeah, yeah. No prob.'

Dave wrote his number on the back of a receipt and gave it to Muff. Everyone but Brains left. There were hugs between some people, and handshakes between others. When they were gone Brains let out a sigh of relief.

'I am so glad that's over,' he said. 'Oh, no offence Dawn. The soup was great. And the cake was incredible.'

'Not a problem,' said Dawn. 'I know what you mean. You're a brave lot, you know.'

*And you're amazing*, I thought, picturing Muff going home. If he told his gran what had happened today, then Dawn stood to lose a friend. In the end, it was even worse than that.

# Chapter 42

'He said *Spread the word. Saturday night on the boat.*'

'He must've said more than that!'

'That's all I could pick up.'

Stevie B. and Brains were eating chips in the canteen.

'How are they even going to get out to that ship?' I said.

'I dunno, but Johnny's dad's a bazillionaire, someone said he's got a speedboat or something.'

'Aye, that won't be conspicuous at all,' said Brains. 'A load of metal-heads zooming out to a cruise ship on a Saturday night.'

'Well, I don't know what they're planning. But they're planning something.'

By the end of the day the story had spread and everyone was talking about it. Johnny Douglas was organising a party on the cruise ship before it got towed away. It was going to be the *gig of the century*, apparently, although nobody seemed to have any clue how they were going to get electricity or amplifiers or a drum kit over to the enormous ship. It was something to talk about, though, and everyone jumped on board. By the middle of the week the *gig of the century* had turned into a party which the whole of the upper school had been invited to. There was talk of drugs and booze and possibly another seance. I reminded myself to tell Robin about the one we'd had for him in the temple. It seemed so long ago now. I was pretty sure that the boat party wasn't going to go ahead because nobody was organising anything, it was all just talk.

'But think about it,' said Stevie B. 'How class would it be? And I bet there's a load of booze on that ship too.'

*Less booze than there was two months ago*, I thought.

'And Gillian Beattie's going. And there'll be cabins, know what I mean?' He nudged Brains but he had one eye on me, gauging my reaction.

'She's not my type,' said Brains.

'I know that, doofus. I meant for me.'

'Like Gillian Beattie would ever get in a cabin with you,' Brains teased.

'Snogged her last week, *actually*,' said Stevie B., sitting up straight.

'You did not.'

'I friggin' did. Ask her!'

And on it went.

I went to the library after school to finish some coursework and stopped on the way back to the estate with Brains and Stevie for pizza. By the time I got in it was eight p.m. and the house was quiet.

I turned on the light and jumped when I saw Jacky in his chair.

'Jeez, Jacky, you scared me there. I thought nobody was here. What are you sitting in the dark for?'

'I was having a wee pray,' he said. 'It got dark and I didn't bother getting up to turn the light on.'

'Wow, OK. Sorry if I disturbed you.'

'That's OK, love.'

But the house was so silent.

'Is everything OK, Jacky? Where's Dawn?'

'She's in bed, love. Not feeling the best.'

That wasn't like her.

'What's wrong?'

Jacky sighed and got up from his chair.

'I suppose you deserve to know. I'll put the kettle on and we'll have a chat.'

Jacky's tea wasn't as good as Dawn's. It was weaker. But we had the rest of the cake, at least. I listened as Jacky told me what had happened that evening. Dawn had gone out to her mid-week prayer group. She might have expected that Muff's gran would be concerned if Muff had told her about the lunchtime meeting. But what she hadn't expected was that not one person would speak to her. The church ladies had sat in their prayer circle and nobody said a word to her. Through their prayers to Jesus they asked forgiveness for those who *lead young people astray*, and strength to *cast out the devil*. When Dawn tried to say hello to some of them afterwards as they drank tea, they pretended not to hear her and swiftly turned to talk to someone else.

'It was very hurtful, you know,' said Jacky in a sad voice.

'It's *horrible*,' I said.

'They're very set in their ways.'

'I know, but there's no need to full-on freeze someone out. That's awful.'

He nodded in agreement. 'It's worse than you think, love.'

'What do you mean?'

He set down his teacup.

'Well, I can't tell you the whole thing. It's Dawn's story to tell. Let's just say that there was a time when she went through something. Something bad. And the prayer circle was very good to her at that time. So kind. They're like family to her now, you see.'

'And now they're turning their back on her?'

He had tears in his eyes.

'Looks like it, eh.' He shrugged. 'People can be hard to understand. I suppose they felt she'd overstepped her mark.'

'Because we had Muff over?'

'Yes, love. They would've seen that as the pastor's business, you see. Not ours.'

So we'd made everything worse by trying to help Muff. It wasn't fair.

'Listen, though,' said Jacky, 'don't you go worrying about it. The Lord will sort it out. He always does. Everything will be fine, and they'll come around eventually.'

He got up and as he walked past me he squeezed my shoulder and said goodnight.

The Lord will sort it out? Fat chance, Jacky. You have to sort things out for yourself, otherwise everyone else decides what happens in your life.

Alone in the living room I turned the TV on and texted Jessica:

**Hi Jess. Did you know the prayer ladies have cut Dawn off? She's gutted. It's not fair. If people want to blame someone**

then they should blame me – it was my idea to invite
Muff over.

I got a reply back immediately, as if Jessica had been sitting
by her phone waiting for me to contact her.

Dawn knows our church better than you. She shouldn't
have gone behind Pastor Ky's back. And you shouldn't
interfere either.

Are you high? I wrote back. You were there, Jessica. You
saw what they did to Muff. That was sick. Really sick. I can't
believe you're all cool with it.

Another quick reply:

Actually I think he went too far, and I apologised to James
for it. But guess what, Cariad? James can make up his own
mind about things, and he wants to be a Christian, not a
gay, so why don't you just butt out.

I threw my phone across the room and instantly regretted it
because Jacky called down to ask if everything was OK.

'Yes,' I lied. 'Just dropped my phone. It's all fine.'

How could Jessica be so dense? And how come Muff was willing to just let them do this to him when we'd just shown him a
way out? It didn't make sense. And now I'd got Dawn involved
and she'd lost all her friends. Shit. Shit. Shit.

I wished I'd never met Jessica or any of them. It would have been better for Jacky and Dawn and Brains and Muff if I'd never come here in the first place. Well, at least I had a way out this time. I'd messed it all up, yet again, but I didn't have to wait for Madge to come and get me. I was old enough now. I could make my own way in the world. I didn't need to wait for *the Lord*, or anyone else, to sort it out. It was time.

# Chapter 43

The next two days were so full of chatter. Even with my best efforts to make plans to run away with Robin, I couldn't drown it out. I tried avoiding Stevie B. and Brains, but I couldn't – they kept on finding me at lunchtime or in the library: Stevie wanting to share gossip about Gillian; Brains wanting to ask questions about coursework. Even during class I had to hear the constant blah blah blah about the big boat party as everyone seemed to be whispering across me to one another, making arrangements, sharing their fantasies about how it might all end up:

*I heard Gillian's going to lose her virginity to Stevie in one of the cabins.*

*I heard that Johnny's dad's in on everything and is gonna let him do shuttle runs with the speedboat!*

*I heard Jason's gonna bring his dad's generator.*

Even the Christians were gossiping when they thought I couldn't hear them:

*I heard that they've organised a drug gang from Belfast to come and supply them all with Marijuana and Cocaine!*

*I heard that they're planning to have another black mass – a proper one with actual goats' blood from Christine's dad's butcher shop.*

*I heard that they're going to play Marilyn Manson songs and invoke the devil. We should do something.*

*We really should.*

Right then I had to say that I didn't care about any of it. Everyone's gossip seemed boring and childish and I almost wished I could take part in it or at least be interested. Saturday night would be fun for all of them, but for me it would be the night that I left Ballybaile for good.

# Chapter 44

Everything from the ship was in odd-shaped bags. A big red rucksack. A small embroidered holdall. A black bin bag. When I arrived at the cave Robin was packing everything up. He smiled when he saw me and then his smile got wider when he saw my bag.

'You're coming with me?' he said.

'Yep.'

He stood up, grinning widely, and kissed me.

I slung my backpack down next to his. I didn't have as much stuff as him. A couple of changes of clothes. My phone and charger. A bottle of water.

'Travelling light, aren't you?'

'Well, we don't *all* have boats to rob.'

The mood was light. Seeing him had lifted a weight. He could always make me forget about everything and I liked that. Maybe this is how it would be from now on. Living in our own little world, not bothered by the outside, not bothering anyone else.

'Where are we going then?' I asked.

He put his hands on my shoulders. 'Anywhere we like, Cari. Where do you want to go?'

I didn't know how to answer that. I had been to so many different families but I didn't feel as if I'd seen anywhere really different. Always just schools and streets, always ending with me moving on. I didn't really care where we went to next. I shrugged.

'Well, never mind,' he said, going back to his bags. 'It'll be great. We've got plenty of stuff which means we'll have ages before we need to sort out money or whatever. We can take our time and see what suits us.' He stopped again and looked up. 'You didn't tell anyone that you were going, did you?'

I froze. 'Em. Not exactly . . .'

'What?' He dropped his bag. 'What do you mean *not exactly*?'

I couldn't have gone without letting Brains know that I hadn't done anything stupid. He was depressed enough as it was. And it wasn't fair after what had happened to him. He deserved to know. And maybe he'd pass it on to Dawn and Jacky that it wasn't their fault as well. Ultimately, I knew that they'd all be better off if I wasn't around to muck things up for them, but I wasn't stupid. I knew that in the short term they'd blame themselves.

'I just told Brains I was planning to move on, and that I'd be grand and not to worry.'

'Cari, I told you to keep it quiet. You've risked our plan!'

'I'm really sorry,' I said. 'I had to. And Brains will be cool with it. I mean, he wasn't when I told him. But he will be. He won't tell anyone, I swear.'

'Fuck *sake*!'

It was the first time he'd ever been angry with me and it made me feel stupid and small.

'Here,' he said, coming over. 'I'm sorry. I'm sorry.' He hugged me. 'It's OK. You just scared me, that's all.'

Over his shoulder I noticed a sharp shadow and I broke apart from him.

'What?' Robin said. 'What are you staring at?'

In the doorway of the cave stood Brains.

'What the ... what's he doing here?' said Robin, his voice raised.

'I need to talk to Cari,' said Brains.

'Well, of course you bloody do. Oh my God ...' Robin was grasping his hair, pacing about. 'This is why, Cari! This is why it was a secret!'

I ignored him.

'What are you doing here?' I asked Brains. 'How did you even find us?'

'Followed you,' he said, still standing in the doorway looking in, fascinated.

'Why? You can't change my mind. Did anyone follow you? Come in, for God's sake.'

'No, nobody followed me. Everyone's heading down to the beach to go over to the ship.'

'What?' Robin stopped pacing.

'I forgot to tell you,' I said. 'A load of kids from school are heading over to the ship tonight for a party.'

'Shit! I left the canoe out! They'll take it!'

'How come you left it out?'

It wasn't like Robin to forget something like that. He was so obsessed with being careful.

'I had to ditch it and run. I did one last trip out last night.

252

As I got back to the shore I heard something, and then I saw a light some way off. I think it was a speedboat out near the ship or something. Maybe they were scoping it for the rescue. I couldn't risk them catching me, so I left the canoe on the beach and ran for it.'

'It was Johnny Douglas. His dad has a speedboat. That's how everyone's getting out to the ship tonight, so I wouldn't worry about your canoe – they'll not need it.'

I'd never seen Robin look so stressed.

'I need a smoke,' he said, hunting through his bag.

He offered one to me and then, grudgingly, to Brains.

We sat on the stone floor of the cave, lighting up. Robin's body relaxed and he sprawled back onto a bag. Brains's long legs were folded, his knees tucked below his chin.

'I know I can't stop you,' he said, looking at me, 'but I wish I could. Dawn and Jacky really love you, you know.'

Bloody hell. Why did he have to go and say that? I tried to keep myself composed, taking a long drag on the cigarette.

'It's just time,' I said. 'Everything has to come to an end sometime.'

'Why?'

'It just does.'

I hoped that I'd said it firmly enough for him to stop going on about it. It seemed to work for a while, at least. Then Robin broke the silence, looking stern.

'Well. Let's have a drink, and then we'll be off, OK?'

I nodded. Robin dug a bottle of brandy out of one of the bags. Brains got up and walked to the mouth of the cave.

'Hey, look at this,' he said.

I got up to join him and Robin brought the bottle over. I flicked my cig over the edge of the cliff. The cruise ship was lit up on the inside. Coloured lights flashed on and off.

'Idiots,' said Robin. 'The cops'll be right over as soon as they get wind of this. Drink up, guys, we're gonna have to get on our way.'

He passed the bottle to me. I drank deeply and passed it to Brains. A shape in the distance moved closer to the shore. Above the wind there was the loud buzz of the speedboat, and then only shouts of laughter and squeals as the buzzing stopped and the boat came to a stop on the sand. We moved back from the edge of the cave, afraid of being spotted, but we needn't have worried. The kids piling into the boat, cracking open tins and pretending to push one another in, were completely wrapped up in their own adventure. I could just about make out Stevie B., his arm around someone, on the boat, and there was a bunch of other kids from school. Once they were all packed on board the speedboat took off towards the ship.

'What a bunch of dicks,' said Robin.

'Hey,' I said, taking the bottle off him and having another drink. 'They're not all bad. They're just having a bit of craic, like.'

Robin shrugged and I wondered if he was partly annoyed because they all had one another. He was nervous about moving on, I could tell by the way he was shifting from foot to foot. He wanted to rip the plaster off and leave as soon as possible, not stand here thinking about all the kids our age having a good time and messing about. I suppose even a cold cave was a home of sorts. I took his hand, thinking he might shrug me off, but he didn't.

'Hey,' I called to Brains. 'You OK?'

He looked serious, gazing out of the cave.

'Yeah.'

He wasn't, though. I wondered if he was wishing he was on his way to the cruise ship party with Muff. One last big party before the mock exams. It was probably going to be a good laugh. Brains hadn't laughed in ages, I reckoned.

'Well,' said Robin, dropping my hand and starting to clear up the drinks. The cork squeaked as he forced it back into the bottle. 'This seems like a good time to head on.'

He stood up and put his hand on my arm. 'You ready?'

'Wait!' said Brains, just as I was about to get up. 'Look at this.'

Voices below us grew louder but they were too far away to hear properly. Five people were standing around the canoe. Then they began pulling it towards the sea. The light was dropping. They stood on the tip of the shore. One got in the canoe.

'Shit! My canoe,' said Robin. 'Wherever we go it'll be by land, then. Probably have to leave some of this shit here.'

'It's Muff,' said Brains softly.

I looked. It did look like Muff.

'Are you sure?' I said. 'It might not be.'

'It is. It's all of them. The Youth Fellowship.'

'Bloody idiots,' said Robin. 'It's not big enough for all of them.'

I squinted my eyes. He was right; it was the Youth Fellowship. They were going to protest at the party. To save people. As they pushed the boat out onto the water and climbed in we could hear them, faintly, starting to sing. The little boat bobbed on the tide and moved out slowly in the direction of the cruise ship. Goodbye, Jessica, I thought. Goodbye, Martha and Gemma and Alicia. Goodbye, Muff.

When the boat was halfway to the ship Brains stood up beside Robin and me.

'Well this is really goodbye, then?' he said.

'Yes, it is,' I said.

I hugged him, hard, wishing I could have said goodbye to Dawn and Jacky too.

'Tell them it's nothing personal, OK?' I said.

'That's it? *Nothing personal?*' he said.

'It's all I've got,' I said.

I was good at goodbyes. Even the ones who deserved tears wouldn't break me. It's how you manage.

'OK,' said Brains. 'I'll miss you.'

'I'll miss you too,' I said.

I turned away, not wanting to look him in the eye, and that's when I saw Robin, staring out to sea. I followed his gaze to see what he was watching. The canoe was a black shadow, but it had stopped moving towards the boat. It bobbed on the water, free from its cargo, face down, like a floating body.

# Chapter 45

'I won't be able to reach,' I said. 'I can't swim that far!'

But they had left the cave already, and I was pleading to nobody. I watched, pathetic, from the cave as Brains and Robin tore down the narrow path to the shore and ran headlong into the water. They raced the quickly fading daylight to the canoe, the only noise was the water, eerie in its calm rhythm against the rocks.

When I lost sight of them I ran down to the beach, hoping that to be closer might give me an advantage. But it was useless. I was useless. And alone.

My phone buzzed. My phone! It was Dawn.

'Dawn! There's been an accident! I'm on the beach beneath the temple. I'm OK but there are people in a boat and it's tipped over. Get an ambulance. And the coastguard. Please, please. Quickly.'

She gasped and told me not to move, that she'd send help. She hung up.

Across the black sea the ship's lights flashed. Orange. Red. Blue. Green. Everyone on board oblivious. I waited.

Orange. Red. Blue. Green.

*Come back*, I thought. Come back. *Come back.*

Orange. Red. Blue. Green.

It seemed to go on for ever.

'Cari!'

To my left, a voice, weak but urgent. It was Robin. I ran and ran towards the sound. There were more voices as I got closer. Crying. Wailing.

*'Help! Oh God! Oh God!'*

And then alarms. And torches. Men running past me on the beach. A siren on the water. A circle of light rippling towards the ship.

Jessica was on the beach, lying still, surrounded by four others – Martha, Alicia, Gemma and Muff. Crying. The men broke their circle. Firm. Loud. Calm. Talking to Jessica's body. Pushing on her chest. Pushing and commanding her to breathe again. Pushing until she gurgled finally, puking salt water on the sand and wheezing her body back to life. More crying. Two of the men turned to calm the others. One called to me but I moved away. I stumbled back into the shadows at the foot of the cliff and a hand grabbed me and pulled me in, a voice saying *Ssshhhhhh* before I could cry out.

'Robin!'

He held his finger to his mouth.

'Sorry!'

It hurt to whisper. Everything in me wanted to cry out.

'You saved them!' I said. 'You saved them!'

He nodded. 'Me and Brains. We got them into the boat and I paddled it back.'

'But,' I said, 'where is Brains?'

His eyes were dark and wide. I remember that the most. The fear. The real fear as he said, 'I'm sorry. I don't know. I couldn't see him, and we had to get back to shore. Jessica was ...' He looked over to where the police officer was rubbing Jessica's back. She was wrapped in a big tin foil sheet.

'But he's still out there then!' I said. 'We have to go! Come on!'

I went to run to the canoe and he grabbed me back into the shadow.

'You can't.'

'But we *have to*!'

Why didn't he understand? Brains was still out there. He was waiting for us.

'Look.' Robin pointed out to sea. A helicopter buzzed above the cliff face. 'It's coming to get him,' said Robin. 'They'll have proper lights and things.'

He was holding me fast. His clothes were soaking and he was freezing. I knew, really. I knew that it was stupid to think that I could paddle out into the night and rescue Brains. I knew that I'd never be able to find him. But every part of my body wanted to break free and run to that boat.

'Listen to me,' said Robin. He was out of breath, but his voice was firm and calm. He turned my body around to face his. 'Listen.' And then he said, 'I can't stay, Cari.'

'No!'

'I have to leave. Right now.'

'You can't! Don't!'

'I've got to. If I stay here it's over for me.'

There were tears coursing down his face now, and I felt myself starting to cry too.

'What about Brains? What about *me*?'

'Come with me, Cariad. Please.'

But I knew I couldn't. And he knew it too. Both of us just stood there for a moment, face to face, wordless. And then he took a sharp breath in and pulled me tightly into his chest. I tried to hug him back but my arms felt so weak. He was really leaving.

'Goodbye,' he said.

'No,' I whispered.

And then he was gone. I curled up in a wet ball on the sand. Trying to be quiet, needing to be small.

He was gone, and I knew he was gone for good, and something inside me swallowed my heart and the void was full of pain.

# Chapter 46

That is where Dawn and Jacky found me; in the shadows on the beach. The paramedics had rushed past me where I was hidden by the rocks, taking the others to hospital. I had dialled 999 and told them there was a boy in the sea. I had to start the sentence four times but they already knew. The others must have told them. I could hardly breathe. I was on the sand, looking out into blackness. The canoe, empty and abandoned, looked so innocent and ordinary. Maybe I should get into it and paddle out, just to be closer to Brains. He was there somewhere. Treading water. Injured. Maybe there was a chance.

But I knew really that there wasn't. I knew that when Robin left everything had changed for good. It was like I had felt the whole world shift from something mundane into a nightmare.

When Dawn and Jacky arrived they wanted to take me to the hospital straight away, but how could I go? If I left, then Brains wouldn't have anything to return to. He'd be alone on the beach, and he'd be lost, or confused. He would have rescued everyone for nothing. If I left, like Robin had left ... then there'd be nobody here for him. Everyone couldn't leave. Why does everyone always leave?

They found his body later that evening.

People had gathered on the cliffs and at the beach to watch the helicopter winch someone down to reach him. One person lowered into the water, and two returning. They were already talking about bravery and a sacrifice and Brains being a hero, even before his body had reached the land.

Dawn and Jacky wanted me to leave with them. They didn't want me to see him, or to see his parents breaking down. Maybe they didn't want to see it themselves. But I had to know that it was real; that he was gone.

I don't remember much after that. I went to the hospital. They gave me a pill to take. I got in the taxi with Dawn and Jacky and woke up in my bed with a pounding headache at lunchtime the next day. That was the first day of everything being different.

# Chapter 47

The days that followed were quiet and empty.

Dawn and Jacky smiled gently, all the time, constantly smiling. *Why are you smiling?* I thought. *There is nothing good any more.*

But I knew they weren't happy. The smiles just meant, 'This is real, but you will be OK.' And I knew it wasn't true, but I didn't mind it because I knew they were trying to be kind. *I will try to be kind too*, I thought. But the idea of being anything was exhausting.

They made me go to the shops for them so that I had something to do. It was all they could think of. I went to the shops so often that we ended up with far more food than we normally had. I walked into the kitchen and there were four loaves of bread on the counter and part of me wanted to cry because that bread was there because of me, because they were trying to help me. And part of me wanted to scream and throw the neat white slices all over the kitchen because it was useless, and I didn't need bread, I needed Brains, alive, and I was so angry at him for dying and so angry at Robin for running away.

Dawn used all the food. I suppose she didn't want to give in and admit that it couldn't really help. She made soups and stews and sandwiches to take to Brains's parents. No cakes, though. Nothing sweet.

I did not switch on my phone. I did not go to school. I walked to the shops. I peeled the vegetables. I did the dishes. I tried not to think.

On the fourth day, the day before the funeral, Dawn asked me if I wanted to go to the wake. I didn't. But she thought I should. We were in the living room with the TV on but nobody was watching it. I asked her if she had another one of those pills from the hospital, but she didn't. I asked her to get one for me, but she said no. *Some things just have to be faced*, she had said. *But you don't have to face them alone.*

'What does that mean?' I said.

She did not reply. Her mouth began to tremble, and she said, 'Excuse me,' and left the room.

I spent the day in the same spot, staring at the TV, trying to take in the words and understand them, and make my brain have thoughts about them, and not all the other things.

In the evening the doorbell went, and it was Dave. Dawn let him in and they hugged for a long time in the hall.

She showed him into the living room. Jacky nodded to say hello and Dave nodded back. He sat down beside me and asked me how I was. I looked at him and started to cry. He shifted closer and put an arm around me, and maybe he was crying too, I wasn't sure. When I had stopped he said he was going to take us to the wake.

'I'm not going,' I said.

'You should,' said Dave.

'I don't want to see him lying there. I can't.'

Dawn was standing in the doorway with her coat on, ready to go. 'Put your coat on, Cariad,' she said. 'We're going to go and say goodbye to Brains now.'

'I can't!' I said, looking up at her.

She came into the room. 'Dave,' she said, 'would you let me talk to Cariad on my own for a little minute?'

Dave and Jacky went into the kitchen, shutting the door behind them.

'Don't try to persuade me, Dawn,' I pleaded. 'I just don't want to. And I don't want to feel guilty about it.'

'I'm not going to make you feel guilty, Cariad. I want to tell you something. Something very personal. Can I trust you?'

Her words made me catch my breath. I wiped my eyes and she handed me a hanky. Sitting up straight on the sofa, beside me, she spoke calmly, as if it was something she'd practised saying many times. 'When I was twenty-five, I was raped.'

'Oh!' I hadn't expected this. 'That's terrible, Dawn!'

'Yes. It was,' she said, calmly. 'I don't normally tell people this, Cariad. It's in the past and I don't like to think of it. But I wanted to tell you about it.'

'You don't have to,' I said.

'I want to.' She took a deep breath in, and then out again. 'It was the pastor of the church. He raped me.'

'Pastor Ky! Oh my God!'

'No, not Pastor Kyle. Another Pastor.'

I decided not to interrupt her again.

'Jacky and I were newly married. Pastor Larry had been the pastor at our wedding, actually. I trusted him completely.'

There were tears in her eyes now. I wanted her to stop. I didn't want her to be hurt all over again. But she went on.

'That morning I was in the church, arranging the flowers for the service the next day. I was alone in the building, or so I thought. But then he came out of the office. He complimented the flowers. He complimented me. And that is when it happened.' She closed her eyes, clasping her hands together. 'It was quick,' she said, 'but it felt like for ever. And Cariad.' She opened her eyes and looked at me. 'I thought my life was over. I thought it was all over.'

I didn't know what to do. I reached out a hand, maybe to touch her arm or something, but as I reached out she took my hand in both of hers.

'I'm telling you this because it's important. It is hard to live with something as big as this. You've had a tough life, Cariad, I know that. Nothing that happened to you will really ever go away. But we are here for you. And Dave is here for you today, as well. You don't have to make sense of Brains's death. But all of us have to face it. That's just the way of it.'

The way she was gripping my hand I wondered if she needed me to go to Brains's house more than I needed to stay away. I wanted to ask a hundred questions. What happened to the pastor? Why did she still go to that church? Why go to *any* church after that? But I knew she had finished talking about it for now. I nodded to let her know that I understood.

I put my coat on and Jacky locked up. We drove to Brains's house, which wasn't Brains's house any more. Now it was just the place where he used to be alive. Standing on his doorstep as Dawn rang the bell, I knew that his body was inside, but that he wouldn't be there.

Part of me wanted to run away, like Robin. In that moment I wished I could have another life. I wished I was somebody else. And at the very same time I also didn't want to be anywhere other than here with Dawn and Jacky, and Dave who did not leave my side from the moment we left our house to the moment we returned to it. Even standing beside the coffin, looking at my friend, asleep, as I broke down, Dave was there.

I knew that there were other people at the house too. People I knew. The Youth Fellowship girls were here somewhere. Muff would be here too. But I didn't look for them. I let Dawn and Jacky talk to Brains's parents. I asked Dave to talk to me so that I didn't have to speak to anyone else. And that was all. We said goodbye and left.

'Well done,' said Dave, as we walked back to the car. 'You survived.'

'But I shouldn't have,' I said. 'I knew I couldn't swim that far out. So I didn't try. And that's why I survived.'

'I meant the wake,' he said.

I knew what he had meant, but now *survival* only meant one thing. It meant me-alive and Brains-dead, and I couldn't think of anything else.

# Chapter 48

On the fifth day I sat in the back pew of the church with Dawn and Jacky and Dave. Everyone was in dark clothes, looking as neat and tidy as they could. Dave looked weird in a suit, his black hair tied back in a ponytail.

'OK?' he whispered.

'Yeah,' I said.

He held my hand because he knew it wasn't true.

The Youth Fellowship sat in the front row. Jessica had her head on Muff's shoulder. Jacky told me that it had been Brains who had saved her. He and Robin had upturned the canoe. Robin had sat in the little boat and pulled the others in as Brains helped them to find their way. Then he had swam out to get Jessica who was drifting a longer way off. He had turned her over in the water, only just reaching the boat where the others could pull her in, before disappearing himself. Robin had jumped in to try to find him, but by then it was dark, and the others were freaking out because Jessica was unconscious. He had had to make a decision.

The police had wanted to know about Robin. I told them I'd seen him that night but not about everything else. They came back a few days later and Dawn shooed them way, telling them off for harassing a bereaved young woman. They didn't argue. They had stopped the party on the boat and arrested a few kids for drugs. Jessica and the others had filled in all the details they needed. The boat was towed the next day.

The music in the church stopped and Pastor Ky began to speak. He said everything that I suppose everyone expected to hear about how clever Brains was. How he would probably have gone to Oxford to study physics. How good he was at sports. How brave he was to save the young people. *Thinking only of others and not of himself*, the pastor said. There were comparisons with Jesus. He would've hated that. I was half listening, half trying not to listen. And then I heard Pastor Ky say something, and it woke me up.

'What a tragedy that this young man was cut down in his prime. He would undoubtedly have gone on to have a successful career. He would certainly have had a wife and a family of his own ...'

I sat up. Dave squeezed my hand. He had heard it too. Pastor Ky couldn't say that, could he? Surely everyone who knew Brains knew by now that he was gay. *Everyone knew it*. The Youth Fellowship knew it. Pastor Ky would have known it if he'd talked to anyone about Brains. A minute ago he was comparing Brains to the son of God. Now he was Tippexing out a whole part of his life, as if there had been something embarrassing or wrong about him.

I wanted to stand up. I wanted to say something. I wanted to make it right. Dave squeezed my hand tighter. I knew he was trying to tell me not to. But come on. This was *so wrong*. As I wondered whether or not to speak I saw Muff getting up at the front of the room. I guessed he was going to walk out. Poor Muff. I felt a pang of guilt at having been about to make a scene at the funeral of his boyfriend. *Shut up, Cari*, I told myself. *For once this isn't about you.*

But Muff didn't leave. He stood in front of Pastor Ky's podium, facing the congregation, and over the pastor's droning he began to speak. We couldn't hear his words at first but then Pastor Ky stopped speaking. Muff's voice was quiet, but it was clear.

'Brains was ...' He started again, clearing his throat. 'Brains was ... my best friend. And. He was my boyfriend.'

The room was silent. Muff paused. Jessica's face was distraught but, like me, she was frozen to the spot.

'He was my boyfriend. He wasn't going to get a wife. He'd never have done that. He was gay. Really, really gay. And I'm gay too. And now he's gone ... and I think ... I think we should tell the truth about him.'

My heart filled my chest until the feeling overflowed and I was crying. I wanted to stand up, or to applaud, or just to go to him. I felt Dave's firm hand squeeze mine again, keeping me calm and still. Someone else was getting up. It was Brains's mum. She put an arm around Muff. He looked so small beside her, like she was holding him up.

'That's right,' she told the open-mouthed onlookers. 'My son was gay. And he was a good boy.' Her voice cracked. 'We were, we *are*, very proud of him.'

That was all she could say before her shoulders began to shake as well, and Muff's mum got up to give her a hug. The three of them helped one another to sit down together at the front of the church.

Pastor Ky cleared his throat and announced the end of the service. There was a hymn. Some people sang along but most were whispering to one another. There was a short prayer and Brains's dad and Big Gay Dave and Muff helped to carry his coffin out of the church. The wooden box passed us with Brains's mum following behind.

Dawn got up. 'Look after Jacky for me,' she said to Dave and me. 'I'm going to walk beside Mrs Baxter.

# Chapter 49

There were eleven of us: Me, Big Gay Dave, his partner Wee Gay Dave, Danny, Muff, Gemma, Stevie B., Dawn, Jacky, Brains's mum and Muff's mum.

It had been exactly one year since Brains's funeral.

We started at his grave, leaving flowers – red and white and yellow and pink roses. Brains's mum had requested colourful things. Everyone took it in turns to say something about Brains or to share something he would have liked. I read a poem I'd written on my college course. Muff played a song by John Grant on his phone. We all cried.

Then we lifted our banners and flags.

I had worked on my sign the whole of the previous day. It said QUEER LIBERATION NOW in huge pink glittery letters. Muff's sign said SUPERGAY. I laughed when I saw it and he smiled. I had forgotten what he looked like when he was happy. He had taken a day off his university course and come home for the memorial. He had put on weight since the start of term and he'd started growing a beard. He looked healthy.

'Well,' announced Big Dave in a loud voice, 'let the first annual Ballybaile Pride march begin!'

We left the graveside quietly but as soon as we got out on the footpath the Daves began blowing their whistles and leading us in a series of chants.

*WE'RE HERE! WE'RE QUEER! GET USED TO IT!*

People doing their shopping on the other side of the street stopped to stare at us. Big Dave waved at them and blew kisses. One woman blew a kiss back. A man in a car slowed down and yelled *PAEDOS* through the window and then took off at speed. Big Dave and Wee Dave looked at each other and laughed but I saw Muff wince. Jacky saw it too and he put a hand on Muff's shoulder.

Dawn and Jacky carried a sign between them which read STANDING WITH OUR LGBT FRIENDS. When Wee Dave started singing 'I Am What I Am', Dawn sang along with him. She was the only one who knew all the words. Jacky nudged me.

'Big fan of the musicals,' he said, winking. 'She'll take you some day if you like. Not my cup of tea, personally. I prefer the football.'

The song took us to the Jenny Haniver, still nailed to the tree, dripping slightly from yesterday's rain. Here, we stopped for a breath. As Dave's performance came to an end, two women in their twenties across the street started clapping and cheering. Wee Dave curtseyed to them and we all laughed. The next part of the journey would take us off the street and up into the forest and then to the cliff's edge. I hadn't been back there since the night I watched Brains and Robin run into the sea together.

'You OK?' Muff whispered.

'Yeah,' I said. I was unsure, though. 'You?'

'Not really.' He smiled, tears in his eyes. 'Brains would have loved all this, though.'

'He totally would've. He'd be so proud of you, Muff.'

Muff sniffed. 'Thanks,' he whispered. He paused. 'I'm gonna need a drink after this. You up for it?'

'Yes. He would've liked that too. Us hanging out together again.'

'And you too?' Muff said to Stevie. 'You coming out later?'

'Try and stop me,' said Stevie.

We made a plan to meet, and then we climbed the hill. When we got to the top everything looked the same as it had done a year ago. I wanted to shout out for Brains. Just in case we'd been wrong. Just in case it had all been a mistake somehow. But the hardest thing, the thing that everyone was thinking, was that it was real. This place was still here, and Brains wasn't. The sun was still on the cliffs. The cave was still there, underneath us. The beach was still below it. The seagulls cried. The light glittered like diamonds on the water. We could feel the peace of what was living and quietly carrying on without him.

A seagull landed on the ground near us and started tearing at an old ice-cream wrapper. I thought about Robin. Robin who had left deliberately when we needed as many to stay as possible to rally against death and emptiness. Robin, who was always running to a safer place. I wondered if he had found it. Nobody had heard from him. I had spent months wondering if he might come back, or even just send a message. But, nothing. Nobody was talking about him any more. He had moved on, and so had everyone else.

Still, when he crept into my thoughts I let him exist there for a while. I let myself remember his words. I let myself get angry at him. I let myself be sad. I let myself miss him and I let myself be with him again in quiet memories. He was here in this way today, in this circle of private prayers and wishes that was binding us together in silence. What we had, all of us standing there, was something I finally understood as holy.

'Is it OK if I join you?' said a soft voice.

Everyone looked towards the voice and then at Muff.

'Of course it is,' he said quietly.

He held out a hand to welcome Jessica into our space.

As we looked to the north, two seals tipped their bald heads out of the sea and floated side by side for a while, the black length of them like an *equals* sign in the water. Then, in unison, they curved their backs and ducked under to disappear between the gentle waves. *See you next year*, I thought. The sky darkened with a passing cloud and, as the first snowflakes of winter floated to the ground, we made our way back down the hill, towards home.

# Note

Ballybaile is a fictional town on the north coast of Ireland. As with a lot of my stories, there is a mixture of real places and entirely fictional places in *Every Sparrow Falling*. Mussenden Temple is real, as are the cliffs, and the Albert Clock in Belfast. But Ballybaile, its people and its church are all fictional. That is not to say that there isn't some truth in the events that take place there.

I have several friends in NI who, when they told their churches that they were gay or transgender, were offered 'reparative therapy' – a pseudoscientific practice which attempts to change someone's sexual orientation or gender, often with deeply damaging results. In *Every Sparrow Falling* I wanted to include a character who felt, as my friends did, torn between faith in God and the feeling that their sexual orientation was problematic in light of that faith.

Of course times are changing in NI. LGBTQ visibility is increasing. We have more politicians than ever who want to work for LGBTQ rights. Our Pride marches are huge. We have excellent support and advocacy organisations and brilliant queer artists, musicians, playwrights, novelists and poets. Schools are beginning to think about how best to support LGBTQ students and young people are in the middle of all of these things, challenging our culture, and making it better all the time.

However, as we work towards being a country that young people want to stay in, I did not want to forget those who still feel shamed by their communities and their churches. We all bear a responsibility to turn a light onto the dark corners of this place. There is still work to do.

If you are an LGBTQ young person who has been affected by any of the issues in this book, please contact any of the following organisations who will listen to you without judgement and may be able to help: www.cara-friend.org.uk; transgenderni.org.uk; www.rainbow-project.org.

If you want to support LGBTQ young people in Northern Ireland then please spread the word about these amazing organisations and, if you can, consider donating. As someone who has worked with LGBTQ young people for several years I know first hand the positive impact they have had on the lives of young people here. They offer practical support, and hope.

If you are a Christian who is looking for a church which affirms LGBTQ lives, here are some places you can look online and on social media for more information: All Soul's Church, Belfast (Non-Subscribing Presbyterian); St George's, Belfast (Anglican); Spectrum LGBT Christian Fellowship, Belfast; Harbour Faith Community, Carrick; the Corrymeela Community (NI); Quest (LGBT Catholic group); Inclusive Church; Diverse Church.

This is not an exhaustive list. The number of groups which support LGBTQ Christians is growing. You might find that leaving the church altogether is the right thing for your mental health, but if not please know that you do not need to choose between God and your sexual orientation or gender. You're good the way you are, and there are places, in real life and online, where people celebrate diversity and where you can find support without being asked to change who you are.

## A note for straight/cisgender young people

Here are some ways that you can support your LGBTQ friends:

- Challenge homophobia and transphobia in your school. Let other people know that you're not cool with homophobic or transphobic jokes. Don't make those jokes yourself.
- Support your LGBTQ friends when they talk about their experiences or when they organise events or meetings. Ask them how you can best support them.
- Listen to your LGBTQ friends. If they say something is hurtful then take it on board. If they just need to talk then be the trustworthy friend who will listen and help.
- Go with your LGBTQ friends if they have an appointment they're nervous about, or if they need to come out to someone and they want some moral support.
- Essentially, being a good ally is about listening and supporting. It's about doing what you know is the right thing, even if nobody's watching (people are always

watching, though). You won't always get it completely right, but all relationships are about learning the best ways to help one another and ourselves, so keep going. We all need one another.

# Acknowledgements

My deep and wide thanks to the following for their help.

Ian and Justin and Eoin. Thank you for taking good care of one another and occasionally letting me hide so that I could write this book. Thank you for your good humour and endless positivity when it comes to my work. Shantay, you stay.

My agent, Jenny Savill, and the editor of this book, Olivia Hutchings. Thank you once again for looking after my story so well.

Peterson. You're the best reader/writer friend a gal could have.

My other writing friends. I am so grateful for your support and encouragement. Thank you for answering my endless questions and for letting me know that it's not just me.

And to everyone else who has been supportive over the last year. Thank you so much for letting me in.

X